GENTLEMAN SEEKS A LADY

TWO PREVIOUSLY PUBLISHED REGENCY NOVELLAS

GRACE BURROWES

GRACE BURROWES PUBLISHING

Architect of My Dreams

Copyright © 2018 by Grace Burrowes

A Is for Amorous

Copyright © 2019 by Grace Burrowes

A IS FOR AMOROUS

Originally published in **Love by the Letters**

DEDICATION

To those who've done battle with the mean girls

CHAPTER ONE

To Miss Adelicia Beauvais,

The honor of your presence is requested in the offices of Mr. William Carruthers, solicitor, at the date and time noted on the enclosed card. The purpose of this appointment is to discuss the transfer of a sum certain into your keeping, and to discuss further terms relating to additional consideration. Time is of the essence, Miss Beauvais, thus the favor of a reply to this letter would be appreciated. I remain,

Your Obedient Servant,
William Carruthers

~

"BUT SIR, what am I *do* with the money?" Adelicia Beauvais had a fine grasp of mathematics, natural science, history, and literature. Mr. Carruthers's daft scheme left her utterly flummoxed.

"You spend it," the solicitor replied. "You will need to bide in Town, socialize, attend formal functions, and otherwise do the pretty if you're to raise a substantial sum for St. Jerome's. You will require a carriage from time to time, and you'll certainly want to buy a few frocks. The initial money is intended to finance your fundraising."

Ada remained seated when she wanted to pace and shout. "I do not *bide in Town*. I do not *attend formal functions*. I do not *socialize*, if by socialize you mean stay up until all hours discussing the weather while wearing fashions too confining to be comfortable, and dancing with any gouty old fool brave enough to ask me."

Mr. Carruthers had perfected that bland, interested expression which was probably the first skill taught in solicitor school. Nonetheless, Ada suspected she'd amused him.

"If you are successful," he said, "you will make a lot of deserving children very happy."

For an educated man, he was a font of irrelevancies. "I have not met these children you speak of, and if their origins are as unfortunate as you imply, then a few more spoonfuls of porridge or a new pair of shoes will hardly alter their expectations."

That sounded cruel, and yet Ada was not being intentionally mean-spirited. People thought a happy childhood consisted of adequate nutrition and shelter from the elements. A child could be well provided for and still be miserable, as these cast-off children must be.

Mr. Carruthers opened a drawer of his desk—a massive edifice as desks went—and unrolled a paper across his blotter.

"That's a recent painting of Hopewell Grange. This perspective is from the park as you come around the curve of the drive."

Ada nearly walked out without even peeking, but her curiosity got the better of her, as it was ever wont to do. She leaned two inches forward in her chair.

"I will own this, if I can raise the money for the orphanage?"

"Those are the terms of the gift, provided the money you raise is received in hand by St. Jerome's before the thirty days are up."

The manor house was four stories of golden sandstone set amid a green park. A swan floated placidly on a pond in the curve of the drive. A fountain in the center of the pond and colorful beds of tulips completed a picture of rural elegance.

"Whose terms?" Ada murmured, while mentally counting windows. Twenty-six full size windows and one door. Twenty-six places to sit and read by natural light. Twenty-six windows in which to grow plants for botany experiments. Twenty-six vantage points from which to gaze out upon lovely acres while simply thinking.

"I am not at liberty to say who has set this challenge before you, miss, but I can assure you that St. Jerome's is deserving."

"Tenancies?"

"Six tenant farms, plus a home farm. The estate is entirely self-supporting and makes a tidy profit."

Self-supporting was a lovely term. One of Ada's favorites in fact. "I have a month to raise how much?"

The solicitor named an outlandish sum, and Ada let the painting curl in on itself. "Do you grasp how impossible a chore you have set for me, Mr. Carruthers? I know nobody. I am invited nowhere. I have no propensity for begging, charming, or wheedling, all of which appear necessary to fulfill this bargain. The money you give me today will be wasted if I spend it on fripperies and dancing slippers in hopes of waltzing polite society out of its coin."

Mr. Carruthers let the painting remain on the blotter like some ancient scroll. "You are from a titled family, Miss Ada. You went to a proper finishing school. You have cousins and connections, aunts and uncles. I daresay you have correspondents. You are not without resources."

Ada rose and collected her gloves and bonnet. A tidy little ginger cat guarded them on the sideboard, and squinted at her as she retrieved her accessories.

"I have family. That cannot be helped, and some of them are even reasonably decent people." Aunt Kitty was a love, if something of an original, and several of the cousins were good company in small doses. "I cannot say you have wasted my time—you apparently have an eccentric client putting demands upon you—but I also cannot accept the sum you offered earlier. I refuse to be a party to a doomed scheme that will waste needed coin. Donate that money to the orphanage, and we'll spare Mayfair my pitiful attempts at small talk."

Mr. Carruthers was on his feet before Ada could gain the door.

"I am unable to do as you wish, miss. The bank draft is made out to you and you alone. You may keep this initial sum and do with it as you please, or you may use it to raise additional funds for the orphanage. Those are your options."

Twenty-six windows... on one façade alone. Ada pulled on her right glove. "Does Hopewell Grange have a conservatory?"

"Of nearly five thousand square feet."

She had to brace herself against the sideboard. Her entire cottage was about one-third that size, and while she loved it, she did not own it. She rented, which limited the modifications and modernizations she could make.

She donned the second glove, which needed darning on the index finger. "What of a stable? Does it have a stable?"

"Eight loose boxes, eight straight stalls, plus a carriage house."

Days cantering the countryside in search of botanical specimens called to Ada. Long afternoons studying geological formations, charting temperature and wind measurements. She undertook those activities now, but not on the scale of a true scientist.

"I am an utter failure at waltzing, Mr. Carruthers, and I do not enjoy it."

He tucked his hands behind his back. "You must do as you see fit, of course."

Ada's finishing governess had used the same excruciatingly indifferent tone when she'd known Ada's resolve was crumbling. Mr. Carruthers was nothing like Miss Gladshaw. She'd been a fluttery blond, while he was dark-haired and dark-eyed. Miss Gladshaw's bombazine and taffeta had announced her every move. Mr. Carruthers raised silence to a high, manly art.

Ada unknotted her bonnet ribbons, a clumsy undertaking when

she'd already put on her gloves. "I am the worst possible candidate to raise money for a lot of hungry children."

"If you say so, miss." Mr. Carruthers held a piece of paper out to her. "The bank draft is yours to do with as you please."

Ada had no delusions about herself. She was a charmless blue-stocking of plain appearance and blunt speech, but she had scruples.

"If I take that money, I must at least try to do what I can for those children. I cannot simply accept funds from an unknown benefactor and indulge my fancies with it."

"No conditions attach to the surrender of this initial sum, Miss Beauvais. I've merely made suggestions that should improve the chances of putting Hopewell Grange into your hands."

Six tenant farms upon which to experiment with various strains of sheep, poultry, and bovines. Horses to ride, acres to roam... Endless supplies of manure with which to experiment on the ideal composting process, too.

"Does Hopewell Grange have a library?" *Say no. Please, please say no.*

"Of course. I can show you the schematics if you like. The library measures sixty feet by twenty feet, if I recall correctly. Not the largest collection in the shire, but a commodious space housing a good four thousand bound volumes."

Ada might have resisted the farms—her family seat was a vast bucolic fiefdom. She might have resisted the conservatory, for it was nearly too big for her to fathom. She might have resisted the stables, because she could after all only ride one mare at a time, but the library...

Defeated by the bound volumes. "Tell me again the name of the orphanage?"

Mr. Carruthers passed her the bank draft and several other sheets of paper. "I've written the name and direction for you, and included a letter of introduction to the current headmaster. Lord John Waverly lives on the premises, and can explain all you care to know about the children and their needs."

"They are children, which is enough bad news for the moment. I have thirty days to tilt at this windmill?"

"Thirty days to make Hopewell Grange your home."

"When water buffalo levitate, Mr. Carruthers. I'll bid you good-day."

He remained by his desk, a tall dapper man impeccably attired for his station. "A word of advice, Miss Beauvais?"

"Please. I have never wasted a large sum of money before. Any insights you care to share will be appreciated."

"Be yourself. Don't undertake this challenge as you think you ought to do it. Raise the money in the manner that is true to your nature."

"Interesting." Ada plunked her bonnet onto her head. "You advise me to stand in Hyde Park bellowing at the lords and ladies to give me their money. Perhaps if I waved a pistol about they'd take me seriously. But no, then I'd be arrested. Can't have that. Even Aunt Kitty would look askance at criminal behavior. Good-day, cat. Good-day, Mr. Carruthers."

Mr. Carruthers bestirred himself to hold the door for her, while the cat remained squinting on the sideboard. Perhaps squinting was the feline version of laughter.

~

"CORA HAD AN ACCIDENT." Henrietta reported that development with the longsuffering of an eight-year-old who'd been making the same announcement nigh daily for a month.

The smaller girl stood holding Henrietta's hand, staring at the floor of the front foyer and sniffling.

Lord John Waverly knelt, and still all Cora risked was a peek at him.

"I'm very proud of you, Cora."

She dropped Henrietta's hand to wipe at her nose with her finger. "I accidented again."

A minor accident this time, if the olfactory evidence was any indication. "But Cora, look at the time. Can you tell me what time it is?"

She stared at the clock in the foyer, her lips moving silently as she counted to herself. "Three."

John poked her gently in the belly. "Exactly right! Three in the afternoon. You went all morning, and halfway through the afternoon without an accident. That is excellent progress. I hope you are proud of yourself."

Over Cora's head, Henrietta was looking at him as if he were daft.

"I'm wet," Cora said, bottom lip quivering. "Again."

"What's a little wet when you nearly lasted until afternoon sunshine without a slip? The Lord in his infinite wisdom made laundry tubs, and nobody is quicker than you are at changing out of a damp dress. Upstairs with you now and then you can join us in the garden."

Her bottom lip stopped quivering. "I can still play in the garden?"

"Of course. In fact, I think you and Henrietta ought to get five extra minutes as a reward for your great progress."

"C'mon, Cora," Henrietta said, grabbing Cora's wrist. "I'll help you get into a clean smock."

Henrietta led the way up the steps, Cora peering down at John dubiously all the way to the first landing.

Cora had been apprenticed to a cook, though what cook could have mistaken such a tiny girl for a seven-year-old? When the cook had pronounced Cora too simple to be of use in the kitchen, a pastor had brought Cora to John, declaring St. Jerome's a far safer environment than the one the child had come from.

"And you *are* making progress," John muttered as the girls' footsteps faded above. "Albeit very slow progress."

He had thirty minutes before he'd be called upon to supervise the children's afternoon time out of doors. Half an hour was sufficient to jot off at least two heartfelt letters imploring the patrons—

A hard triple thump suggested a stranger on John's doorstep. The regular deliveries went around back, and callers were non-existent. He swiped his fingers through his hair, buttoned his coat, gave his hopelessly wrinkled cravat a fluff, and opened the front door.

A small, plain woman in a straw hat that had seen better days stood on the steps. She was attired in a gray wool cloak fit only for shepherds in rural Christmas plays, and wore spectacles that seemed too big for her face.

"Good-day," John said. "Do you need directions?"

"If this is St. Jerome's Charitable Hospital then I've been given all the directions I could possibly wish for. Might I come in?"

She had the look of a crusader, so John stepped back because crusaders could be angels in disguise—or that was the theory.

"John Waverly, at your service."

She drew off her gloves and stuffed them into a beaded reticule. "*Lord* John Waverly?"

Oh, dear. *Lord* John, in that tone, never boded well. "My father is the Marquess of Gandham, though in these surrounds, the title seems superfluous. I am vastly honored to be headmaster of this humble establishment, and the children refer to me in that capacity. May I take your cloak?"

As angels went, the lady was *very* well disguised. Beneath her cloak was another drab garment that might once have been a dress, though it would have served equally well as a horse blanket. When she removed her bonnet, a lock of dark hair tumbled free, only to be tucked haphazardly back into the bun at her nape.

The errant tress only half-heeded the guidance of her fingers, and draped itself against her neck as she peered around the foyer.

"I am Miss Ada Beauvais. What is that smell?"

"That is the smell of progress."

"A very odd sort of progress, my lord. I come bearing a letter from Mr. William Carruthers. Might we discuss its contents somewhere less malodorous?"

The hint of Accident in the air was so faint John could barely detect it, but then, women were said to have delicate noses. Miss Beauvais's proboscis was more heroic than delicate, though it served well to hold up her spectacles.

"Let's use the garden," he said. "The day is fine, and my duties will soon require me to bide there." The name Carruthers rang a distant bell, which was a relief. Had Mr. Carruthers been a bill-collecting sort of fellow, John's mental bells would be tolling more loudly than St. Peter's ever had.

"This was a fine house once," Miss Ada said, peering about as they traversed the corridor. "With some effort, it could be lovely."

"With a lot of effort. We prefer to shine the walls with laughter and polish the floors with the joy of learning. The children all have regular chores, but they are small children and the house is quite large when viewed from the perspective of one wielding a mop."

The house wasn't dirty, though. Worn, tired, and aging, but not dirty.

John led his guest through the library and into the side garden. "Welcome to our humble tribute to nature." Also to economy, otherwise St. Jerome's would never have been able to afford kitchen spices or the simplest of medicinals.

"Somebody tends your beds conscientiously," Miss Beauvais said, snapping off a sprig of spearmint. "You should group the sage, rosemary and lavender together, though, because they all prefer dry soils. Your chervil would rather be in the shade and have moist soil." She withdrew a sealed paper from her reticule. "Mr. Carruthers's letter."

The missive was written on good quality paper, the wax a rich claret color.

John scanned the tidy script as Miss Beauvais sniffed this plant and untangled that one from its neighbor.

The news was not bad: Miss Ada Beauvais boasted ducal family connections, and had been challenged to raise money for St. Jerome's by an anonymous benefactor. A small sum (an enormous sum by John's lights) was in her keeping to facilitate fundraising. Further details would be forthcoming from Miss Beauvais if she chose to attempt the challenge. If she was successful, she'd be granted owner-ship of a modest country estate.

"This is most interesting," John said. "Won't you have a seat?"

The only place to sit was the bench the boys had built as a Christmas present for John. They reasoned he spent many hours supervising children out of doors, and at the great age of seven-and-twenty, he might well relish a place to rest his ancient bones.

The children were right, as usual.

Miss Beauvais took one side of the bench. "Feel free to join me. The scents here really are intriguing." She withdrew a short pencil and a crumpled piece of paper from her reticule and scribbled some-thing. "I felt I owed it to you and your institution to make your acquaintance. I have no ability to raise funds, my lord, nor do I aspire to acquire that talent."

She put him in mind of Henrietta, reciting facts and allowing them to speak for themselves in all their unimpressive glory.

"May I ask how much you are supposed to raise?"

She named a sum so far beyond John's wildest dreams that if he'd coveted that much money, he would not have sought forgiveness, for surely desire of such outlandish proportions would be a product of mental imbalance.

"I can see why you are disinclined to make the attempt," he said. "With that kind of money, I could ensure the security of every child on the premises with a significant sum left over for their siblings."

Miss Ada scooted about on the bench. "I never said I wouldn't make an attempt, but the matter is one of probabilities."

He did not know another woman in all of England who used the word *probabilities*, much less with that much assurance. "In what sense?"

"I have a tidy sum in hand. I can simply give it to you, and then you'll have a bit to put by. That is a certain benefit, no risk to you or to me. In the alternative, I can use that money to attempt to attract more money. Mr. Carruthers seemed to think that were I to social-ize, chat up the ladies I went to school with, beg for their pin money, and exert myself to be charming, then the larger sum might materialize."

She spoke with precision and certainty, which was at complete variance with what John expected from a proper lady. Upon closer inspection, she appeared younger than he'd first thought, and sitting beside her, he detected a faint fragrance of lemon verbena.

"And the risk involved in the latter scenario?" he asked.

She removed her spectacles and polished them on her sleeve. "The probability that I will fail at such an undertaking approaches absolute certainty." She stared at the brick cobbles the same way Cora had stared at the floor of the foyer, as if anticipating a deserved blow.

"Why will you fail?" John asked.

She turned serious blue eyes on him. "Because I lack charm, my lord. The best governesses and masters of deportment in England were defeated by my lack of charm, and matters have only deteriorated during the geological epoch since my come out. The case is hopeless, I do assure you. I'll have the smaller sum delivered on the first of the week."

John could hardly fault her reasoning or her self-assessment though some sentiment lurking in her honest gaze tempted him to argue. Did she *want* him to meekly agree that she was without charm? Miss Beauvais was blunt, unconcerned with her appearance, and highly intelligent. How did that add up to a lack of charm?

And yet, the decision had to be hers.

"I will most gratefully accept any charity you care to bestow on us," John said. "The children will remember you in their prayers and so will I."

An awkward silence sprang up amid the sounds of a London neighborhood on a pleasant afternoon. A cart clattered past in the alley beyond the garden. Out on the street, a man called a friendly greeting in West Country accents. The sum Miss Beauvais offered was much, much needed, and nothing short of the very miracle John had been hoping for.

And yet... Miss Beauvais was not charmless any more than Cora was hopeless. John was about to render that opinion to his guest when a brisk salutation rang out over the garden.

"Good day, your lordship! Good day. A moment of your time, if you please!" Mr. Bushrod P. Hewitt let himself through the gate and churned up the walkway. "I am so glad I've caught you at your leisure, my lord. We have much to discuss."

"I'll just be leaving," Miss Beauvais murmured, rising unassisted.

"Please stay," John muttered. "He's timed this invasion for when the children will soon be underfoot, and for that alone, I might do him an injury."

The lady sat back down.

CHAPTER TWO

Lord John looked familiar to Ada, though perhaps because he had the open, genial countenance of every country curate she'd ever met. Goodness beamed forth from him, but like the sun's brilliance, Ada found his virtue uncomfortable to behold directly.

People that open-hearted were all but demanding to be taught hard lessons in betrayal and disappointment.

Then the portly fellow had come through the garden gate, and any trace of the friendly headmaster vanished. In his place stood a tall, determined man ready to hurl righteous thunderbolts from parapets of personal indignation.

"Mr. Hewitt." Lord John stopped on the path and barely inclined his head. "Your timing is inopportune. Not only are the children about to have their afternoon sunshine, you find me in company with another caller. The lady has the prior claim on my attention, and you will have to make an appointment for another day."

"Not another day. Today." Hewitt hooked his thumbs into the waistband of his breeches. "I have been more than patient with you, my lord. I've written to you and left my card and written to you again.

Your rent is three months past due, the coal man says he'll extend you no more credit, and I have it on good authority that—"

"Hewitt, you will not spout your grievances with me here in the open air, like a fishmonger berating his competition."

Had Ada not heard with her own ears the frigid tone Lord John had adopted, she would not have believed him capable of such banked fury.

"Here is as good as anywhere," Hewitt said, widening his stance. "All of London knows you couldn't make a go of vicaring despite having a nob for a papa. Now you exploit these poor waifs, pretending to provide for them when the money goes heaven knows where, for heaven knows what. I've half a mind to set a parliamentary commission on you."

Ada knew that sneering tone, knew when an insult was intended to land with maximum injury to the victim's dignity. She came up on Lord John's right.

"Your manners are disgraceful, Mr. Hewitt. Lord John kindly gave me a few moments of his time, and now you have interrupted. You hurl nasty threats in public, when any civilized man would never have this conversation anywhere but behind a closed door. Be off with you."

She shooed him and he took a step back.

"And who, may I ask, are you, madam?"

"You may not ask," Ada said. "We have not been introduced, and I am a lady. Have the grace to slink back into the alley from whence you slithered. Your business will keep until another day."

Though his kind seldom waited an entire day to strike again. They delighted in destruction and nobody ever seemed to hold them to account.

Two small girls had come out of the building and stood holding hands further up the walk. What struck Ada about the girls was the contrast between them. One was taller, with round, rosy cheeks, a bold stare, and confident posture. The other was small, deathly pale, her gaze riveted on the walkway. Her little cheeks were gaunt, and if she had any confidence, the mildest breeze would waft it into the countryside.

"Please leave, Hewitt," Lord John said. "I never discuss business in front of the children. They've faced horrors enough in their short lives without you threatening to toss them into the streets."

Hewitt drew himself up, putting Ada in mind of a hot air balloon filling with gas.

"I would *never* be so unchristian," Hewitt retorted. "They'll go to the parish, where the proper authorities will oversee their care and education. No more of this larking about in the sun, wasting time, and cavorting the afternoon away. No more sparing the rod where these little—"

Ada marched up to him. "Go frighten some other unfortunate children, kick your hapless dog, or berate your servants, for that's how shriveled souls like you feel important. These children are not yours to bully."

Hewitt took another step back. "Who did you say you were?"

"You'll find me in Debrett's along with a large, distinguished family—just like his lordship here. They will be very interested to know what variety of charity you espouse, Mr. Hewitt, and what a sad reflection you are on your upbringing. Now, begone."

Hewitt looked like he wanted to say more.

"If you do not quit these premises now, Hewitt," Lord John said, "I will treat you to language unfit for a lady's ears. You may call upon me Wednesday morning at ten of the clock, and we will discuss any arrearages you care to mention."

Hewitt jerked down his waistcoat, an ugly yellow affair with buttons straining at their buttonholes. "You may be sure I will be punctual."

"Delighted to hear that you can tell time in addition to frightening children," Ada said. "The gate is that direction."

He huffed away just as a stream of children gushed forth from the building.

When Lord John turned to greet the noisy horde, he was smiling again. "Children, good afternoon! Grant me a few minutes peace with my caller and I'll be right with you."

The taller girl pounded down the steps, leaving her smaller companion and joining the throng tearing and shrieking across the garden. The little girl simply stood abandoned, staring at the ground.

Nobody came over to her, nobody noticed her all alone off by herself.

"Who is she?" Ada asked.

"That is my dear Cora," Lord John replied, his tone suggesting the child was dearly exasperating. "She's new, and progress is often slow at first. Children like Cora have to learn how to play."

"She doesn't *know how* to play?" The scientist in Ada tried to fathom such a concept and could not. "How can a child lack a grasp of play?"

Lord John offered his arm, and Ada took it automatically. She had male cousins, and such courtesies were second nature with them.

"We take play for granted," he said, "thinking our proper childhoods bleak and miserable because our recreation was limited by hours of instruction. Cora probably never saw a doll before she arrived here. I can tell you for a certainty that she had to be shown how to hold a pencil and what it was for. Hide and seek makes no sense to her, because hiding and remaining absolutely still and silent are necessary skills in her view, not part of a game for whiling away an afternoon."

"And Hewitt spewed his venom where that little girl could hear every word?"

They'd reached the bench but Ada was in no mood to sit.

"He chooses his moments like a thespian. The children will be on an outing next Wednesday with their instructors. None of them will see Hewitt calling on me."

Ada paced away from the bench.

She paced back.

She paced away, though there was no out-distancing the folly she was about to commit. "I cannot abide a bully, my lord. I cannot—I *loathe* bullies of every stripe. No more contemptible vermin has crawled out of the Pit since Lucifer took up residence in his feculent lair."

His lordship remained by the bench, far calmer than he should have been while Ada was battling old wounds.

"Bullies should be held in universal disregard," he said. "We are agreed, but rent should also be paid. Thanks to you, I can address the arrearages on Wednesday."

"But what of the coal man?" Ada asked, gaze on the solitary child at the top of the steps. "What of the chandler, the butcher, and the mercer?"

"They can all be given some coin for the present," Lord John said, "and I am hopeful, with Polite Society gathered for the Season, that others like yourself will be charitably disposed toward us."

"Hope never lit a candle," Ada muttered. "Hope does not add beef to the soup. Hope... oh, what's the use. I must try to raise St. Jerome's some money, my lord. I must at least try."

Lord John's smile was not the benediction of a godly man engaged in good works, but rather, the smile of a handsome fellow intent on excellent mischief.

"I was hoping you'd say that, Miss Beauvais. I was very much hoping you'd say that. Come, I'll introduce you to Cora and she can show you around our garden."

"That won't be necessary," Ada said, "and I can see myself out. If we're to mount a forlorn hope besieging the charitable impulses of better society, I need to do some research. I can return tomorrow afternoon, if that is convenient."

"Come back anytime," Lord John said. "A call from you will always be convenient."

"Headmaster!" cried a high voice. "You have to help us choose teams!"

"You're needed," Ada said, dipping a curtsey. "Until tomorrow, my lord."

He tossed her a bow. "Until tomorrow, and make no mistake, Miss Ada. You are needed too, and very much appreciated."

Ada stalked off, for nonsense such as that merited no reply. She went back through the doors that led to the corridor rather than pass the solemn little girl standing sentinel on the steps.

"BUT AUNT KITTY," Ada said, "I am to call upon *people*—people who move in polite circles. I haven't any notion, not the slightest, least, scintilla of a hint of a notion, how to go about such a task."

"Well, that is most odd," Aunt Kitty replied. "I distinctly recall taking you with me when I paid a call on Lady Haysmith just last year." She turned a limpid gaze on Ada, all innocence and charm, as usual. Kitty was only ten years Ada's senior, but worlds more sophisticated when it came to social subtleties.

"I spilled tea all over myself." Ada could still feel the heat scalding her through her sleeve and the mortification of having ruined yet another walking dress.

Aunt's embroidery needle moved in a steady rhythm, unlike the beat of Ada's heart.

"The dog bumped your arm, dearest, which is why no social call should involve canines. You can't take one isolated incident—"

"I tripped on the carpet and fell flat on my face when we called on Mrs. Dagenhart," Ada went on, finishing her fifth circuit of Aunt's private parlor. "At Lady Morehouse's soiree, or whatever it was, I caused a footman to upend a whole tray of glasses."

"His fault, darling. It's always the footman's fault. Anybody who says otherwise is simply mistaken."

Loyalty was one thing, but Aunt's recollection went beyond fanciful.

"At Sir Bolton Chiswick's dinner," Ada said, "I got into an argument with Lady Ffyle. Had you not intervened, her ladyship and I would have met over pistols at dawn."

Aunt's needle moved in the same serene rhythm. "And had you done her an injury, every hostess in London would have cheered your success. You know how to pay social calls, Ada. If that expensive finishing school taught you nothing else, you do know how to serve tea, swill tea, and discuss tea."

Ada came to a halt before the pier glass positioned between two sets of French doors. Everything about Aunt's abode was light and elegant, the exact opposite of the comfy clutter Ada preferred. And yet, Aunt Kitty was her favorite relation, half doting older sister, half fairy godmother.

"I look a fright," Ada murmured. "It's a wonder the children didn't run from me."

"Which children would that be?"

"At St. Jerome's. I visited there before agreeing to take on this challenge." Now that Aunt had mentioned tea, Ada was hungry. "Do you suppose we might ring for a tray?"

"Two tugs on the bell pull. Tell me about the children."

Aunt Kitty made spinsterhood a pretty business full of delicious secrets and private freedoms. On her, the unmarried state was defined not by the lack of a husband, but by the presence of endless possibilities.

Ada tugged the bell pull twice. "The children are noisy."

"Happy children generally are."

"I wasn't noisy as a child."

Kitty held up her needlework, an elaborate pastiche of flowers and leaves that brought to mind exotic jungles and rare birds. "You were also unhappy. Are you happy now?"

What had that to do with raising a king's ransom in thirty days? "I am content, or I was before Mr. Carruthers involved me in this demented scheme."

Aunt tucked her embroidery into her work basket, and even her work basket was a cunning little wicker confection with silk roses braided into the handle. "The name is familiar. He's one of my solicitors, I believe."

Half the men of business in London handled some part of the family's vast financial holdings.

"Mr. Carruthers explained the challenge to me," Ada said. "If I raise the money for St. Jerome's, then I shall have a manor house of my own."

Kitty rose, ever graceful. "And if you fail?"

"*When* I fail, I'll return to my experiments and my books. I'll catch up on all my correspondence, I'll…"

The tea tray arrived, sparing Ada from more babbling. After she'd wasted thirty days trying to raise funds for the orphanage, she'd resume her life. Not a bad life, compared to the inane years spent battling boredom at school, or a childhood that had consisted mostly of avoiding and enduring various governesses.

"Please do pour out," Aunt said, settling into a wing chair. "Other than noisy children, did St. Jerome's have anything to recommend it?"

"The architecture is lovely, though the appointments are old-fashioned. The children spend time in the garden on fine days, and they even take lessons out there when the weather obliges." Would that Ada's governesses had allowed her even a single hour twice a week to wander out of doors. At least fresh air had been among the offerings at school.

Ada passed Aunt Kitty her tea, then fixed a plate with a tea cake and a square of shortbread.

"And what of the staff at St. Jerome's?" Kitty asked. "What was their reaction when you proposed to raise money for this venerable institution?"

"I met with the headmaster, who assured me that St. Jerome's is in want of funds."

Kitty dipped her shortbread into her tea. "Headmasters can be such dreary people. I hope he wasn't prone to lecturing. You are the last person to placidly endure a lecture."

"Lord John doesn't lecture," Ada said, pouring her own tea. "He explains. He loves those children, and I do believe they love him."

They should love him, all but little Cora, who would love him in time.

Provided St. Jerome's could keep its doors open.

Kitty made eating shortbread a sybaritic delight. "Grandfatherly, is he, this Lord John?"

Not exactly. "Devoted to the children, well educated." *Overwhelmed and more than passingly attractive.* Not that his looks mattered.

"Does he present well? I mean, no odor of mildew about his wardrobe, no threadbare cuffs?"

"He presents very well," Ada replied. "His papa is a marquess, and Lord John comports himself like a gentleman."

"So why not take him with you on these social calls? He knows St. Jerome's better than anybody, he's probably danced with half the women you went to school with, and two heads are better than one."

"Whoever said that never spilled tea all over her new dress." Or fell on her face, tripped a footman, or provoked a near-shouting match at a formal dinner. Ada wasn't sure if making calls with Lord John was worse or better than making them on her own.

Probably worse.

Kitty set down her cup and saucer. "Ada, you have spent the past ten minutes pouring out for me, handling some of the finest china in Mayfair, making conversation all the while. You've spilled nothing. You've broken nothing. You didn't raise your voice, though I gather the whole business with St. Jerome's is rather vexing. Take this Lord John fellow with you on one call, and if it ends in disaster, then you needn't persist. Admit defeat and return to your weather studies or compost heaps or whatever has your fancy these days."

Such sound, sensible advice, as always. "This is why I came by, because you are always so reasonable. More tea?"

"Please." Kitty steered the conversation to what various cousins and neighbors were up to, and Ada paid attention as best she could. Compared to the prospect of importuning former schoolmates for money, Great-Aunt Helen's gouty toe was a less-than compelling topic.

"You'll see," Kitty said, as she walked Ada to the door thirty minutes later. "Some polite conversation, a few hints, an earnest fellow by your side, and St. Jerome's will soon have a full exchequer. Then I will be calling upon you at your country estate."

She offered Ada the same confiding, *we-know-interesting-things* smile that had been so fortifying when Ada had been banished to boarding school, and only Kitty had ever come to visit her.

The smile wasn't as magical now. Ada took her leave, still pre-occupied with the who and the how of these social calls she was supposed to make on behalf of the orphanage. Kitty made asking former acquaintances for money sound so easy, but in this, dear Aunt Kitty was wrong.

Parading around Mayfair in hopes of raising funds for needy chil-dren would be even more difficult than getting back on one's feet after sprawling face-first before half the gossips in Mayfair. Ada had risen, dusted her skirts, and joined in the general laughter, though her knees had smarted for weeks.

And yet, Ada would try. She'd given her word, the children were a worthy cause, and if by some chance she ended up with a home of her own, that would indeed be a wish come true.

"I'VE MADE A LIST," Miss Beauvais said. "These are women I went to school with, and I would not be mortified to call on them."

John unfolded the piece of paper she passed across the table in his office. "Six names? You went to school with only six other ladies?" The curriculum must not have focused on penmanship, for Miss Beavais's hand was as bold and plain as any tradesman's.

She jammed the ever-drooping lock of hair back into her bun. "I went to school at Henderson's Select Academy, not the most exclusive establishment of its kind, but among the better ones. We did more than parrot French idioms and mince about with books on our heads. Those are the six women I am willing to pay a call on."

Six names, even if all were moved to charity, would not come anywhere near the sum Miss Beauvais had been challenged to raise.

"You have a countess on this list. I think I know her." Lady Barstow had been Miss Elspeth Morrison, making her bow as John had completed his theological studies. "She's quite shy."

"She will receive me."

John had consulted his tattered copy of Debrett's, and found that Adelicia Beauvais claimed a close connection to a ducal family. She was sufficiently well placed in society that nearly any household in Mayfair should graciously welcome her.

"Miss Beauvais, is there something I should know regarding the social circles you travel in?"

She searched in her reticule, a voluminous sack sporting cobbler's last for its drawstrings. "My social circle is quite small. One might even say tiny."

"Tiny?"

"Miniscule." More searching. "Microscopic, vanishingly small. I don't go out much. Socially, that is. I attend lectures, I have been to the theater once or twice, and I do enjoy a good Shakespearean tragedy, provided the villains aren't overdone."

She set a pencil and a folded piece of paper on the table. "I have cousins, but I am loath to ask them for money. I thought perhaps you might have some suggestions." She sent him a hopeful glance then jerked the ties on her reticule closed and took up the pencil and paper. "I'm prepared to make a list for you."

"St. Jerome's has patrons, of course." At Yuletide, those patrons sometimes sent along a few pounds or a basket of comestibles. "We managed adequately until last year, when one of our most generous benefactors went to his reward. He left us a sizeable bequest, but the family is contesting it."

Then too, John's own means had gone toward keeping St.

Jerome's doors open, and the inheritance he'd received upon his majority was all but gone.

Miss Beauvais rose and studied the shelves along the office's inside wall. "Contested—because that family begrudges children a safe place to sleep or bowl of warm porridge on a winter morning, children who have lost even the comfort of a family to shiver away the winter with. If Chancery is involved, you will never see that money."

John's father had said the same thing, more than once, and not unkindly. "Hence, the need for additional funds."

"You have Lind's treatise on the prevention of scurvy."

She made it sound as if John had a treasure map lurking among his books. "Do you have cards, Miss Beauvais. Calling cards?"

She faced away from him, her nose buried in Lind's experiments. "I suppose I do."

"One can't call on a countess without leaving a card, miss."

"Scurvy is a terrible illness."

John walked up beside her, extracted the monograph from her hands, and reshelved it. "Might we save the medical discussion for later, when we've addressed St. Jerome's financial hemorrhaging?"

She smelled good. Grassy with a hint of lemons. Standing this close to her, John realized that she was really quite petite.

And nicely shaped.

"I'm not precisely afraid to make these calls," she said, "but I have to confess that the prospect of socializing makes me a bit uneasy."

She was related to a duke. Social calls should be as simple for her as rattling off the Ten Commandments was for him.

"A bit uneasy, Miss Beauvais?"

"Nervous, might be more accurate."

The lady seemed uncertain, self-conscious, *shy*. "Why would you be nervous? You are gently bred, articulate, well educated, and well motivated. St. Jerome's is a deserving cause, and those who have been generously blessed have an affirmative—"

She put gentle, ink-stained fingers against his lips. "I'm the problem, my lord. I have a talent—a genius—for social bungling. I gave up trying to fit in well before my come out, and life has been much more peaceful for all as a result."

She'd given up? What force of nature, what act of God, could have inspired Miss Adelicia Beauvais to *give up*? Peering down into slate-blue eyes, John saw banked misery and something else—longing? Loneliness? He could not be sure, though it hurt his heart for her sake.

"You didn't think I'd expect you to make these calls on your own, did you?" John asked.

He'd expected exactly that. The children kept him busy from dawn to midnight, and entire afternoons spent taking tea and making small talk were not on his schedule.

"You'd come with me?" Miss Beauvais asked, surveying the books arranged in author-order on his shelves.

"Would you like to have my escort?"

"One doesn't want to impose, but two heads are better than one, and you present quite well. I, by contrast, generally look like I've been dragged backward through a bramble patch in a high wind."

He turned her gently by the shoulders. Good sturdy shoulders, but delicate too. "Are you quoting somebody?"

She stared at his cravat. "My favorite aunt."

That's how her *favorite aunt* described her? "My father calls me hopelessly idealistic and a waste of good tailoring."

Miss Beauvais patted his cravat. "You are a very fine use of good tailoring, in my opinion. Will you pay these calls with me, my lord? I never know what to say, I spill my tea, I trip and stumble and bring up the wrong topics. I talk about compost, which one is not supposed to mention, and I neglect to remark upon the weather, which one is supposed to do, and... I am babbling."

She was anxious about simple socializing. "Nobody likes asking for money, but many people take pleasure in supporting a worthy cause. To bestow an appreciated kindness feels good, and I believe we are meant to be kind to one another."

Miss Beauvais studied him for a curiously long time. "I wish you were right about that. Upon whom do we call first?"

"Lady Barstow," John said. "My sisters consider her a friend, and she's sweet-natured, but Miss Beauvais?"

"You'll come with me? Truly? You won't make me do this alone?"

She beamed at him with such feminine benevolence, such... such warm-heartedness, John nearly lost his train of thought.

"An unmarried lady typically does have an escort, and it would be my pleasure to serve you in that capacity. There is one thing, however."

"No, there is not. There is nothing except my immense relief to know you will be at my side. I've never had to ask anybody for money, you see. If I can't be self-sufficient, I simply do without. Life is easier, and nobody is bothered with my importuning."

She was still smiling, even as she recited circumstances no well-born lady should be familiar with.

"Perhaps that explains the difficulty," John said, "because surely straitened circumstances have played a hand in your wardrobe selection."

Miss Beauvais's smile dimmed, then flickered, then winked out. "I am decently covered."

She was trying for a brisk statement of fact, but John heard the defensiveness lurking in her words.

"You are not dressed to receive callers, much less make calls, not as you deserve to be. I have sisters, and if you have no other plans for the rest of the afternoon, I'd like to introduce you to them."

Miss Beauvais bowed her head. "They will fuss at me. They will say I am too short, and too stout, and my hair is mousy, and I need to smile." She grimaced at him, putting straight white teeth on display. "I am altogether hopeless."

John fell in love. He was well acquainted with the sensation because it visited him regularly. He fell in love with the sound of a small boy puzzling out new words for the first time, with a fresh pot of tea first thing in the morning, with the laughter of rambunctious children charging into the garden to play knights, Valkyries, buccaneers, and castaways.

This time, he fell in love with the vulnerability and hope in Miss Beauvais's eyes, and with the fact that she was trusting *him*—the marquess's despair, unfit for the church, behind in his rent, *him*—to aid her to achieve her objective.

"Nothing is hopeless," he said, "and my sisters will say you are intelligent, comely, and possessed of a fine feminine figure."

"They'd lie to you?"

He took her by the hand. "Somebody has been lying to you. Come along, Miss Beauvais. Time is of the essence, and the fate of St. Jerome's might well rest on your selection of new bonnets."

CHAPTER THREE

Ada moved carefully to the mirror to survey the damage wrought by two hours closeted with Lord John's sisters. New stays, petticoats, underskirts, and lace were an unfamiliar hindrance to her movements, far more confining than the worn versions of the same items she usually donned.

"I rustle when I move," she said, scowling at the frothy image in the mirror. "I *swish* when I walk. My clothing never ceases whispering unless I remain as still as a statue."

Lord John's sisters were much like him: Tall, confident, and cheerfully determined. The eldest, Lady Thalia, stood smiling behind Ada.

"Your attire whispers of elegance and ladylike self-possession."

The middle sister, Lady Clio, joined them at the mirror. "Your outfit also whispers of money. Money begets money, Papa says, and he ought to know."

"We must do something about your shoes," said the third sister, Lady Polyhymnia.

"Polly is right," Lady Thalia said. "You can't attire yourself in the first stare of fashion, and then clomp about in jack boots."

Ada felt surrounded by titans, though Lord John's sisters had been named for Greek muses. "My boots add two inches to my height. I refuse to give them up."

An unreadable look was exchanged over Ada's head, reminding her that the ways of women had never made sense to her. At school, all the girls had known when to laugh and when to remain silent, while Ada had never learned those cues.

"Your petite stature is an asset," Lady Thalia said. "Your earnestness and intellect are more formidable for being housed in a delicate temple."

I am not a temple. Rather than make that retort, Ada considered her reflection. "I look... *female.*" Her figure was in evidence, though more in a suggestion of curves and contours, rather than a cinched waist and up-thrust bust. The effect was womanly rather than girlish or flirtatious.

"You look feminine," Lady Polly said. "What if you wore heeled slippers?"

"You won't clomp," Lady Thalia added. "But you'll have an inch or so of added height, enough that none of your hems will have to be taken up, and you can be about your calls immediately."

A compromise. With these women, compromise was a battle tactic. Ada would surrender her beloved and comfortable half-boots, and a selection of slippers would be presented. Not a one of them would have even an inch of heel, but she'd concede, because one must wear something on one's feet, and half an inch of heel was better than nothing.

Then too, their ladyships asked so reasonably, so prettily. They seemed genuinely kind, not at all like the conniving minxes Ada had gone to school with.

"Very well," Ada said, "I will try slippers for a day. If they give me blisters, I get my boots back."

"Oh, of course," Lady Clio said. "One cannot waltz with blistered feet. Perish the notion. Let's show Johnnie your new frock."

Ada let the mention of waltzing pass, for these good women

could not know her dread of mincing around Almack's. She would leave the marquess's mansion with boxes of new frocks, or new-to-her frocks most of which were cast-offs of some Waverly cousin or in-law. She would most assuredly not be waltzing.

She was propelled on a sea of smiles, muslin, and silk into the sitting room where she'd surrendered her reticule and her dignity. Lord John occupied a loveseat, rising when the ladies entered the room.

"And what," he asked, looking quite severe, "have you done with my dear Miss Beauvais? I yield her into your care, wait for days, and now you return without my friend." He bent as if to turn a quizzing glass on Ada. "Though who is this lovely creature? I vow I have never seen her before."

"Isn't Miss Ada magnificent?" Lady Thalia said. "Truly exquisite."

Ada let the cooing and fussing go on, because she was not sure who was jesting and who was in earnest. That familiar confusion was more than half the reason why taking Lord John along on these begging calls was prudent.

"We forgot the slippers!" Lady Polly said. "Johnnie, you must wait another eternity while we decide on slippers for this outfit."

He subsided onto the loveseat with a dramatic groan. "Not the slippers! Purgatory was invented by men waiting for their sisters to choose a pair of slippers."

Jesting, then. Ada was almost certain he was jesting.

"Dante left slipper-hell off of his list," Lady Clio said. "Even he quailed at the thought of describing such a chamber of terrors."

"You read Dante?" Ada asked.

Lady Clio left off fluffing Ada's hems. "Doesn't everybody?"

Ada understood that smile, understood it to be proof that she and Lady Clio shared membership in at least one exclusive club.

"All ladies of refined intellect enjoy the Divine Comedy," Ada replied.

"We must discuss it over tea," Lady Clio said, rising. "I've done some of my own translations and—"

Lady Polly fluttered back into the sitting room. "Let's try these first." She held up a pair of slippers that might as well have been a bouquet of flowers, so richly were they embroidered. "They have one-inch heels, and they are only slightly worn. You will not suffer blisters, though your ladylike toes, peeping from beneath your hems, will attract the best kind of notice."

"I did not hear that," Lord John murmured, looking vastly amused. "Selective hearing is the first duty of any loving brother."

The heels were three-quarters of an inch, probably the best Ada would do. "I will try them on. If they don't fit, I get my boots back."

"Now, Miss Ada," Lady Thalia chided—smilingly, of course. "We have others you should try on, and in fact you will need more than one pair of slippers if you are to be *au courant*."

I do not want to be au courant. I want to be home, measuring the heat of my compost heaps, trying to recall if I've had my luncheon.

Ada was about to make that announcement when Lord John caught her eye. His gaze held understanding, and a promise of some sort. *Tolerate this,* he silently asked, *because my sisters are trying to be helpful.*

He rose from the love seat. "Allow me."

"John, you are awful," Lady Polly said. "You make everything into a parlor play."

"Which is why the children love him," Lady Clio added, as John led Ada to the love seat.

"If you'd please be seated, miss?"

Ada had no idea what he was up to, but he was the most familiar element in this whirlwind of gracious commanders. Ada even remembered to smooth her skirts as she sank to the cushion, her hand in Lord John's.

He dropped to one knee before her, and before she could recoil in protest, he was unlacing her boots. He didn't precisely reach beneath her hems to perform that office, but Ada was more mortified than if he had.

"Please don't trouble yourself, my lord." *Please just let me disappear between the seat cushions.*

"Do you know how many shoes I lace and unlace in the course of a day?" he asked. "I teach an entire demonstration to the five-year-olds on how to tie shoes, because when a child is raised without footwear, that skill is a mystery." He set aside her first boot without even looking at it, a small mercy. "I can tie shoes faster and more tightly than any nanny, and untie them with one hand."

The second boot followed, and amid all the finery and porcelain of this airy parlor, Ada's comfy boots looked worn and homely. *Like me.*

"Johnnie taught us all how to tie our shoes," Lady Thalia said. "He is the best of big brothers."

"He showed us how to use a bow and arrow too," Lady Polly said, passing Lord John the flowery slippers. "And if you need a dance partner whose toes have been smashed by three sisters and four cousins, John is your man."

His lordship appeared embarrassed by this praise. Either that or, he was fascinated with the lacey ties on the ridiculous slippers.

"Left foot," he said, holding up a slipper.

Ada cautiously extended the requested appendage, and Lord John eased her foot into the slipper. The moment should have been awkward—the entire afternoon had been awkward—but instead Ada was put in mind of a children's tale, about a handsome prince who'd lost his dearest love and had only a glass slipper with which to find her.

To have a man kneeling before her, taking on the mundane business of assisting with her shoes was personal. Touching, humbling in a way.

"John also checked under our beds for dragons when we were too frightened to bother our nanny," Lady Clio said.

"Some of our nannies were quite formidable," Lady Thalia added, as Lord John tied the bow on the first slipper.

"Some of your nannies," Lord John muttered, "were worse than anything a child could imagine lurking beneath any bed. Other foot."

Ada complied, and felt as if she were not only allowing Lord John to assist her with her slippers, but also walking in those slippers for a few hours, surrounded by the caring and goodwill of his sisters. He'd grown up with these young women, loved by them and loving them. No wonder the children at St. Jerome's thrived in his care, for he'd seen that business about *love one another* first hand.

"I'm sure his lordship was the very best, bravest, and most noble of brothers," Ada said, as John tied the bow on the second slipper.

"I wouldn't go that far," Lady Clio said. "Though we weren't exactly exemplary sisters on a few occasions."

Lord John rose and extended a hand to Ada. "I will refrain from comment, because I am, as Miss Ada so perceptively notes, the best of brothers. Ladies, we thank you."

"I had a thought," Lady Clio said. "If your objective is to raise money for the orphanage, and Miss Ada is familiar with Dante's work, you really ought to call on Uncle Bascomb."

"He's wealthy," Lady Thalia noted, oh so casually.

"He and Papa don't get on," Lady Polly added, gaze on Ada's old boots. "He's quite the curmudgeon."

"Uncle Bascomb is an expert on hell," Lord John said. "He can discourse about the literary qualities of the Pit until you have the fullest flavor of the experience while sitting in his parlor. I offer this by way of warning, Miss Ada."

Lord John was not keen on visiting his uncle, clearly. Optimistic, cheerful, forthright Lord John, did not want to call on Uncle Bascomb.

"I deal well with curmudgeons," Ada said. "Let's add Uncle Bascomb to the list, my lord."

Lord John's gaze held no humor. "You're certain? He can be vexatious and spiteful. Polly is absolutely right that he and Papa don't get on."

Ah, so Lord John's entire family was not cut from the cloth of merriment and goodwill. "I'm quite certain," Ada said.

She was certain of something else: Lord John's touch on the silk stockings covering her feet, had felt in every way respectful, but not— she was *quite* sure of this—at all brotherly.

JOHN TOOK the coach's backward facing seat out of habit, also the better to behold Miss Beauvais on the opposite bench. His sisters had peeled away more than frumpy attire when they'd taken her wardrobe in hand the previous day.

Her gaze was still boldly direct. Her movements were still purposeful, and she still spoke either with authority or not at all— witness the silence in the coach—but something else had been revealed that eluded simple description.

Curves. Not the coltish immaturity of the newly fledged, but rather, a petite woman full of energy and intellect, and well blessed with feminine endowments, too.

"I should not have worn this bonnet," Miss Beauvais muttered. "I can accept all the noisy frills and whatnot, but millinery that restricts my very vision is inexcusable. Men are never subjected to such an impediment to their safety."

As bonnets went, her hat was fairly simple—a straw scoop with a few silk violets adorning the brim and blue ribbons tied in an off-center bow.

"The bonnet affords you privacy," John said. "It allows you to shield your expression from nearly anybody."

"My house affords me privacy. This,"—she waved a hand clad in a blue crocheted glove—"merely obstructs my vision."

The coach, a loan from John's sisters, slowed to take a corner.

"If it's any consolation," he said, "I dread our call on Uncle Bascomb. He and my father barely speak."

"Consider that a blessing, my lord. My esteemed uncle speaks only to ask when I'll marry and have a few babies, as if that dangerous prospect should loom as my dearest ambition."

"Perhaps he doesn't know what else to say? My own father has been known to put similar queries to my sisters."

That earned John a pensive perusal. Miss Beauvais wore a blue dress with a lavender spencer today. Her eyes looked less gray and more the color of forget-me-nots.

"That your family has a curmudgeonly Uncle Bascomb, and a papa who occasionally says the wrong thing is a relief," she observed. "I would have liked to have had sisters like yours, though. They were quite kind."

She turned to gaze out the window, which left John unable to see, much less decipher, her expression.

Time to change the topic. "Lady Barstow is a decent sort. She was a good choice for our first call. She might refuse to aid us, but she'll be gracious about it."

Miss Beauvais speared him with an expression far from sanguine. "We won't be refused. We'll be promised funds that are either never remitted, or are so modest as to afford little progress toward our goal."

John's father would have arrived at those conclusions. "Shall we give up then, Miss Beauvais? Shall we say my orphans aren't worth even a day's effort?"

The questions bordered on rude, but they had the curious effect of making Miss Beauvais smile. "I do not give up on a goal once I set it, sir. You are doomed to be dragged about Mayfair for the next month, and there's nothing you can say to it."

The coach came to a halt. John nearly informed his companion that a month of touring Mayfair's guest parlors with her would be no hardship at all, but Miss Beauvais had snatched up her reticule and her parasol and scooted to the edge of her seat.

"This is not a battle we're charging into," John said gently. "We're merely making a social call."

"There are battles," Miss Beauvais replied, "and battles." She pushed open the door as if she intended to storm Lady Barstow's citadel at a dead gallop, but a liveried footman stood in her way, his gloved hand extended.

She allowed him to assist her from the coach, and before she could march off, John climbed out and winged his arm at her.

"Nobody intent on victory rides into battle alone," he said.

Her chin rose, she took a firm grasp of his arm, and then John was rapping Lady Barstow's knocker against an imposing front door.

"I will trip," Miss Beauvais muttered. "I will trip and fall on my face."

"I will catch you."

Her grip on his arm tightened. "I will spill my tea."

"You needn't drink any."

"I will spill *your* tea."

"Do you know how many noisome substances have been spilled on my person? Never underestimate the impact a three-year-old can have on a man's laundry."

Ah, he'd made her smile, and that was fortunate, because the door opened at that moment, and a tall, white-haired fellow was ushering them into a soaring, oak-paneled foyer.

"My lord, miss." The butler bowed with the particular grace and gravity of one well suited to his lofty office. "If I might have your bonnet, miss? Her ladyship said to take you upstairs straight away."

Miss Beauvais untied her bonnet ribbons and grasped her millinery by the brim. She'd apparently forgotten the pin that secured her hat to her hair, because as she raised the hat, a lock of dark hair behind her left ear uncoiled from her chignon.

"Oh, drat the luck," she muttered, the hat held half-off.

"Allow me," John said, slipping the pin free of her hair.

She passed over the bonnet, and sent John an I-told-you-so glance that also hinted of misery.

"Hold still, miss." John removed his gloves and hooked a finger through the drooping curl, easing it free of the bun at her nape. "There. You are fashionable. Have a look."

He turned her to face the mirror, so she could admire the dark, silky locks that now rested fetchingly against her shoulder. Her hair was thick and fine, and the style John had effected suited her well.

"Very becoming," the butler said, "if I might say so. This way, or my lady will chastise me for making her guests tarry at the door."

He led them up the grand staircase, and by the time they reached the top, Miss Beauvais's grip on John's arm had become desperate.

The butler showed them to a parlor done up in shades of rose, green, and gold. The carpet alone would have brought a sum equal to St. Jerome's rental arrearages, and the silk on the walls would have paid the coal man for twice as long.

"Miss Beauvais." Her ladyship crossed the room, arms outstretched. "How wonderful to see you. How very, exceedingly wonderful." She enveloped Miss Ada in a hug, then burst into tears.

~

ADA DID NOT KNOW what to do when people hugged her. She generally held her breath, looked past the person into whose embrace she had stumbled, and silently counted in Latin, but Lady Barstow's grasp was too tight to allow those strategies.

"I should have written to you, I know," her ladyship said, finally stepping back. "You were all that made Henderson's Hell bearable, but I hadn't your direction once we left school, and you appeared so seldom in society. I assumed you were anxious to put the whole experience behind you, as I was. Lord John, you will think my wits have gone begging."

While Ada reminded herself to breathe, Lord John bowed over the countess's hand, as if sniffling women were of no moment.

"To reunite with old friends is a dear pleasure, isn't it?" he said. "Even if the memories shared aren't all that happy."

The countess drew Ada by the hand to a sofa done up in cabbage roses. "Henderson's wasn't awful, not for most people, but I am mortally shy. I dread public occasions, and don't even like to leave my house. Without Miss Beauvais, I might well have succumbed to the dramatics for which young women are infamous. Shall I ring for tea?"

"Tea would be lovely," Lord John said, just as Ada murmured, "We wouldn't want to trouble you."

Her ladyship overlooked this contradiction and beamed at Ada as if they were indeed, long-lost friends—and that made no sense whatsoever.

"Tell me more about Henderson's," Lord John said. "The school is in the Midlands, I take it?"

"Oxfordshire," Lady Barstow said, tugging a bell pull. "Just far enough away that my family could forget me. I was desperately lonely. I was the oldest girl in my family, and for the first year at Henderson's, I hadn't even a sibling to share the experience with. Then Miss Beauvais arrived, and all of that changed."

Ada felt increasingly as if she'd walked into a drama, but nobody had apprised her of the plot. "My lady, I confess I don't recall that we were more than cordial."

The countess patted her hand. "Nobody was great friends there. It took me years to see that. We were all managing as best we could, pretending happiness, friendship, and dutiful interest in our studies. You were the genuine article, however."

Lord John took a wingchair and looked on as if her ladyship's prattling was the most fascinating recitation ever to grace his ears.

"Genuine in what way?" Ada asked.

"You challenged the teachers who weren't in thorough command of their subjects. We went through three Latin instructors after your arrival, and no less than four French tutors. The maths professor didn't last a fortnight after you came, but the best part of all was that *you sat with me.*"

"I sat with you."

"At luncheon and at breakfast. We had assigned seats at dinner, but at other meals, at least half the time, you took the chair next to me. You'd start the conversation with some observation about pickled cabbage and scurvy, and then the other girls started chattering and changing the subject—that was your strategy: Say something to get the others gabbling. I never needed to say anything. It was marvelous."

Don't cry, my lady. If you cry about cabbage and catty females...

Her ladyship dabbed at her eyes with a silk handkerchief. "You will forgive me. My condition has made me a watering pot. I have thought of you so often, Miss Beauvais. You had such fortitude, and once you arrived, the nasty older girls turned their sights on you, but you never seemed to mind."

I minded. Ada thought back to the frogs put in her bed—poor fellows; the time she'd woken up to find the last foot of her braid had been cut off; the mud smeared inside her shoes when Aunt Kitty had sent her a new pair of white silk stockings.

"Bullies thrive on knowing their prey is intimidated," Ada said. "Are you well, my lady?"

The countess put a hand over her middle. "I am in excellent health, but his lordship and I are anticipating a miraculous event."

She blushed as she poured the tea, she grew weepy again as she served the cakes, she blotted her tears as she sipped from delicate porcelain and inquired regarding John's sisters.

"We are actually here on behalf of his lordship's young charges," Ada said, lest the conversation degenerate into a recitation of John's sisters'—the Muses' in his parlance—endless social schedule. "St. Jerome's is in need of friends, my lady, and you came to my mind."

John's genial expression faltered, but he certainly hadn't done anything to steer the conversation in a productive direction.

"Friends?" the countess inquired.

"Friends with means," Ada clarified. "You and I received a proper education at Henderson's, despite all that other nonsense. Lord John has dedicated himself to St. Jerome's, where children who have no other hope of a decent upbringing can thrive. They have nobody to sit with them, my lady, nobody to read to them, nobody to care for them, save Lord John and his staff. I am moved by their plight, and I hope you will be too."

Her ladyship set down her teacup. She turned the handle of the teapot. She folded her handkerchief into perfect quarters.

"Will you ask Emily Deevers to contribute?"

Emily Deevers had been the leader of the meanest group of girls. Her father had no title, but she had made up in arrogance what she lacked in social standing. She'd been very pretty, and the headmistress had doted on her.

"I will call upon Emily tomorrow if it will inspire you to generosity today."

Lord John all but stared at Ada, then took a hasty sip of his tea.

"I can put Emily to shame in this," the countess said. "Not very Christian of me, but then, Emily terrorized any who were weaker than she. You tell her I've given you goodly sum—one hundred pounds should do—and she will know the mortification of being bested at last. Her family's fortunes have declined since we left school, and she's had no offers of marriage for the past two years."

One hundred pounds? *One hundred pounds?* Ada's heart sped up simply to hear the sum spoken of aloud.

"That is exceedingly generous of you, my lady," Lord John said. "When shall we expect your bank draft?"

"His lordship will send it over within the week. He expects me to handle the charitable disbursements, though he did not explain to me exactly how I was to go about that."

One hundred pounds...? "Can you think of anybody else upon whom we might call?" Ada asked. "Your generosity is extraordinary, but St. Jerome's is a large institution, and many needs have gone unmet there in recent years."

"I will give it some thought," the countess said, "and I will impose on my husband to do likewise. What do you think of the name Elizabeth for a girl?"

Half the women in England were named Elizabeth. A more

insipid choice did not come to mind. Ada would have said as much, except that Lord John spoke first.

"Elizabeth is a marvelous name. Stately, feminine, regal, and yet it lends itself to affectionate nicknames. A fine choice, my lady. Might I have some more tea?"

~

JOHN'S AMBITIONS had been humble: Take Miss Beauvais around on a few calls and possibly raise some coin for St. Jerome's.

Don't get your hopes up. As he handed Miss Beauvais into the coach, his hopes weren't merely *up*, they were soaring thousands of feet above Mayfair. This gruff, unprepossessing woman had in a single day solved all of St. Jerome's pressing bills with a tidy sum left over.

"I cannot believe she did that," Miss Beauvais said. "I cannot believe, on the strength of a few girlhood trivialities, the countess committed a fortune to St. Jerome's."

"To have a champion is not a triviality," John said, rapping on the coach roof. "You were decent to a shy young woman when others weren't decent to you. Was Henderson's horrible?"

"We learned to manage," she said, drawing off her gloves. "That was probably the point, to provide us a place to practice the skills we'd need in the greater world."

How much heartache did those calm words hide? John had gone to public school, but he'd attended as a marquess's spare. He'd also been taller and stronger than most of the boys in his form, and he'd been academically competent without blundering into the sort of brilliance that made a boy an outcast.

"I will manage a great deal more easily at St. Jerome's if Lady Barstow produces that bank draft," John said. "You cannot imagine my relief."

"Do you ever worry that you'll fail?" Miss Beauvais asked. "Ever worry that the children will end up in the poorhouse, worse off for having known some comfort and security?"

"You ask the most fearless questions."

She was trying to tuck the errant lock of hair back into her chignon, but the curl wasn't obliging. John switched seats and stuffed his gloves in his pocket. "Let me, though I think the softer style suits you well." He twisted the coil snugly about his finger, then tucked it up at her nape. "Have you a spare hair pin?"

"What do you think?"

"If it comes down again, let it fly free. You have very pretty hair."

She scowled at him and pulled her gloves on. "Tell me about Uncle Bascomb."

That question wasn't so fearless, but John opted for an honest answer. "He is the embittered younger son, unfit for the military by virtue of physical limitations, unfit for the church due to moral short-comings. I have two illegitimate cousins that I know of, thanks to Uncle. He and Papa had grand rows about it when I was growing up."

"I like him already. Did he take responsibility for his children?"

"Of course, rather too openly. Papa wanted some discretion about the business. Uncle scoffed and told Papa that a man who ignores his own children isn't worth the name. I'd never heard anybody address the marquess so bluntly."

"And yet, you have made it your life's work to look after children other people have discarded."

Well.... Yes. John pondered that coincidence—surely it was coincidence—until he and Miss Beauvais were sitting in Uncle's cluttered, stuffy parlor. Uncle sat with his foot propped on a pillow, and he made no effort to rise when Miss Beauvais entered the room.

"So why are you here, young Johnnie?" Uncle asked. "You come around flashing a bit of muslin at your old uncle, and something must be afoot. Are you in trouble, young lady?"

Oh, ye leaping imps, he was getting worse.

"Not in the sense you mean," Miss Beauvais replied. "But I do know a number of young ladies who could use some assistance."

"The Waverlys are a lusty bunch," Uncle said. "Sit down, the pair of you. Am I to be a great uncle, Johnnie?"

"That happy adventure is not to befall you yet," John said. "Miss Beauvais refers to my charges at St. Jerome's."

Uncle snorted. "I have a bet going with your Aunt Selma. She says the doors to that place will close by Christmas. I say she's wrong."

Selma was a maternal aunt, and not a warm woman.

"You will win," Miss Beauvais said. "Though you might consider hedging your bet."

Bushy eyebrows rose. "Speak plainly, miss."

"St. Jerome's needs help," she said. "You are in a position to assist. If a doting uncle doesn't support his nephew's good works, why should anybody else?"

Bascomb glowered at his propped foot. "My damned brother refuses to help, is that it? I vow he's the most stubborn, irascible, ungrateful wretch ever to sit in the Lords, and that is saying a very great deal. He will be furious if I donate to your cause."

Miss Beauvais glanced around the room, at paintings dark with age, a carpet in need of beating. "Isn't that just a shame? I am furious when children freeze to death on London's streets each winter. Your art collection is fascinating, though you are missing the second circle of hell."

"Perceptive chit, ain't you? My favorite is the eighth circle, with its special accommodations for fraudulent politicians. As for the second circle, I have yet to find an image of lust that does justice to the pleasures afforded by the transgression."

For Uncle, that was put delicately, though once started on his favorite subject, he could not be dissuaded.

Miss Beauvais rose to re-arrange the pillow beneath Uncle's foot. "You should elevate your leg if the issue is inflammation."

"The issue is I got stepped on by a bedamned horse when I was fourteen years old. Had to spend a year on my arse, though thanks to a decent tutor, I put that year to good academic use."

A year in purgatory? "I wasn't aware of the origins of your injury," John said.

"It's not an injury, pup. It's a mishap. Fifty years on, and your father still refers to a serious maiming as a mishap because it was his damned horse that got loose."

John hadn't heard that part either. "A groom lost control of the horse?" His mother referred in passing to "poor Bascomb's riding accident," though never in Papa's hearing.

Uncle regarded the painting that depicted endless combat on the surface of the River Styx. The perpetually angry souls made up the fifth circle of hell, and their fate was eternal discord.

"His Almighty Lordship let the beast go," Bascomb said. "He had no idea I was about to walk through the stable door and be trampled, but he'd neglected to wear gloves, you see. As he attempted to wrestle the horse into submission, the leather reins scored the flesh from his palms. The whole situation was damned lamentable."

Fifty years on, that was still true. Uncle's language was lamentable too.

Miss Beavais sat back down. "Is there a circle of hell for those tormented by regret?"

Uncle's smile was for once devoid of bitterness. "I suppose that circle would be life, but we can't judge the marquess too harshly for wanting to see St. Jerome's fail."

"*Whyever not?*" John's question was rife with honest anger. "If St. Jerome's fails, then I fail, which matters not at all, but forty children will be left to the dubious generosity of the parish, where they will doubtless fall prey to consumption or worse."

Ada's lock of hair had come loose again. John focused on that, on the silky, shiny coil, on the memory of its warmth against his fingers. He'd never quite admitted that his own father wanted him to fail, and the pain of that betrayal cut deeply.

Bascomb twitched at his lap robe. Of all the room's appointments, that one item was pristine, with a border of embroidered laurel leaves and strawberries.

"Your Uncle Simon died of consumption," Bascomb said. "He and Pompeii were thick as thieves, while I was the extra spare who came along eight years later. When Simon died, he took a part of Pompeii with him. A year later, I'd been brought to bed with my injury, and two years after that, our dear Mama succumbed to pleurisy. Pompeii has a mortal fear of lung ailments, and you cannot blame him for that, boy."

And yet, John's father enjoyed robust good health. "I'd always been told Uncle Simon had weak lungs." A portrait of a smiling young man with overly-rosy cheeks was John's sole association with an uncle he'd never met.

"He did have weak lungs," Uncle Bascomb said. "Very weak. He was a good lad, though. Kind-hearted, like you. I'm sure Pompeii fears to lose you to a similar affliction. You're not much older than Simon was when he succumbed. Miss Beauvais, would you please ring for tea? The scalawags passing for servants in this house must be roused from their dicing if a man isn't to starve."

Miss Beavais obliged, while Uncle quizzed John about each sibling and the marchioness. When Uncle's conversation drifted toward grousing, Miss Beauvais diverted him with questions about his art, until the tea pot was empty and the afternoon shadows long.

"Young Johnnie, you have brightened my day, as have you, Miss Beauvais. Forgive me if I do not see you out, but do come around again. Perhaps I'll have found my portrait of lust when next you call."

Naughty old scamp. "Or perhaps you will have found some manners," John said, offering his hand. "Shall I give your regards to the family?" *And what about St. Jerome's?*

"You shall do no such thing," Uncle said, sitting up on his chair. "If Pompeii wants to know how his only surviving brother goes on, he can damned well take an afternoon away from his infernal committees and drop by for a brandy. You may give my love to your sisters and your mama, but his perishing lordship... Tell him I gave you two hundred pounds for your brats. He'll come around to harangue me about my meddling, which is a sure tonic for my every ailment. Somebody needs to sound the hue and cry on Lord Pomposity from time to time, and you lot are too timid to do it."

Lord Pomposity? This visit was just full of revelations.

"When I return," Miss Beauvais said, "we can argue about anything you please. I love a rousing disagreement and I respect a generous and forgiving nature."

"Uncle, I do believe the lady is in earnest." Which had the old fellow looking downright merry. "Thank you very much for your support, and we'll see ourselves out."

Miss Beauvais was quiet through the sorting of wraps and gloves and parasols, then John was handing her into the coach.

"You needn't sit over there as if I'm some maiden auntie," she said. "What an interesting family you have, my lord. Whatever became of your uncle's paramour?"

"She is his housekeeper." John switched seats, because sitting in the backward facing direction after tea and sandwiches was uncomfortable.

"Why did they never marry?"

"Possibly had a husband somewhere once upon a time. More likely, she was simply beneath Uncle's station. I'm not sure."

"They should marry," Miss Beauvais said. "And Lord Pomposity should be your uncle's best man."

She smiled, then she snickered, then she laughed outright until John went off into whoops with her, and the coach was filled with their mirth.

CHAPTER FOUR

Emily Deevers had put on weight. Ada beheld this development with a curious disappointment. One wanted adversaries to be worthy, to be formidable and in need of vanquishing.

Not downcast and self-conscious. In the week since beginning her quest, Ada had faced the imperious, the indifferent, and the indecisive—also more than a few who were generous—but nobody she'd called on had been less than confident to receive guests.

Clearly, Emily Deevers was no longer the most popular girl in any class.

"Miss Beauvais, a pleasure." Miss Deevers curtseyed. "And Lord John. I haven't seen you this age, sir. How are your sisters?"

She hadn't seen Ada in at least four ages, but the lady's entire focus was on his lordship. For him, she had a smile that hinted of her former vivaciousness, and for him she had endless questions regarding the Muses.

For Ada she had sidelong glances that varied from anxious to sheepish. The inevitable tray arrived, plain blue porcelain, a single dish of shortbread to accompany the teapot. On close inspection, the guest parlor was going a bit shabby around the edges. A water stain marred the low table, a reading chair sat before the fire at an awkward angle, probably to hide a defect in the carpet.

The candlesticks were brass rather than marble or crystal, and the curio cabinet held barely three items per shelf.

"Did you know that his lordship is the headmaster at St. Jerome's Hospital?" Ada asked, when the topic of Lady Polly's shoe collection had been exhausted.

"So kind of you, your lordship, to take an interest in the less fortunate. Would you care for more tea?"

John passed over his cup and saucer. "More tea would be delightful. My duties at St. Jerome's have afforded me so little opportunity for socializing, that I can't expect you to know how we go on there. I can tell you honestly, that nothing prepared me for the challenge of caring for forty rambunctious children."

Miss Deever's hand shook slightly as she poured him another steaming cup. "Forty rambunctious anythings would be a challenge, I dare say. Miss Beauvauis, more tea?"

The topic of a donation was not finding its way into the conversation, so endless had been Miss Deever's chatter. Ada wasn't sure it should.

"Half a cup," Ada said. "I am still prone to spilling, tripping, and starting arguments, you see."

Miss Deever set down the empty cup. "You didn't start arguments, you merely corrected those instructors who lacked a grasp of their subject matter. Miss Henderson herself said that. She said the quality of education at her academy had improved because of one stubborn girl. Shortbread?"

"One piece, please." *Miss Henderson had said what?*

"Miss Beauvais has a ferociously vigorous intellect," Lord John observed. "I'm getting up my nerve to ask her if she'd like to take on some duties at St. Jerome's."

Was he really? Or was this idle conversation intended to move the discussion sideways to the topic of a donation?

Miss Deever filled the cup half-full, while Ada mentally fumbled for something to say. "If you never ask for my assistance, my lord, you will never hear my reply."

"I might enjoy spending some time at St. Jerome's," Miss Deevers said, chin coming up. "As a charitable activity. Ladies do."

We don't want you, we want your money. That retort seemed like something Emily Deevers would have said to a much younger Ada Beauvais.

"When I was a child," Ada said, "one of few joys in my life was when my Aunt Kitty would visit. She'd read to me. Sometimes, we read the same story over and over, but when she brought me a new book, she eclipsed Father Christmas in my affections."

Mention of Aunt Kitty had Miss Deevers setting the cup and saucer down on the tray rather abruptly.

"Your aunt still hasn't married?" she asked. "Such an attractive woman, and one has to conclude she's well dowered."

The question held a hint of the catty schoolgirl, but also genuine bewilderment. "Lady Kitty has particular tastes," Ada said. "We still get on very well."

The moment begged for somebody—Lord John, say—to mention that St. Jerome's was not getting on well, but Miss Deevers sat forward, clearly intent on seizing the conversational reins.

"Do you recall when your aunt lost that letter you'd written to some dashing swain?" she asked. "I vow, I've never heard such impassioned prose before or since. I knew you excelled at maths and natural science, but I had no idea you were of such a literary bent. My lord, this letter was such a paean to manly virtue, that no mortal fellow could possibly have measured up."

John regarded Ada curiously. "And you wrote this missive? How did your personal correspondence become common knowledge among the other girls?"

"The tale is long and not worth repeating," Ada said. "Suffice it to say, the letter was never sent, and Miss Henderson forbade me to use the school's library for the rest of the quarter."

A terrible punishment at the time, but one Ada had borne proudly.

"Miss Beauvais spent her afternoons roaming the grounds instead," Miss Deevers said. "We were very concerned she'd develop freckles."

Oh, of course they had been. "Speaking of Henderson's," Ada said, "we called on Lady Barstow yesterday. She sends her regards."

Miss Deevers set two pieces of shortbread on her own plate. "I have heard she isn't much of one for socializing."

"She is quite retiring," John said, "but she received us graciously."

Miss Deevers crammed a piece of shortbread into her mouth.

"She wished to be remembered to you specifically," Ada added, which wasn't exactly a lie.

"Have you allowed *her* to read to your orphans?" Miss Deevers asked. "Of course you have. Why have a plain miss read to the children when a countess is on hand to lend her cachet?"

That was the Emily Deevers whom Ada had gone to school with—petulant, unkind, and self-centered.

Insecure, in other words. *To be pitied*.

"The children don't care who holds what station," Ada said. "They would be just as pleased to hear a story from you as from his lordship here."

"More pleased to hear one from you," Lord John added. "I'm forever reading to them and bleating on about penmanship and Cromwell and Ceylon. You would be quite the fresh face, miss, if you're really interested."

She set down her plate of sweets and looked around the shabby parlor as if the windows were barred and the door locked from the outside.

"We couldn't get vouchers for Almack's," she said. "Mama tried everything, but Papa isn't... he doesn't... We were *denied*. My parents spent all that money seeing me properly educated, and I have failed them utterly."

Such misery lay in that admission, such mortification. "I'm sorry,"

Ada said, meaning it. "I would have given anything to have been spared the ordeal of waltzing at Almack's. Their punch is truly awful."

Miss Deevers rose. "I have wondered if spinsterhood isn't to be my punishment for having been such a horrid girl."

Ada glowered at John: *Say something. Be charming. Do something,* but he had apparently developed a fascination with the pattern of faded irises on the carpet.

"I don't think Henderson's brought out the best in any of us," Ada said. "St. Jerome's is a very different sort of place."

Miss Deever considered them from across the room. "Different how?"

"St. Jerome's is loud," Lord John said. "If you came by on Thursday afternoon, you could join our local curate, Mr. Addison Palmer, when he reads to the children. The children are very good for him, so don't be deceived by their apparent docility. Turn them loose in a garden, and they are hooligans."

Miss Deever looked away. "Would they ever cut off a girl's hair in the middle of the night just because she'd taken a first in maths?"

Ada got to her feet. "*That's* why you cut off my braid? Because I like math?"

Miss Deever nodded, a tear trickling down her cheek. "I was awful. I'm sorry. I will never get a first in anything, and I think I knew that even then."

The moment should have been... triumphant? Vindicating? Gloating, even? But how sad, to be denied intellectual confidence, and have only spite to fall back on.

"My hair grows quickly," Ada said, "and I have never set much store by elaborate coiffures. Will you read to the children?"

Lord John was on his feet as well. "They are much better behaved when they know they will have a story later in the day. Please say you will come."

"I have no talent for dramatic reading," Ada said. "I suspect you excel at it."

Miss Deever wiped at her cheek with her fingers. "What time on Thursday?"

"Four of the clock," Lord John said, passing over a card. "Mr. Palmer is punctual, or we have rebellion in the schoolrooms."

"I can be punctual as well," Miss Deever said. "My thanks to you both for calling. Please do come again."

Not perishing likely. Except that clearly, Miss Deevers was lonely. "You mentioned that Lady Barstow hardly ever goes out." Ada said. "She is something of a recluse, but she seemed very pleased to receive us. You might drop in on her, while you were out and about."

"You think she would receive me?"

If Ada wrote her ladyship a note explaining the circumstances, then she would.

"Of course she would," John said. "You and Miss Ada weren't the only ones struggling to find solid footing at Henderson's. Until Thursday, Miss Deever."

She saw them to the door, and they left her smiling, while Ada wasn't quite certain what to feel.

"She is not the gorgon I made her out to be," Ada said, as Lord John settled beside her on the forward-facing coach seat. "She is in truth a rather sorry young woman."

"While you were and are magnificent."

Ada took off her bonnet and set it on the opposite bench. "You have taken leave of your senses. We didn't get a penny from her, and I doubt she'll show up on Thursday, meaning the children will be disappointed."

"Mr. Palmer will keep his appointment, and he's a prodigiously jolly fellow. His father is an earl, and Palmer has a true vocation. He and I knew each other at school."

"He's an honorable?"

Lord John's expression was utterly solemn. "Also an eligible, who has no use for waltzing at Almack's."

"Then I suppose," Ada said, "that I must concede that you were magnificent too, my lord."

They shared a smile. Lord John patted her hand, and then the coach lurched forward, the horses trotting on to the next call of the day.

~

THE TIME SPENT with Miss Deevers didn't appear to have unsettled Miss Beauvais, but it had certainly left John with much to ponder.

"Was Henderson's really so awful?" he asked when he and Miss Beauvais resumed their calls three days later. Their next call was likely to be awful.

"I have no basis for a comparison," Miss Beauvais said. "I attended only Henderson's, as my mother did. She is not afflicted with a *ferociously vigorous intellect*, and thus her experience was different from mine."

He'd meant those words as a sincere and high compliment. "Perhaps your mother does have a vigorous intellect, but she lacked the courage to display it. My mother would never put herself forward as any sort of genius, but she generally reads three books at once. She instilled a love of learning in all of her children, and Papa respects her command of all things literary."

"Tell me about Mrs. MacHeath," Miss Beauvais said. "Will she donate?"

A smooth change of subject, that was *not*. "Mrs. MacHeath will be mortally offended if I call on the other patrons and leave her off my list, but I doubt she'll donate a farthing. We needn't stay long. Tell me about the dashing swain who moved your girlish heart to love letters."

What sort of man could inspire Ada Beauvais to an infatuation, much less a passionate correspondence? John was more interested in that conundrum than in how to pry a few groats from Mrs. MacHeath.

"He wasn't my swain," Miss Ada said, her smile wistful. "I agreed to post that letter for my Aunt Kitty, because she did not want the object of her affections to suspect her direction. The mail from Henderson's went through Oxford, a large enough town that she'd be guaranteed anonymity, and I was happy to do her the favor."

"Your aunt should not have imposed on you like that. You were a child, and she was... she involved you in her intrigues."

"I was sixteen, my lord. Women marry, become engaged, and have children at sixteen. Kitty is only ten years my senior, and I was pleased to do a kindness for her. She has certainly done many for me. Besides, I went from being the butt of jokes and pranks to a sophisticated level of notorious because of that letter, and I gained the freedom of the school grounds."

Now, John wished he was on the opposite bench, because Miss Ada Beauvais, for the first time in his experience, looked *pleased* with herself.

"You turned defeat into victory."

"Not defeat," she said, waving a hand. "Never that. I should have known the girls would rifle my reticule. They were forever snooping and snitching, which I now see as evidence of vast boredom. Mrs. Henderson should have had some of the braver Oxford scholars come read to us."

Was that a jest? A humorous aside?

"You bore your punishment without betraying your aunt," John said. "I admire family loyalty."

"I'm tempted to call on your father," Miss Beavais replied, her smile disappearing. "I understand that our families want us to be safe, my lord, but you are fully grown, the children at St. Jerome's are healthy, and your father's protectiveness shades very close to sabotage."

There was her ferociousness again. "Papa provided me an education and a more than decent upbringing. He owes me no more, if he even owed me that."

"If somebody offered to provide your orphans three meals each day and textbooks, would you consider all of their needs met?"

"Of course not. Children need love and affection, they need moral guidance and good examples. They need recreation and rest. They need friendships and a sense of security. They need much more than mere food and lectures."

An uneasy insight hovered at the edge of John's awareness: *He had needed more than lectures, primers, a safe place to sleep, and punctual meal times, and his father hadn't known how to provide much more than that.*

Still didn't.

"You asked about Mrs. MacHeath," John said. "She's a terror. She knows everything, she has yet to part with more than five pounds annually for St. Jerome's, and nothing we do for the children is up to her standards."

"Does she have children?"

"Not a one. Is that significant?"

"I don't know, but I suspect Mrs. MacHeath and I will get on quite well."

Nobody should get along well with Lorna MacHeath, but John could not afford to offend her. "If you can do that, you will be the first to accomplish it."

"We must seek out an area where her expertise is genuine," Miss Beauvais said. "Just as Miss Deevers can be of use by reading to the children, Mrs. MacHeath has something of value to offer us. We need only be clever enough to discern what it is."

"I applaud your strategy," John said, for it closely matched how he took on difficult children: Find what they excel at and start there. "I will applaud even more loudly if you can make it work."

Miss Beauvais pulled on her bonnet, sitting docilely while John arranged her hair over her shoulder. She was again smiling the pleased, self-satisfied smile that brought out all of her best features: Her forget-me-not eyes, her direct gaze, her pretty mouth, and her determined chin.

Good lord. When she wore that serene, confident expression, she wasn't simply pretty, she was quietly *stunning*.

ADA FOUND the décor in Mrs. MacHeath's house remarkable for its unrelenting masculinity. The art was all heroic and military. Blunderbusses, swords, and daggers adorned the walls. The furniture was heavy and dark, as were the volumes lining the bookshelves in the parlor.

A stuffed animal that resembled a small, furious bear glowered down from a corner of the room, its mouth open in a perpetual snarl.

"What on earth is that creature?" Ada asked. "It is the embodiment of all that is fierce." *Fierce and tormented.*

"That is a wolverine," Mrs. MacHeath replied. "The colonel shot it in lower Canada on his second campaign. I doubt there's another like it in all of England."

And thank the Deity for that.

"Such a creature would give me nightmares," Lord John said. "I was forever imagining dragons and the like in my wardrobe and under my bed as a child."

Mrs. MacHeath paused before taking a seat. "And do you allow such fanciful notions in your young charges, my lord? An overactive imagination is a sore trial for a child who must bend his attention to every scrap of learning he can find."

She was a stout, gray-haired lady whose attire would have made Quakers appear festive by comparison. Her bun looked lacquered into place, and the lace at her collar was blackwork.

For whom or what does she mourn? Her parlor looked like an estate office, with more weaponry on the walls, more heavy, dark furniture, and more martial art.

"It's about those young charges that we'd like to consult you," Ada said, taking a seat on a horsehair sofa. "St. Jerome's has come through the winter in need of all available support, you see."

Mrs. MacHeath settled into a large reading chair. "Please do sit down, your lordship, and explain to me how St. Jerome's comes to be at such a pass. Is it not your job to ensure adequate funds are on hand? Perhaps what's needed is sounder management. The colonel always said the regiment's success was more often in the hands of the quartermaster than the generals."

"Even a brilliant quartermaster cannot control the elements," Ada said. "Children need coal and candles, though if you're concerned that St. Jerome's is not well run, perhaps you could join us for a tour of the facilities? His lordship has never experienced the economies necessary on a military campaign, and you might have insights to share that could benefit the children and the exchequer."

Lord John was seized with a coughing fit.

"My lord, are you well?" Mrs. MacHeath asked.

"Just a tickle," he managed. "Springtime, you know."

"You should have a nip of rum. The colonel swore by a flask of rum for most ills, and he lived through many a difficult march."

The colonel, the colonel, the colonel. Perhaps Mrs. MacHeath's grief was like that wolverine. All teeth and tenacity. "How long since he went to his reward?" Ada asked.

Mrs. MacHeath sat up quite straight. "Eight years, four months, and three days. He died peacefully in his sleep, though he was taken much too soon. After all the bullets, the horses shot from beneath him, the dysentery and worse... he simply slipped away. I should be grateful, but my gratitude is bounded by sorrow."

Ada pulled off her gloves, for surely such a proper lady would soon be ringing for the infernal tea tray.

"I suppose that's why you have such concern for Lord John's charges," she said. "Like you, they have all known loss and hardship, and they struggle under a burden of grief, even in the midst of blessings."

"They do," Lord John said. "They've lost their homes and their families, and when our years are tender, so are our hearts."

Had Mrs. MacHeath ever had a tender heart for anybody but her colonel?

"I wonder what the colonel would tell us about how to bring the children along?" Ada asked, glancing around the room. "Their enemies are ignorance and ill-health, but also despair. How does one combat such a foe when one is small, sad, and alone?"

"But that's the thing," Mrs. MacHeath said. "That's the very thing about army life. One is never alone. One never marches alone or makes camp alone. One always has comrades who become dearer than family. For them, one would make any sacrifice. The colonel rode at the head of his troops into every battle, he'd visit the injured before he broke his fast and after he took his supper. He made sure the recruits were taught more than how to march and salute, and his men had decent boots or the generals got no peace. People think army life is brutish, but this civilian society, where we hardly know our neighbors, and have nothing more important to do than pour tea and gossip... this is the true disgrace."

Mrs. MacHeath's pale cheeks had acquired a hint of color and her tone had become spirited.

"What skills did the colonel ensure his men had, other than marching and saluting?" Lord John asked.

"Why, how to start a fire without flint and steel, for one thing. Many a bivouac takes place in rustic surrounds, and many's the time a raging river stole our cook's supplies. Everybody, from the lowliest piper to the colonel's aide had to be able to start a fire from wood and tinder."

"What else?" Ada asked, for it would not have occurred to her that soldiers might lack such a skill.

"How to sew a straight seam," Mrs. MacHeath went on. "What manner of soldier will bring glory to his regiment when his trousers are gaping, I ask you? And yet, some of the most fierce fellows, the most curmudgeonly sergeants, had no idea how to wield a needle and thread. Let me tell you, I addressed *that* oversight whenever I came across it, and I heard some of the most marvelous stories from those old soldiers."

"You taught them to sew?" Lord John asked.

"And darn their socks, my lord. An army might march on its belly figuratively, but men march on their feet literally, and one small blister can render a soldier useless after twenty miles of open country."

She launched into a story about how a strategic use of laxative herbs in the enemy's supper on the eve of battle had seen British forces victorious without a shot fired the next day.

"The children would love that story," Lord John said, when Mrs. MacHeath had brought her tale to a conclusion.

"The older children would also love knowing how to start a fire without a flint," Ada said. "I would like that skill myself."

"I could show you," Mrs. MacHeath said. "I taught that trick to many officers' wives and they had reason to be grateful."

"Perhaps when you tour St. Jerome's, you could make a list of practical accomplishments we could teach the children." Lord John dangled that possibility like yarn before a bored cat. "We can't have their little noses in books every hour of the day, and some of the boys will grow up to take the king's shilling."

The conversation was interesting, though as far as Ada could see, none of this talk was putting any shillings in St. Jerome's coffers.

"Save up your mending for the next week," Mrs. MacHeath said. "I will pay a call on you on Wednesday, and you will provide me a tour of the facilities. In addition to advising you on possible economies, I will begin instructing the children in the rudiments of sewing."

Hold your horses, Mrs. Colonel. "My lord," Ada said, "do you have sewing supplies for forty children? That's rather a lot of thread, not to mention needles, thimbles, sewing boxes—"

"Never mind that," Mrs. MacHeath said. "If I put out a call to the officers' wives, we can assemble you enough supplies to outfit an army, and enough cast off fabric to make quilts for every child three times over. We could sell a few of the prettier ones at the regiment's annual charity auction. You leave that to me."

"You can *sell* quilts for St. Jerome's?" Lord John asked.

"Oh,my, yes. Anybody can stitch together squares of fabric, my lord, and the officers' wives will cheerfully do the batting and backing until the older children learn that skill. With forty pairs of hands to support the effort, you could have a quilt shop, if you only had somebody to manage such an undertaking.

"The children could earn a bit of coin," she went on, getting up to pace, "and when, I ask you, is it a bad idea to provide a child valuable skills? The colonel always said that marching and fighting were fine on the day of battle, but where would the regiment be without its cobblers and seamstresses?"

Lord John rose as well. "I will look forward to your tour of the facilities, Mrs. MacHeath. Please send a note around letting me know what time suits you."

"Might I join that tour?" Ada asked, rising, lest she be the only one left in camp. "And should we invite some of Mrs. MacHeath's friends to come along?"

"Not too many," Mrs. MacHeath said, coming to a halt beneath the wolverine. "An abundance of generals makes for a poor battle plan, the colonel used to say. I will invite Mrs. McMurtry, and Mrs. Pine. Lady Platcher's brother owns linen mills, so we should invite her as well, but no more than that."

"I will look forward to your note," Lord John said, "and you will doubtless want to be about planning St. Jerome's quilting projects. The children will benefit from the skills you can teach them, but please also give some thought to the marvelous stories you've collected as wife to a career officer."

Mrs. MacHeath put a pale hand to her throat. "Stories, my lord?"

"Those herbs," Ada said. "That is the greatest exercise of cleverness I've heard of in years. The children will love it. I'm sure you have a story associated with the wolf-bear creature too."

"The wolverine? The colonel called him Wellington. I don't suppose the children should hear that."

John bowed over her hand. "I suppose they should. His Grace would be flattered as well. Miss Beauvais, shall we be on our way? I cannot wait to tell the staff of Mrs. MacHeath's ideas."

They took their leave, and when they did, Mrs. MacHeath was smiling and waving as if parting from her dearest friends.

Ada wasn't sure what, exactly had transpired in the course of that call, but Lord John was also beaming as if his most precious dream had come true.

"I am astounded," he said, settling onto the bench beside Ada. "I am dumbstruck, and I will go to my grave having witnessed at least one miracle in my life. That was amazing."

"What amazed me," Ada said, "is that she forgot to order the tray once she began talking about her dear colonel." Something Ada might do, though her present passions were butterflies and compost heaps.

"Who needs tea when we can have a quilt shop instead? She can supply the fabric, teach the children the skills, and find ladies willing to take on the finishing work. St. Jerome's will have *income*, Ada. Not a lot of income, and the children will have to demonstrate ability before they can work on the fancier quilts for sale, but we'll also save money because we'll no longer have to buy our blankets. Oh, this is marvelous."

He was gushing like a young scholar appointed to captain his cricket team.

"You are pleased, then?" Ada asked.

"I am thrilled, and this only came about because you got her maundering on about her sainted colonel. That was brave of you, but then, you are brave, and wonderful, and oh,"—he smiled at her so warmly, Ada felt it in her middle—"I could just kiss you, Ada Beauvais."

"So why don't you?"

Those words were out, unplanned and unladylike, but if anything, Lord John's smile became even more brilliant.

JOHN WISHED Ada had been present when he'd written Mr. Hewitt a bank draft for all rental arrearages plus two months in advance. Uncle Bascomb's money had been the first to arrive, and the first to depart, but two weeks after Miss Ada had begun her project, other pledges were steadily arriving.

Miss Deever had come to read for the first time, and Mr. Palmer had walked her home.

Mrs. MacHeath's network of officers' wives had begun sending over sewing supplies and fabric, and those were accumulating in the unused gallery. The great quilt project was scheduled to get under way by week's end, and all of the patrons upon whom John had called had offered some sort of support.

"Cora had an accident."

Henrietta stood in the doorway to John's office, a shame-faced Cora beside her. Cora had the occasional dry day, but she made up for that progress by having the occasional wet night.

"She had an accident yesterday," Henrietta went on, "and she had one the day before. Miss Gillian despairs of her."

A single tear hit the toe of Cora's boot.

"Well, I do not despair of our Cora," John said. "Cora, when you've tended to your clothes, I'd like to have a chat with you."

Henrietta looked like she wanted to say more: *Can somebody else be Cora's honorary big sister?* But John wasn't about to have that discussion while Cora was damp and uncomfortable.

"Thank you, Henrietta."

Henrietta huffed a sigh and led Cora by the hand into the corridor.

"Girls." Miss Beavais met them at the doorway. "Greetings." She curtseyed, and Henrietta bobbed while Cora continued staring at the floor. "Not having a good day today, Cora?"

Cora shook her head.

"We all have trying days, but they pass. Don't let me keep you."

Henrietta dragged the smaller girl toward the stairs. "Good-day, Miss Beauvais."

Miss Beauvais watched them go. "The olfactory evidence

suggests that Cora is still having difficulties. Did you try putting her on a schedule?"

"As brilliant as that suggestion was, after more than a week, it has yielded no results." John rose and rolled down his cuffs, glad for some bit of busyness. Ever since he'd made a passing remark about kissing Miss Ada, his mind had fixated on that idea.

Her reaction had been to interrogate him: *Why don't you?* she'd asked.

Because one doesn't presume on a lady's good graces, he'd said, and that answer had been so inadequate that he'd commenced babbling about Aunt Selma's collection of porcelain shepherdesses.

He'd not kissed Miss Beauvais because he was a penniless younger son with forty children to support, and Miss Beauvais deserved her country manor.

"Where are we off to today?" she asked.

"Another one of your old schoolmates," John said, "but I wanted to show you first how much progress we've made."

Miss Beauvais took off her bonnet and gloves, a simpler undertaking now that she'd styled her hair with tresses curling over one shoulder.

"We've used up more than half our time," she said. "I can't imagine a dozen calls have resulted in all that much money."

John drew her over to the window, the better to enjoy how morning sun found red highlights in her dark hair.

"This is the list of pledges," he said, "and the tally at the bottom is the funding we have collected. We have made enormous progress toward our goal." Part of that progress was simply because Ada compelled him to leave the orphanage, call on his patrons, and state St. Jerome's position to them plainly.

The patrons *did* want to help, apparently, but they also needed a gentle reminder. John had been too absorbed in accidents, cricket squabbles, and rental arrearages to offer that reminder.

Miss Beauvais took the list from him. "This cannot be right."

"Adelicia Beauvais, I am an Oxford-educated scholar, and simple addition is within my grasp. You have raised an enormous amount of money in a very short time."

She sank into his reading chair. "But this is... this is nearly half of what I had to earn in the thirty days. This is... *a lot of money.*"

For the first time in their acquaintance, Miss Beauvais looked uncertain. Bewildered, even.

"In two weeks," John said, "you have created more wealth and security for St. Jerome's than I was able to generate in all my tenure as its headmaster. You tried harder, you brought more ideas to the undertaking, and you have been prodigiously talented at inspiring people to open their purses."

She stared at the paper in her hand. "You've checked these figures?"

"Several times each day."

"I have simply been my un-charming, un-beautiful, blunt-to-a-fault self. I don't understand this."

John sank to the hassock before her, for they were no longer lord and lady, standing on manners moment by moment. They were allies, possibly even friends.

"You are honest and forthright," he said. "You are willing to admit that St. Jerome's needs help. You don't dissemble or posture, and that makes you trustworthy. I'd still be avoiding a call on Uncle Bascomb but for you, and I'm his favorite nephew."

Miss Beauvais set the tally down as if it were a royal decree from a far away kingdom. "I don't know what to say. I took on the situation at St. Jerome's because it was asked of me. I never expected I'd be able to make a difference. I have arrived at the place in life where people ignore me, you see. They aren't trying to educate me or *finish* me or marry me off. Now, all that's wanted is for me to retreat some-where obscure and quiet, where I won't bother anybody and nobody will bother me."

John sensed her words had ramifications beyond the obvious, and the moment didn't call for a cheerful rejoinder. Cheerful rejoinders could be just another way to ignore a woman who should never have been overlooked.

He put his arms around her, slowly and gently, lest he mistake her mood. She rested her head on his shoulder, and he resumed breathing.

"I would miss you," he said, "if you retreated to the countryside. Promise you won't abandon us when your thirty days are over."

Abandon me. He allowed himself to stroke her hair, to brush his thumb over the silky warmth of her nape and for a moment, he allowed himself to hope that he and she might have more than a few shared memories and carriage rides.

Ada sighed—another first from her. "I doubt I will ever see that country retreat, my lord. Time grows short and we have far to go. You need not worry that I will decamp to parts distant anytime soon. Besides, Mrs. MacHeath has yet to teach me how to build a fire from old linen and magic herbs."

For Ada, that was a cheerful rejoinder, and it left John's heart aching.

CHAPTER FIVE

Oh, to be held, not simply grabbed in a passing hug. Lord John's embrace was shelter and warmth, security and a steadying sort of closeness. He wasn't offering perfunctory social affection, he was filling a need for which Ada had no words.

His hand on her hair was both soothing and stirring, and his touch made her want to reciprocate with similar caresses.

She sat up, because foolish fancies served no purpose. "We should be on our way."

A timid knock sounded on the door jamb. "I changed my dress."

Cora hovered in the doorway, Henrietta nowhere to be seen.

"Come in, Cora," Lord John said, "and please close the door."

Cora did as she was asked and came to stand by his hassock.

"Cora, are you happy here?" he asked.

She darted a glance at him, and even Ada could read her puzzlement: *How does headmaster want me to answer?*

"Cora, come here," Ada said, gesturing for the girl to stand beside the reading chair. Ada fished her silver comb from her reticule and turned the child by the shoulders so she would not have to face Lord John during this inquisition.

"How can you be happy," Ada asked, "when you have no friends?" She undid Cora's braid and drew the comb carefully through curly golden locks.

"Cora?" Lord John asked. "What have you to say to that?"

"I stink. Nobody wants a friend who stinks."

Clearly not the reply his lordship had been expecting. "I stink too sometimes," Ada said, dividing Cora's hair into three shiny strands, "when I've been working with my compost heaps."

"What's a gone-post heap?" Cora asked.

"Compost," Lord John said, "is a combination of dirt; vegetable matter such as dead weeds, straw, or rotten potatoes; and other organic matter."

Ada leaned close to Cora's ear. "He means manure. Manure makes everything grow, though some object to the smell."

Cora twisted about, though Ada kept hold of her hair. "But if you stink, miss, you won't have any friends."

"I wash my hands, I change my clothes. I tend to my ablutions, and the scent fades. Lord John is my friend, despite my interest in compost heaps. I suspect he is your friend too, Cora, so you'd best find another strategy if you're trying to keep us all at arms' length."

The little girl's reasoning was brilliantly simple, also heartrending.

"You have accidents to keep people away," Lord John said. "Who are you trying to keep away, Cora?"

"Everybody." She fell silent, while Ada retied her hair ribbon. "Mostly boys, especially *big* boys."

"Is it working?" John asked.

"Yes. Nobody wants to be my friend. I have my bed all to myself every night, no matter how cold it gets. Nobody kicks me all night long and steals the blankets. I pee on my clothes so nobody else wants to wear them. Nobody wants to sit near me so nobody can steal my pudding. Because Henrietta says I stink."

Ada had to blink to keep from weeping.

His lordship appeared quite composed. "Cora, thank you for explaining this to us, but now I have a few things to explain to you."

"Will you send me back to Cook?"

"No, I will not send you back. Not ever. St. Jerome's is your home, whether you are fragrant or noisome."

Cora brows knit.

"He means," Ada said, "whether you smell like a flower or a compost heap."

Cora said nothing. She was very good at holding her peace—too good. Even if the other girls cut off her braid in the middle of the night, she'd probably just get up the next day and roll her tresses into the usual bun without saying anything.

"Your bed is yours, nobody else's," Lord John said. "Your clothing belongs to you, which is why we sewed your name into every article you've been given. Your pudding is served to you alone. If somebody trespasses against your property or your privacy, then you apply to Matron, to me, to a teacher, to—"

"Or to me," Ada added. "To an adult."

"Right," Lord John said, "to an adult, and the matter will be addressed."

Cora twiddled the end of her braid and faced her headmaster. "Will you send the boys to Cook if they steal my pudding?"

"No," Lord John said. "I will remind the transgressors that we have rules at St. Jerome's, and we respect each other's privacy and property."

"The transgressor is the thief," Ada said. "Lord John means he'll remind the person who steals your pudding about how the rules work. I daresay the thief will also do without his or her own pudding for a few days."

Cora regarded John in silence, and Ada felt as if the fate of St. Jerome's might hang on the child's next words.

"Will you *tell* them?" she asked. "Will you *tell* the other children what the rules are so they know that my clothes are for me and my bed is for me?"

"I will make an announcement at supper tonight," John said. "I will remind everybody, and you will try to stop having accidents. Are we agreed?"

Ada doubted it would be that simple.

"I will try, Headmaster."

"Fair enough, now run along to the gallery and see if you can help sort the fabric for Mrs. MacHeath's quilts."

Cora would have scampered to the door, but Ada caught her in a hug. "I'm proud of you, you clever girl."

Cora hugged her back, and then skipped away, grinning gloriously.

"I cannot imagine what that child has been through," Ada said, subsiding into the reading chair. "But you must make that announcement, my lord. Promise me."

"I do so solemnly promise. You made her smile."

"You made her feel safe."

While Lord John left Ada feeling half hopeful, half worried, and entirely at sea.

"YOU'VE PUT the Bonhoff sisters at the end of your list," John said. "Are they the easiest or the most difficult of your old school acquaintances?"

He and Ada had taken to sitting side by side in the coach as a matter of course, and when next he paid calls on his patrons, he would miss her sorely. She was effective at raising money, she kept the social calls to a reasonable length, and she kept John company.

As the horses trotted from one house to another, John had taken to trotting out the petty triumphs and frustrations of his days. Cora hadn't had an accident since he'd made his announcement at dinner last week, Mr. Palmer and Miss Deevers appeared to share a lively interest in orchids. Mrs. MacHeath's first quilt would be ready by the end of the month.

"You needn't chatter, my lord," Ada said, as the coach turned down a wide Mayfair thoroughfare. "I know we will likely fall short of our goal."

"Ada Beauvais, we still have three days to go. Anything can happen in three days." Three short days and then he'd likely be bidding her farewell.

"Much has happened in the past few weeks," she said, "all of it good. I do believe I've acquired a taste for frivolous slippers." She stuck out a dainty foot adorned with flowered embroidery and wiggled her toes. A month ago, John would likely not have remarked the sight—he'd seen many a slippered foot.

But that was Ada's ankle turned so gracefully. That was Ada's lemon verbena scent wafting through the coach. Those were Ada's skirts brushing against his boots and swishing through his dreams.

"I will never acquire a taste for stale shortbread," John said. "But I will bless the day you knocked upon St. Jerome's door, Ada Beauvais. The whole building is a lighter, happier place for your efforts, and I hope you will—"

The coach hit a pothole, always a hazard in springtime.

"You hope I will—?"

I am a penniless younger son who has nothing to offer you. "I hope you will recall us fondly. Tell me about Hopewell Grange."

"I've told you about Hopewell Grange," Ada retorted. "It's a typical country manor and I will very likely never lay eyes on it. I put the Bonhoff's at the bottom of my list because they were witnesses to the worst of my clumsiness."

"You are no clumsier than any other woman of my acquaintance. I've squired you about on a year's worth of social calls, and you never put a foot wrong."

"Because with you, I'm not nervous."

She wasn't exactly cheerful in his presence lately either. "So what great faux pas did you commit that you still recall it to this day?" Recall it, and regret it.

"I fell on my arse at Almack's, knocked a footman down at the same time, and ended up with my dancing partner and lemonade all over my person. When I attempted to get to my feet, my hand landed on an unfortunate part of my partner's anatomy, and all of Mayfair applauded my mortification."

"Applauded? Metaphorically?"

She slowly clapped her gloved hands together. "My Aunt Kitty made me go back the next week, and produced a few intrepid bachelors for me to dance with, but Mr. Bonhoff wasn't among them. I'm told he had to keep to his rooms for a fortnight, in close proximity to a bucket of ice as a result of the injury I'd done him."

Oh, dear. "Mr. Bonhoff?"

"Horatio Bonhoff, brother to my schoolmates. I half-way fancied him, to the extent I've ever fancied any man."

Could you ever fancy me? "Adelicia, you cannot blame yourself for an accident."

"Horatio was the worse for drink. I could smell it on him, but young men are a bibulous lot and I was enchanted to think he chose to waltz with the awkward Miss Ada Beauvais."

"He got what he deserved," John said. "If a man can't hold his liquor, he has no business taking a lady in his arms, much less in public."

The coach slowed, though John wasn't nearly done with this conversation.

"Then I got what I deserved, too, didn't I? I stood up with an inebriate simply because he smiled at me."

"And your aunt, or whoever was chaperoning you, failed to intervene when she clearly had the wisdom and experience to do so. I hope that she, at least, has found an occasion to apologize."

The coach came to a halt, though for once, Ada did not bound down the steps, parasol at the ready.

"You really are quite fierce," she said, cupping his jaw with her gloved hand. "I admire that about you tremendously."

John caught her hand in his own. "You are fierce as well, Ada Beauvais, and in the loveliest way imaginable. I hope we achieve our objective, not only for the children, but also for you. Hopewell Grange should be yours, and I look forward to visiting you there someday."

He moved nearer, thinking to punctuate that sentiment with a parting kiss to her cheek, but the dratted, benighted footman chose that moment to open the door and let down the steps. Ada descended, all grace and lace, and promenaded with John to an imposing front door.

The footman rapped the knocker and then they were making the last of the calls that Ada herself had scheduled.

~

SOMEDAY WAS AN ANNOYINGLY VAGUE CONCEPT.

Lord John had said he hoped to visit Ada *someday* at Hopewell Grange. What good was a *someday* visit when a Tuesday or a Friday visit could have served instead?

Ada passed her cloak to the Bonhoff butler and checked her appearance in the mirror hanging near the porter's nook. The woman staring back at her was nearly a stranger. Her eyes were alight with purpose, her ensemble was fashionable without being ostentatious. Her cheeks sported a natural blush, and her coiffure was neither a severe bun nor a fussy affectation. A single curling tress lay against her shoulder, a style that Aunt Kitty might have suggested but never had.

"This way, miss, my lord," the butler said, gesturing to a curved staircase. "The ladies are expecting you."

Ada wanted to get this call behind her so she could resume her discussion with Lord John: *When will you call upon me, if I am so fortunate as to acquire Hopewell Grange? Why haven't you pursued that comment you made more than a fortnight ago, about having me take on some duties at the orphanage? Does Cora have any friends yet?*

When will you kiss me?

The butler announced them, and then Ada was curtsying before Miss Daniella Bonhoff and Mrs. Sarah Bonhoff Merriman. They were attired in silk day gowns with tasseled paisley peacock shawls, and the scent of orange blossoms was so thick Ada nearly asked the butler to open a window.

"Miss Ada Beauvais," Mrs. Merriman cooed. "What an age it has been. And Lord John, a pleasure to see you. I would never in my wildest dreams have paired the two of you for any occasion. Do sit down."

John took a seat beside Ada on the sofa. "Miss Beauvais has been kind enough to take an interest in St. Jerome's," he said. "I wish more of polite society had her genuine concern for the less fortunate."

For his lordship, that was very direct speech, indeed. Even more direct than Ada would have been.

"We are very concerned for the less fortunate," Mrs. Merriman replied. "That's why we pull back the drapes whenever we host a ball, right Daniella? We provide a marvelous spectacle at no charge whatsoever and brighten the lives of those of humble stations. Tell me how your sisters get on, my lord."

"My sisters are well. I cannot report as cheerfully on the state of St. Jerome's."

Daniella scooted to the edge of her seat, just as her older sibling waved a hand. "Let's have no talk of dreary orphans, my lord. How is your dear mama?"

Even for the lovely and well-dowered Sarah, that was less than deft.

"The marchioness is well, but I'll thank you not to refer the children at St. Jerome's as dreary orphans."

Daniella darted a glance at her sister. "Sarah meant no offense, my lord. I'm sure your orphans aren't dreary at all. I wonder where the tea tray could be."

Daniella was apparently still a follower rather than a leader, though clearly, the role sat ill on her today.

"I would enjoy a cup of tea," Ada said, mostly to fill a silence during which Lord John glowered—*glowered*—at Sarah. He was her social superior, and without his escort, Ada would likely not have been received.

"I doubt we'll be staying for tea," Lord John said. "Miss Ada has recounted a tale for me involving Mr. Horatio Bonhoff, public drunkenness, and premeditated harm to Miss Ada's person and reputation. I was hoping to hear an apology today—two apologies in fact."

Ada stared at him, his profile a study in heroic resolve. How could this be the same man who'd spoken so encouragingly to little Cora and pitched the slowest cricket inning ever to while away a sunny afternoon?

"I beg—I beg your pardon?" Sarah said, chin coming up.

"Sarah...." Daniella muttered.

Lord John rose. "You challenged your sot of a brother to subject Miss Ada to public humiliation, never thinking she might have twisted an ankle, sprained a wrist, or landed on broken glass. She had done nothing to deserve that sort of abuse, and you are not fit to donate to St. Jerome's. Miss Ada, let's be leaving."

He offered his arm. Ada took it, dipped half a curtsy to the room at large, and returned with him to the foyer, where a surprised butler passed Ada her cloak.

Lord John took his hat, he didn't put it on.

"I can make your excuses," Ada said, leaving her cloak unbuttoned. "I can go back in there and explain that you are under a lot of strain lately, and your chivalrous nature has leapt to unfortunate conclusions."

He did up the frogs of her cloak. "I would hate to be the reason you stooped to dissembling, Miss Beauvais. They aren't worth it. I know Horatio Bonhoff. He's a notorious drunkard who should never have been admitted to Almack's, but his family is old and wealthy. You were ambushed for their entertainment, and I refuse to pretend otherwise."

Ada respected Lord John, the patient teacher and conscientious administrator. She enjoyed the company of the well-bred young man with the courtesy title, and she treasured her friend, the cheerful, honest, hard-working failed cleric. She dreamed of the handsome fellow whose embrace had been so intriguing and longed for.

This *gentleman*, though, who stood up for a lady's honor, who refused to wink at wrongdoing, captured her heart.

"Very well then," she said, accepting her bonnet from the butler. "Let's get back to St. Jerome's, and to blazes with—"

Miss Daniella hurried up the corridor. "You must take this," she said, brandishing a piece of paper. "Sarah is sorry, I'm sure of it, she just doesn't know how to say the words. I am very sorry, Miss Beauvais, but Sarah and Horrie had concocted that unfortunate prank before I got wind of it, and the next thing I knew, Almack's was littered in broken glass and Horrie was being helped into the coach by three footmen."

The butler passed Ada her parasol, bowed, and withdrew.

"So you did ambush me," Ada said. The realization was painful, but not mortifying. "You put your brother up to making a fool of me."

"Mr. Merriman had remarked flatteringly about your figure more than once, and Sarah had set her cap for him. She had no other followers, and thus she went to Horrie. Horrie never has any money, so he agreed to her scheme in exchange for a portion of Sarah's pin money. Now it's Sarah who has no money. She would donate to the orphanage if she could, but she can't."

This recitation was delivered in a near whisper.

"She's a married woman," Ada said. "Why has she no pin money?"

Daniella glanced down the corridor and leaned near. "Gambling. Can't help herself. Mr. Merriman had to *take measures*, but I have money and I insist on donating." She pressed the piece of paper into Ada's hand. "Please take it. Please."

"My lord?" Ada left the decision to John.

He considered for a moment, then nodded. "You have my thanks,

Miss Bonhoff. Miss Beauvais, shall we be going? Miss Bonhoff, good day."

Ada took her place in the coach a moment later, and passed John the folded piece of paper. "I almost feel sorry for them. Almost." She unpinned her bonnet and let a sense of relief wash over her. The visits to schoolmates were done, St. Jerome's was much better off, and Ada would soon be free to return to her compost heaps and butterflies.

Lord John sat beside her, the piece of paper in his hand. "Ada, look at this."

She tossed her parasol to the opposite bench and leaned her head back against the squabs. "You look at it. I'm all visited-out for the day, and probably for the rest of my life. I still think we should call on your papa, though. Your mother and sisters—"

"Ada, *look at this.*"

She opened her eyes and caught his hand, because he was waving a bank note at her. "What?"

"Miss Daniella Bonhoff must manage her allowance very well, because with this sum, you have achieved the goal set for you last month by that Carruthers fellow. You will soon be the proud owner of Hopewell Grange, my dear, the proud and happy owner."

John would not lie to her, or miscalculate, or misrepresent. "Truly? We did it?"

"You did it, with your determination, honesty, and ingenuity. Even a failed call results in funds with you. You are a marvel, Adelicia Beauvais. A walking, talking, marvel."

Ada had the oddest urge to cry, to bolt from the coach and put distance between Lord John's words, and her fluttering, capering heart.

"We did it," she said. "I could never have made these calls on my own. We did it, and oh... Hopewell Grange. I could just kiss you, John Waverly."

He tucked the bank note into his pocket, took off his hat, and set it next to Ada's bonnet on the opposite bench.

"So why don't you?"

JOHN WOULD HAVE SAID that Ada Beauvais's most memorable characteristic was her determination. She marched through life from objective to objective, undeterred by doubt, despair, or dark of night. Her kisses though...

When it came to kisses, Ada was an adventurer. She swaggered into the kiss with a bold press of her mouth to his, then retreated as if she expected that warning shot to draw return fire.

John obliged, gently at first, because a kiss wanted savoring, and because he wasn't certain what manner of kiss this was. Celebratory? Friendly? Both?

But a friendly kiss didn't involve the lady taking a subtle taste of the fellow, did it? Or her hands shaping the muscles of his arms, and her fingers sinking into his hair. Ada tucked in closer, anchoring an arm around John's waist, and he reciprocated by drawing her into his embrace.

The coach might have started forward, the coach might have floated aloft like a hot air balloon. All John knew was that Ada was in his arms, kissing him as if he were her every wish come true.

"A moment," he panted as the carriage took a corner that brought Ada even closer. "The shades..."

"To blazes with the shades. I like kissing you."

"If you merely like it, I'm not going about it properly."

She slanted him a look and sat back. "Properly is a relative term. You are a fine kisser, Lord John."

He ran a hand through his hair trying to bring order to more than his thoughts. "You have kissed enough men to evaluate my relative abilities?" he asked.

Ada passed over a silver comb. "I have kissed *you* enough to evaluate your relative abilities, sir. Will you call upon Mr. Carruthers with me?"

Not in my present state. "To confirm your success?"

"Somebody must. He will never believe we raised all this money. I don't believe it."

John's body had made off with the reasoning portion of his mind. He watched Ada's lips as she spoke, he breathed through his nose the better to inhale lemon verbena, and he imagined her fingers rather than her comb putting his hair to rights.

"Pay a visit to Carruthers," he muttered, returning the comb. "You kiss me like that, and then speak of solicitors and social calls."

Ada reached for her bonnet. "Did I do it wrong?"

Ye saints abiding. "You kiss very well, Miss Beauvais, which I think you know. So well, I am only just now remembering that I have the patron's luncheon tomorrow."

Ada toyed with her bonnet ribbons. "As long as the money was raised within the allotted thirty days, I don't suppose it matters whether we call upon Carruthers today or the day after tomorrow."

John reached past her to pull down the window shade, then he gently pried her bonnet from her hands.

"The day after tomorrow, we'll make a proper morning call on Mr. Carruthers, and I will have all of my documents in hand. I'd like to resume kissing you now."

"I'd like that too."

WHO KNEW KISSING WAS SO complicated? The mechanics weren't all that complex—lips, hands, bodies, breath—but what did it all *mean*? Ada could not ask even Aunt Kitty that question, so she spent the day of the patron's luncheon wandering about her little house, staring off into space, and alternately missing Lord John and dreading her next encounter with him.

Would he think her forward? Backward? Would he kiss her again?

As the hour to call on Mr. Carruthers drew closer, Ada dressed in the finest of her new attire, right down to her flowered slippers, and tucked a few extra pins into her hair. When the coach came by, she was waiting for his lordship in her parlor, though she wasn't prepared for the dapper gentleman who greeted her.

"My lord." She curtseyed, Lord John bowed. "You have troubled over your appearance, sir." His coat was tailored to perfection, his boots gleamed, and his lapel sported a pink rosebud.

His smile was a bit sheepish. "Solicitors can be sticklers for protocol. This is an important day, and I wanted to look my best."

As had Ada, but not because Mr. Carruthers might be a stickler. "Let's be off, then, shall we?"

His lordship handed her into the coach, and then the blighter sat on the backward facing bench.

"John? Are we no longer friends?"

"We will always be friends, I hope."

"So why are you perched over there, when you could be beside me?"

"One doesn't want to presume."

"*One* is behaving very oddly. You kissed me two days ago as if I were the answer to your every dream, and today you are back to being Lord Headmaster. Do you regret kissing me?"

He looked out the window, which he could do, because the shades were rolled up—all the way up. "Of course not, but kissing has an effect on a fellow's humors, and one doesn't want to arrive to a business appointment in a state of... in a *state*."

Ada's grasp of reproductive biology was more sophisticated than most unmarried women of her station, but she also knew an excuse when she heard one.

"You do regret kissing me, at least a little." That was a worse blow than knowing she'd been intentionally embarrassed at Almack's.

"Never." Said with reassuring emphasis. "But I regret that I am merely the headmaster of an orphanage, that I've poured my wealth, such wealth as I had, into St. Jerome's, that I could never abandon the children or entrust their welfare to strangers. I'm all they have, and I can't turn my back on them for... mere kisses."

A thousand retorts sprang to mind:

I am not asking you to turn your back on anybody.

Don't entrust the children to strangers, entrust them to people who care for them as you do.

My kisses are not mere.

And yet, John was being honorable, in his way. "I did not know your personal wealth was spent at St. Jerome's."

"My father nearly disowned me."

"While I esteem you all the more for your commitment." She kissed his cheek, sat back, and promised herself that Hopewell Grange would be everything she could possibly have longed for, even if it was all the way out in blasted, beautiful Surrey.

~

JOHN DID NOT WANT to let Ada go, but he could offer nothing to compare with the glories of Hopewell Grange. He'd made inquiries of Mr. Palmer, whose family seat was in Surrey. The Grange was a gem of a manor house set in a shining tiara of an estate.

Precisely what Ada Beauvais deserved, and exactly what would make her happy. That St. Jerome's had benefited from her good fortune was some consolation, but not as much as it should have been.

"Mr. Carruthers." John bowed before a tall, dark-eyed fellow who looked to have some foreign antecedents a generation or two back. "I am privileged to accompany Miss Beauvais today in the capacity of corroborating witness. You will be very pleased to learn that she has accomplished the goal set out for her thirty days ago."

Mrs. Carruthers's brows rose. "Have you, Miss Beauvais? Have you really? Let's discuss this in my office."

"We raised the necessary sum," Miss Ada said, preceding the gentlemen into a tidy, spacious chamber. "His lordship and I paid calls on my old schoolmates, as you suggested, Mr. Carruthers, and on his patrons. A few of them suggested others who might be generously inclined, and Lord John's family also contributed."

A compact ginger cat sat upon the mantel, so still John at first through it was a porcelain figure. Then the beast yawned, showing a deal of sharp teeth.

"Have a seat," Carruthers said, gesturing to a group of chairs before an unlit hearth. "I am most delighted to hear of your success, Miss Beauvais. I must nonetheless ask for particulars, or I would be remiss in my duty to your benefactor."

Ada settled into her chair with a rustle of skirts, delicately embroidered slippers peeking out from beneath her hems. John handed Carruthers the tally of the sum earned, and admitted to a regret: The sight of those slippers, the memory of putting them on Ada's feet for the first time, was worth more to him than the entire fortune earned for St. Jerome's.

John had considered, in a theoretical, wishful sort of way, if he could transition St. Jerome's to another headmaster, but nobody came to mind. Mr. Palmer was happy to read to the children once a week—and to walk Miss Deevers home—but his ambitions lay with the church. Mrs. MacHeath was content with generalship of the quilts. She was also getting on in years, and had little patience with the children themselves.

"You have accomplished much," Mr. Carruthers said, perusing the list John had prepared. "An impressive feat, Miss Beauvais, and I'm sure much good will result from your efforts."

"That's the best part," Miss Ada said. "All I did was pay a few calls, spend a few weeks pretending I'm not socially backward, and the children's future is secure. I own I am astonished, Mr. Carruthers, and now to think I'll have Hopewell Grange as well seems too much."

"You aren't socially backward," John retorted, "and I don't care if I'm arguing with a lady, miss. You are an original, and to blazes with anybody who says otherwise."

Carruthers watched this exchange with a faint smile. "Miss Beauvais, it appears you have acquired a champion."

"St. Jerome's acquired the champion," John said. "I merely state the obvious."

Carruthers passed the papers back. "While I must refine on a regrettable subtlety. Miss Beauvais you have not, in fact, achieved your objective. The total sum earned is fifty pounds short of the goal. I'm sorry."

John was on his feet. "I checked my math several times, Carruthers. You can stow the lawyerly obfuscation. Miss Beauvais achieved her objective with fifty pounds to spare. You will prepare documents to deed Hopewell Grange to her, or I'll know the reason why."

Carruthers remained sitting, which was shrewd of him. Even furious, John would not strike a man who wasn't standing.

"Please explain, Mr. Carruthers," Ada said, sounding curiously calm. "I verified his lordship's figures myself, and kept my own tally. I reached the same total he did."

"The total is correct," Carruthers said, "but money promised is not money earned. Lady Barstow's pledge of one hundred pounds is not in hand paid, and today is the last day you had to raise that sum. A promise of funds does not meet the terms of the challenge. You could have promised to provide the entire sum at a future date otherwise, and done nothing for St. Jerome's."

As angry as John had been with his father, as frustrated as he'd been with his patrons, he was ten times that upset with Carruthers.

"You cannot be serious, Carruthers. Miss Ada has saved St. Jerome's, and you are denying her the promised consideration. If I had the damned fifty pounds I'd write out a note for it now."

"John, I cannot miss what I never had," Ada said. "We need not take up any more of Mr. Carruthers's time."

Carruthers rose. "Miss Beauvais, I truly commend you for your efforts, and I will convey to my client that you exerted yourself to the utmost for the sake of St. Jerome's. I regret I can do no more than that."

John assisted Ada to her feet, though her composure baffled him. "We will call on Lady Barstow straightaway and obtain the damned funds, Carruthers."

"We can't," Ada said. "She has left Town to take the sea air. Mr. Carruthers, thank you for your time. Please thank your client for providing me with an interesting several weeks. Good day." She curtsied to the lawyer and to the cat, then took John by the hand and led him from the office.

CHAPTER SIX

"I cannot believe that man," Lord John said as he and Ada waited for the empty coach to pull up before Carruthers's office. "I cannot deuced believe him, pardon my language. To mislead you, to waste your efforts, to manipulate you into dealing with the very women who were so unkind to you in your girlhood... I have no words, Ada, other than I'm sorry."

Ada climbed into the coach and patted the place beside her. "Thank you for that, but Mr. Carruthers did mention that I was to raise the actual money, not promises of money. I was not attending him at the time, because I did not anticipate embarking on the venture at all. As it is, I've never even seen Hopewell Grange. I'm only one person. What do I need with twenty-six window seats?"

Ada wasn't dissembling or putting on a brave face. Hopewell Grange was doubtless a lovely estate, but in the past month, she'd seen a household full to the brim with noise, learning, and laughter. What was the point of having all those windows, all those acres, for only one person?

"You need Hopewell Grange because you love your privacy," Lord John said, delivering a hard rap to the roof of the coach. "You need those windows because you will put them all to good use, growing herbs or measuring sunlight or some such. You worked for those windows."

"I will pay taxes on those windows, too," Ada said. "Or I would, if I owned Hopewell Grange, which I do not." She was disappointed, but not devastated. Not even crestfallen. "Perhaps if I remain in Town, I can drop in on St. Jerome's from time to time." She was already planning on visiting Lord Bascomb, and hoped John's sisters would receive her as well. She owed them her thanks and wanted their recommendations for modistes and milliners.

"You're sure Lady Barstow is from home?" Lord John asked.

"She wrote me a note. She won't be back for another fortnight."

"Perhaps Lord Barstow might be in Town?"

"He's with her at the seaside." Was Lord John really so anxious to consign Ada to the wilds of Surrey? "I failed to win my challenge, but you did not fail St. Jerome's. Let's be proud of that."

Some of the ire went out of him. "We came so close."

Close to what, though? "You have your quilting teams. You have Miss Deevers not only reading to the little ones, but giving lessons in deportment to the older children. Lady Noland is offering French lessons, and Her Grace of Anselm is lending you her botanist to re-organize your gardens. I'd say we exceeded all expectations."

Lord John took her hand and brought her knuckles to his lips as the coach drew to a halt before St. Jerome's. The front porch was adorned with pots of salvia now. One of Mrs. MacHeath's lady generals had made that donation.

"You are being more than generous, Ada. Uncle Bascomb is asking after you."

God bless Uncle Bascomb. "You have a visitor," Ada said, for an older gentleman stood at the front door, fist raised to knock. "He looks familiar." Like a leaner version of Bascomb, in fact.

John peered through the window. "My father is paying a call. Surely the realm has come to a dire pass. He will doubtless berate me for going about Town in his crested coach begging for money."

Losing Hopewell Grange was disappointing, but Ada had gained so much: The satisfaction of assisting a worthy cause, the profound peace of having laid the past to rest, and the joy of embroidered slippers. Then too, she'd stolen a few kisses, and they were perhaps the greatest boon of all.

Lord John should have more than regular coal deliveries for all the tea he'd swilled in the past few weeks. Ada climbed down from the coach and marched up to the old fellow strutting about on the porch.

"You, my lord, have much to answer for."

Eyebrows much like John's drew down. "Who the devil are you?"

"I am the woman who will call you to account for sabotaging your own son," Ada said, jabbing him in the chest with her finger. "I am the woman who has seen firsthand how hard Lord John works to provide for these children, to see them kept safe and warm and happy. I am the woman who has the honor to call him my friend, and you are the fool who hasn't the sense to be proud of an exemplary son. You should be ashamed of yourself."

John emerged from the coach and took the place at Ada's side. "Miss Adelicia Beauvais, may I make known to you Pompeii, Marquess of Gandham. My lord, Miss Adelicia Beauvais."

"Might we continue this discussion indoors?" the marquess groused. "I am unused to being harangued in the very street."

"More's the pity," Ada snapped. "If somebody had done a better job of haranguing you, Lord John might not be toiling away here for years with virtually no support from the people who ought to champion his causes. You will please rectify that oversight, or I will know the reason why. Good day."

She hurled a curtsy at the marquess and returned to the coach, proud of herself for keeping her harangue short and mostly factual.

Lord John handed her in, his expression hard to read.

"Don't expect me to apologize," Ada said. "I see how hard you work, I see how the children depend on you, and that man owes you his respect at least. His lack of support has made your life more difficult and somebody needed to call him to account."

Lord John bowed over her hand. "Is that what you call it? It looked to me more like reading the old boy the Riot Act. Well done, Miss Ada."

How she loved his smile, loved the kindness and humor that he never lost sight of for long. "You'd best go patch it up with him. Tell him I'm an original. We are given to expressing ourselves."

Lord John leaned through the coach doorway and kissed her cheek. "You are very much an original. Thank you for everything, Ada. I will never, ever forget your determination and fortitude, and I wish you the very best in all your endeavors."

He stepped back and the footman closed the door. The coachman signaled the horses to walk on, and then Ada was parting from the only man to win her respect *and* her heart, though she hadn't even bid him a proper farewell.

"IF THAT IS the sort of company you're keeping these days, no wonder this moldering pile is about to collapse in on itself." The marquess waited until John ushered him into St. Jerome's to make that observation.

"That *company*, sir, is the reason St. Jerome's will still be standing twenty years from now. Miss Beauvais took it upon herself to raise money for the children, and her efforts were exceedingly successful." On any other occasion, John would have been pleased that the marquess deigned to grace St. Jerome's with a visit.

Now, he hesitated to take his father's hat and coat.

"Big place," the marquess said, glancing around. "Hard to heat."

"But cool in the summer, spacious, and full of light. What might I do for you, my lord?"

The marquess took off his hat but didn't pass it over. "Bascomb mentioned that you'd come calling, you and the young lady."

"We had a delightful visit with Uncle several weeks ago."

The marquess usually spent his afternoons in parliamentary committee meetings. A troubling thought dropped into John's head. "Are you well, sir?"

"Well? Of course, I'm well. Don't you offer your guests any hospitality at this establishment?"

John had just bid a too-hasty farewell to the woman who'd safeguarded St. Jerome's future, the same woman who held John's heart in her hands. To blazes with tea and crumpets.

"Why are you condescending to make a social call now, sir, when all of Mayfair knows you long to see St. Jerome's close its doors?"

Cora slid down the bannister, a first in John's recollection. "Headmaster, we have company!"

"I'm not sure we do," John said, lifting Cora from the bannister and setting her on her feet. "I'm not sure why his lordship, after five years of all but turning his back on us, has decided to pay a call today of all days."

The child bobbed at the knees. "I'm Cora. I haven't had an accident for eight days, because nobody is allowed to wear my clothes or sleep in my bed but me. I don't stink!"

The marquess looked honestly baffled, bringing to mind Bascomb's words: *Pompeii has a mortal fear of lung ailments... he fears to lose you.*

"Shall we repair to my office?" John asked. "Cora, that's enough sliding on bannisters for now, please. I'm sure you're supposed to be in the garden with the others."

"I had to use the close stool," she said, grinning and twirling until her pinafore belled out, "so I wouldn't stink."

"Well done, child, but it's time to enjoy some sunshine. Miss Deevers will soon be here to read and if you are all very good, she might be persuaded to read in the garden."

"Stories!" Cora caroled, skipping off down the corridor. "I love stories!"

"What a robust child," the marquess said as Cora's steps faded. "She puts me in mind of your sisters."

John took the opposite direction from Cora, toward his office. "Did they put you up to calling on me?"

"Nobody put me up to... well, Bascomb might have mentioned looking in on you."

John ushered his father into the headmaster's office, which had a view of the back gardens. The children were in good voice, scrabbling over a game of kickball. Normally, John would have been with them ensuring the match didn't degenerate into fisticuffs.

He wished Ada were on hand to provide the same supervision to him and his father. "What did Uncle have to say? I'd like to make a suggestion regarding his situation."

The marquess pretended to study the books on the shelves, though what Lund's treatise on scurvy had to say to anything, John did not know.

"Speak your piece," the marquess said, "and then I've a few words to impart as well."

"Bascomb is all but housebound because of his bad foot," John said, "but he has yet managed to find somebody in this life who cares for him, who treasurers his companionship. Because that person apparently hasn't met your standards for who should and should not be become a member of the family, he lives in sin. What possible difference could it make to you if your brother marries his house-keeper so late in life? They love each other."

Papa was no longer pretending to study the books. He was staring at John as if he'd never seen him before.

"The children at this orphanage have no family," John went on. "They know better than to turn up their noses at people who offer to care for them and treat them decently. You have a brother—a dear, difficult man who yet spoke up in your defense when last I called up on him. He deserves your loyalty and support, even if you can't see fit to offer that loyalty and support to your own son. Make peace with

Bascomb, Papa, or don't bother calling here at St. Jerome's again. Family is as family does."

The marquess circled his hat in his hands, he cleared his throat. He went to the window so he stood half in profile to John.

"Bascomb said that your female friend had a very salutary effect on a man's disposition. Does she scold everybody the way she scolded me?"

"Ada Beauvais has a tender heart that's been much buffeted by unkindness. She is nonetheless the soul of decency, though she has not the least acquaintance with dissembling. I am honored to call her my friend."

The marquess set his hat on the desk and faced the garden. "Seems to me, if a woman makes your troubles her own and delivers a dressing down to your father for all to hear, she's something more than a friend. I'd like to make a donation to St. Jerome's."

John's heart chose then to start thumping against his ribs. "Why?"

"Because forty children cannot feed themselves. Because... because I should have long ago, but I didn't want to intrude or imply that you needed my help. Nobody likes to be an object of charity, least of all a Waverly." The marquess clasped his hands behind his back. "Bascomb said I had it all wrong, and that the gossips and tattlers took my silence for condemnation."

"Bascomb is correct." Also more blunt than John had ever been able to be with the marquess. "The gossips and tattlers concluded that because I was no sort of cleric, you were ashamed of me."

The marquess glanced up sharply. "Have you taken leave of your senses, John?"

"I repeat what a friendly curate has conveyed to me, and as an earl's son, Mr. Palmer moves in lofty circles. He merely confirms what others have said. *If the marquess takes no notice of Lord John's foundling home, why should anybody else?*"

"Bloody idiots. Bloody, blasted idiots. I've half a mind... Would you entertain a parliamentary committee visit? Perhaps sit on that same committee in an ex officio capacity?"

The marquess had never asked anything of John. He'd made threats and demands, but never requests.

"What committee? I'm very busy here at St. Jerome's, and I haven't time for political frolics."

"A committee investigating the plight of homeless children. They starve and freeze in the streets, you know. Even cabinet ministers, a vastly hardnosed lot, can't continue to ignore that spectacle winter after winter while the realm as a whole is both at peace and prospering."

"May I think about this?" *May I discuss it with Ada? She'd see clearly whether this was a step forward or a stumble.*

"Of course, but I'd still like to make a donation."

An odd, blossoming sensation opened in John's middle. "Can you spare a hundred pounds?"

"Of course I can spare—why that sum?"

"Because if you're willing to write out a bank draft for that sum dated today, then I must ask you to accompany me to a certain solicitor's office. You can tell me about your committee on the way."

The marquess donned his hat. "If I must jaunt across Town to get a moment of your time, so be it, but please assure me you'll take the money. Bascomb said he'd disown me if I didn't make that offer."

"I'll take the money if you'll stand up with Uncle when he says his vows."

"Clearly that outspoken young woman has been a significant influence on you." The marquess moved toward the door, his stride jaunty. "I daresay she and I will get along famously."

"I daresay you had better exert yourself to that very end, sir."

"A FINAL DONATION," Mr. Carruthers said, sliding a sealed document across the desk to Ada. "Very last minute, but the donor himself verified the donation last week. That deed makes you the sole owner of Hopewell Grange in fee simple absolute. May I be the first to congratulate you on having met a significant challenge?"

Ada stared at the florid script covering the paper before her, but the words made no sense. "I don't understand. We came up short. You said so."

"You exceeded the necessary total by the end of the thirtieth day. A final donor accompanied Lord John to my office as I was finishing up my work, and produced a signed bank draft for another one hundred pounds. You exceeded the terms of the challenge by fifty pounds. The donor was very clear that your fundraising efforts motivated his generosity."

Who on earth would turn over a hundred pounds, much less accompany Lord John to the solicitor's office?

"Was it my Aunt Kitty?" Ada asked. "She would part with a hundred pounds to see me securely established on my own property." Though lately, Kitty had been preoccupied, and she certainly hadn't asked Ada for any details regarding the situation at St. Jerome's.

"I'm sure Lady Catherine cares for you a great deal, Miss Beauvais, but she did not supply the final donation. That sum came from the Marquess of Gandham, and he appeared prepared to furnish a much larger sum. Lord John refused anything more than the hundred pounds."

Oh, John. "He should have accepted every groat."

"Perhaps you can tell him that when you invite him for a tour of Hopewell Grange." Mr. Carruthers wasn't smiling, but his eyes were... twinkling? He was an attractive man, in a quiet, solicitor-ish way.

"I'd like to invite my benefactor to the property, if you'd be so good as to inform me to whom I owe my thanks."

The cat, who had been sprawled in ginger splendor across the blotter, rose and ambled across papers to stretch an inquisitive nose in Ada's direction.

"I regret that I am not at liberty to disclose the identity of that person, Miss Beauvais. The benefactor owed you a debt, and that debt has been repaid. I wish you every joy as you take up residence in Surrey."

Ada should be feeling joy, but mostly she was bewildered. Perhaps the joy would come later, when she actually laid eyes on her property. Then too, nobody owed her anything approaching the sort of debt that was repaid with a prosperous estate.

"She's a friendly feline," Ada said, stroking her hand over the cat's head. "She looks standoffish and dignified, but she's actually a good sort, isn't she?"

"Marigold is an estimable lady. When you take up residence at the Grange, I hope you find companions who can match her for wisdom and charm."

John had wisdom and charm. Also humor, generosity of spirit, fortitude, kindness, and excellent kisses. "Why did you wait nearly a week to inform me of my good fortune, Mr. Carruthers?"

"I conferred first with your benefactor, then I spent some time preparing the requisite documents. I am also anticipating extended travel myself, Miss Beauvais, and preparations for my journey required my attention."

"So you won't be on hand to introduce me to my staff at Hopewell Grange?" That bothered Ada. She'd accomplished the dream of a lifetime, and had nobody to celebrate it with her. Was she supposed to tool out to Surrey on her own? Announce herself? Write her own letters of introduction?

"My relatives in India have been exhorting me to come home for years, Miss Beauvais. I dare not put them off any longer."

While Ada's relatives tended to forget her. "Are you married, Mr. Carruthers?" He should be. He had that sort of dignity and self-possession. He was a relatively young man, and he had a lucrative profession.

"I am not yet married. Travel to India might rectify that lonely state of affairs."

Gracious days, his smile was positively buccaneering. "I'll wish you safe journey then," Ada said. "And thank you for all you've done."

"The staff at the Grange is expecting you," Mr. Carruthers replied, rising. "I've also sent letters to your new neighbors and the local vicar, though I left to you the task of notifying your family of your good fortune." He passed Ada a packet of papers tied with a blue ribbon. "Those are the leaseholds, along with a letter of introduction to your steward, and a list of the people who now answer to you, from the butler and housekeeper to the tenants' newest baby. The entire staff is looking forward to having an owner in residence, miss. You should be very happy at Hopewell Grange."

All quite lovely, but why wasn't Ada happy *now*, when she held in her very hands the documents that proved her dream had come true?

~

"ARE YOU LONELY?" Cora asked, peering over John's arm at his latest attempt at a letter to Ada. "If you are lonely, I could be your friend. Henrietta says you can have as many friends as you please. She's my friend, but so are Susan, and Mallory and James—even though he's a boy—and Mary Helen, and Alma, and—"

"I account it my very good fortune to be your headmaster, Cora, and I'm pleased you have so many friends."

"What are you writing?"

My very first love letter. "I'm inviting Miss Ada to come see our quilts."

"They aren't finished yet. Mrs. MacHeath says genius cannot be rushed. Am I a genius?"

Cora was a pest, the most delightful, dear, darling pest ever to destroy a man's concentration. "Of course you are. All of my scholars at St. Jerome's are geniuses. Right now, your brilliant conversation is distracting me from my assignment though."

She patted his arm. "If you got a 'signment, I have to leave you alone. That's the rule. 'Bye!"

She scampered around the desk and pelted for the door, though she stopped short of the corridor. "Miss Ada. Good day. Headmaster wants you to see our quilts but they aren't finished yet. I'm a genius."

"And possessed of such charming conversation too," Miss Ada said, bending down to hug the child. "Shall we practice our curtsies?"

Cora stood very tall, then held her skirts with one hand and bent precisely at the knees while dipping her chin.

"Marvelously graceful," Ada said, doing likewise. "I can tell you've been practicing."

"Mrs. MacHeath says I'm a new recruit. We have to practice. Headmaster has a 'signment. You have to leave him alone."

"I won't be long," Ada said, pulling off her gloves. "I'm only here to convey an invitation."

She was also, whether she knew it or not, showing off a blue velvet walking dress to very good advantage. Her reticule matched her gloves, both straw colored, and from beneath her hem a pair of green embroidered slippers had John's imagination galloping off to picnic blankets and secluded woodlands.

"Headmaster needs friends," Cora said. "I am his friend, but you can be too. 'Bye!" She trotted off, making noises that replicated the sound of shod hooves on cobblestones.

"Our Cora has become quite lively," Ada said. "While I find you at your desk in the middle of a sunny afternoon. Have you been naughty, Headmaster?"

He wanted to be naughty, but he left the door open precisely to thwart that foolishness. "Miss Beauvais, a pleasure to see you. You are looking exceedingly well. I hope Mr. Carruthers has met with you?"

She still bore the scent of lemon verbena, and John was still in love with her, more than ever. St. Jerome's was coming to life in new and wonderful ways, thanks to the funds Ada Beauvais had raised, and while John delighted in those changes, he also realized that a part of him missed Ada and always would.

"I met with Mr. Carruthers at the first of the week. He imparted very interesting news to me."

John dredged up a smile, though the news that Ada was moving out to Surrey, there to frolic with her butterflies and window seats, left him oddly bereft.

"You are the proud owner of Hopewell Grange," he said. "I am so pleased for you. My father took the homily you offered him to heart—Uncle Bascomb had delivered the same message in fact. Papa didn't want me to feel beholden. He wanted my successes at St. Jerome's to be entirely mine, though he'd failed to consider how his distance would look to others. Won't you have a seat?"

Won't you please stay?

"No," she said, swishing across his office. "No, I will not have a seat. Why haven't you asked me to read to the children?"

"I beg your pardon?"

She came to a halt before him. "If Miss Deevers is sufficiently literate to read stories to the children, then so am I."

He recalled the feel of Ada in his arms, the press of her lips to his. "You are very literate." Also brilliant, determined, passionate, and so very dear. "If you have the time to read to the children, they would love a story from you when you find yourself in Town."

She whirled away and John nearly grabbed her by the wrist.

"What am I to do with sixty-eight windows, my lord? That's not including the half-windows at the back of the house that let light into my kitchens, nor the attic windows, which I've yet to count. I have only the one backside, and if I sat in a different window every day, I would make fewer than six circuits of my house in an entire year. That is a ridiculous waste of natural light."

"Ada?"

"My park," she went on, traversing the office in the opposite direction, "the grassy meadow immediately proximate to my house, measures nearly forty acres. I have my own pond—a whole pond—but am I to be the only person who goes wading there? Do I keep a coach and four simply for myself? I find the notion insupportable."

"But you dreamed of a home of your own, a place to call your own and do as you like. That's a good dream, a fine dream. I want you to have your dream and be happy, Ada. I do."

She paused again, the desk between them. "Is that all you want?"

"I want many things. I want the children to be healthy and happy. I want the staff to know they are appreciated. I want…"

John had wanted his father's notice, and more than that, his father's respect. He had that now—he'd always had it—and still he was not content.

"What do you want, John?"

What marvelous blue eyes she had, so honest. "I want St. Jerome's to thrive. I want to watch Cora grow up into a delightful, incorrigible, brilliant scamp of a young lady. I want all of London to know that with love, care, and determination, children discarded from the lowest ranks of society can mature into adults who carry themselves with pride and make a contribution we all benefit from."

"You are a better person than I am," Ada said, coming around the desk to stroke her hand over his cravat. "I want you to have your dream, but I want to have mine too, and greedy woman that I am, dozens of windows and acres of grass won't content me. I've seen Hopewell Grange. It's lovely, but it's not enough."

He took her hand in his, because when she caressed his chest like that, his thinking mind went straight to the happiest corner of perdition.

"I can visit you in Surrey, Ada. It's not so far. I'll bring my sisters." All three of them together might be enough to chaperone his wayward impulses, but only just.

"The Muses are certainly welcome to call, but the problem is you, John Waverly. I want you."

"*Me?*"

"And Cora, and Henrietta, and Mrs. MacHeath. I want St. Jerome's, and I want Hopewell Grange."

Those two objectives were a good twenty miles apart.

That was John's last coherent thought before Ada kissed him, or he kissed her. Whoever started it, the kiss became a mutual expression of wonder, wishes, and desire, until John was braced against the desk, Ada bundled in close, and both of them were winded.

"Ada, what are you saying?"

"I am saying that I want *all* of my wishes to come true, and your wishes too, I hope. I want you, the children, and St. Jerome's to share the Grange with me. I want us to be a family, to learn and laugh, and on fine days we can play cricket in the park, and Cora can climb trees and then—"

"Yes," John said. "Yes, yes, yes, to all of it, and especially to the part about being a family. My father wants a chance to make a better impression on you."

Ada wrapped her arms around him and rested her cheek against his chest. "The marquess saved the day, John. Mr. Carruthers told me all about it. I owe the marquess a great deal."

John stroked her hair, toying with the thick tress that curled at her shoulder. "You gave the marques back his prodigal son, Ada. Papa and I hadn't talked—really talked—for years. Because of you, we walked across half of London as if it was five minutes down to the corner pub. He must sit on a dozen committees, and one in particular deals with London's homeless orphans. He asked my opinion."

"And you gave it to him, I hope. Your honest opinion."

"I did not mince my words, because I spoke to him the way I'd speak to you, without fear of judgment."

Oh, how he loved to hold her, to have her in his arms, to be in her company. And yet... the door was open, the children were soon to abandon the garden.

"We have much to plan," Ada said. "I want to show you Hopewell Grange. I have some ideas, but I'm sure you will have ideas too."

John led her to the reading chairs, and resisted, barely, the temptation to sit with her in his lap. Time for that later—though not too much later. Ada held forth about dormitories and school rooms, a conservatory and a music room, while John's head spun and his heart waltzed.

"Do you know," Ada said, "when Mr. Carruthers put this challenge to me, I dreaded what lay before me, because I had to face a few old nightmares in order to reach for a dream."

"And?" John asked.

"And making me let go of those nightmares is the best gift anybody could have given me, short of the gift I look forward to sharing with you."

She smiled *such* a smile, mysterious, pleased, a bit naughty. "Ada Beauvais, you tempt me to indiscretions."

"Good, because you tempt me to outright scandal."

He rose and closed the door. "Might I tempt you just a little bit more?"

Ada arranged her skirts so the toes of her slippers peeked from beneath her hems, and John's mouth went dry.

"You may, but only a little."

Fortunately for John, *little* was a relative term.

EPILOGUE

The business diary on William Carruthers's desk held only a single entry for the remainder of the day, week, month, and year. His final appointment before quitting England would be with the same client whose business had launched him into his own practice, fittingly enough. Other than the journal, the desk was bare—the blotter devoid of documents, books, and correspondence for the first time in years.

Afternoon light gleamed on bare mahogany, though of course, Marigold sat directly in the path of the sunbeams slanting through the window. She looked quite at home in the empty correspondence tray, as if the shallow box had finally found its true purpose.

"This time tomorrow," William informed his cat, "I will be sailing away from English shores, back to the warmth, color, and beauty of Assam."

Marigold squinted at him, then settled into a sphinx-like pose.

"My mother waits for me there," he went on, pacing before the desk as if composing a legal argument, "along with cousins, aunties, in-laws..." So many years, they'd waited for him to return and yet, the notion of leaving London saddened him.

"Who would have thought that London—stinking, filthy, bustling London—could ever become dear to a boy raised in India?" He took the seat behind the desk, the cushion intimately contoured for his comfort. "But her ladyship loves London, loves the noise and busyness, and even the damned winter snows. I will never recall this place without also recalling the woman who stole my heart. Larceny is a crime, you know."

Marigold, with the vast indifference for which felines are infamous, began to purr. Larceny might be a crime, but harboring a *tendresse* for a client was unprofessional—also pointless.

"She needed a competent solicitor," William said, scratching Marigold's shoulders. "Not another conquest. And as for what I needed..."

To grow his business, to uphold the client's faith in her trusted advisor, to be *honorable*.

"Perhaps a little less honor might have resulted in fewer regrets, eh, cat?"

The answer to that question was a contented rumbling larger than such a petite beast should be able to produce. The clock on the mantel showed five minutes to the hour. Time to put the water on for tea.

William rose to swing a kettle over the coals on the hearth. He measured chamomile into the strainer—the client's favorite—and checked the sugar bowl, for she preferred her tea with a dash of sweetness.

The sound of the heavy outer door opening warned William to gather his composure and assume his customary position behind the desk. A murmur of voices—the clerks all knew this client by name—and then the space of thirty-six confident footfalls to bury the longing he'd carried in silence for years.

"Will she miss me half as much as I will miss her?"

Marigold replied with a toothy yawn.

Lady Katherine Blackmore sailed into the office, her smile radiant, the roses in her cheeks rivaling the season's prettiest blooms.

She'd always exuded confidence, but time had gilded her self-possession with a feminine assurance that William found more alluring for being all too rare among the ladies of polite society.

"Mr. Carruthers, good day."

He bowed. "On time as always, Lady Kitty."

She untied her bonnet and stripped off her gloves, placing them on the sideboard. "You are a busy man. For you, I bestir myself to punctuality."

He moved around the desk. "I will always have time for you, my lady. Shall I take your cloak?" He made certain the office was warm on the days she was scheduled to call, in part because that was mere consideration, but also because the simple act of removing her wrap pleased him.

Silly, that. To look forward to performing a basic courtesy for a woman he'd never see again.

She passed him her cloak—merino wool, very soft, and lightly scented with her jasmine perfume. The feel of it in his hands was exquisite.

"I have never seen your office looking so..." She took her time surveying the room.

"Tidy?" William suggested as the kettle began to hiss. "Clean?"

"Your office has always been spotless," her ladyship said, settling into the chair before the desk. "Now, it looks empty."

"I sail tomorrow. If the new fellow is to move in, the least I owe him is a clean blotter. He professes to love cats. Marigold will soon know if he's telling the truth."

Kitty's gaze—usually forthright to a fault in the opinion of her meddlesome family—was unreadable.

"You returned twenty thousand pounds to my account. Which of my couples failed their challenge?"

William used an ancient potholder to pour the boiling water into his Jasperware teapot. He'd chosen this set for today because the blue of the ceramic had reminded him of Kitty's eyes, more fool he.

"Mr. Sedgewick did not sell enough art. The piece he brought me did not sell in time. He missed the challenge by twenty-five hundred pounds."

Kitty and Marigold indulged in a nose kiss while William nearly poured scalding water on his own fingers.

"He missed by that much?" Kitty murmured. "That is a shame."

"Sedgewick and his lady were happy with the outcome. Two of the challenges were completed according to your terms, for which I congratulate you. That's greater success than I expected."

Marigold turned a smug expression on William then curled up again in his letter tray. *No success for you, old man. Bon voyage.*

"You were skeptical of my approach," Kitty said, sitting back.

"A little." He'd had no blessed idea what she'd been about with these challenges and still did not. "I admire your generosity and your dedication to your family. The funds you disbursed will make an enormous difference to those involved. I've always respected your sense of purpose, and your willingness to risk your assets for the right causes."

"They were all three good causes, and I account them all successful." She was confident of her opinion, as always.

"Even though Sedgewick didn't meet the terms?"

"Mr. Carruthers, this little project was never about money." Lady Kitty spoke quietly.

She knew her mind, though William was still baffled by the motivation behind her "little project." He added a single lump of sugar to her tea and passed the cup and saucer across the desk.

"Perhaps you were concerned with the specific couples," he said, pouring his own tea. He'd packed himself a cannister of chamomile for the voyage, and because he was a sentimental fool.

Kitty saluted with her tea cup. "You are correct."

"So Lady Katherine Blackmore has turned into a matchmaker." Ironic that. "How did you know your schemes would go well?"

She took a sip of her tea, stalling perhaps, or gathering her thoughts. "I've not been successful at love, but did you think it impossible for my ideas to bring couples together?"

Abruptly, they were on difficult terrain. Kitty posed her question with a particular glint in her eyes that William had learned to respect.

"Your engagement to that bleating disgrace of a lordling was hardly a matter of the heart, my lady. The only failure was his inability to cozen his way to your fortune with obvious flummery."

"Or cozen you with his consequence and threats. Have I ever thanked you for convincing me to cry off?"

"I merely provided you advice based on the available facts." That she'd heeded William's guidance had earned him her family's enmity, also their grudging respect.

"I knew Adelicia Beauvais's determination and pragmatism would balance Lord John Waverly's optimism and pride," Kitty said.

"Miss Beauvais, soon to be Lady John Waverly, is your niece. I suppose that would give you insight into her character, but how did you know Waverly?"

"I'm well acquainted with his sisters, and believe he'd do anything for those he cares about. I also knew his orphanage was failing for want of dedicated patrons. Honorable men seldom excel at plainly stating their needs and desires."

She held out her cup and saucer, he refreshed her tea and set the pot down on the tray. Rather than resume his seat, he leaned a hip against the side of the desk.

"Lord John and Miss Beauvais struck me as having little in common."

"Sometimes," Kitty said, "different perspectives are not only desirable but ideal. You and I manage to rub along quite well, for example, though I am entirely lacking in subtlety and you are seldom direct."

Was that a challenge? Kitty finished her tea in silence and passed William her empty cup. If he'd been a fatuous, doting swain he might have drunk from the place on the rim her lips had touched and then sent her a melting glance. Kitty would likely laugh uproariously and bid him to pack up his romantic aspirations along with his chamomile tea.

"And yet," he said, "you remained an anonymous donor, which some might consider the behavior of a discreet if not subtle lady."

Lady Kitty looked around the empty office, a place where she and William had argued, plotted financial strategies, and even laughed together.

"I regret how selfishly I acted in my youth. The heedless way I treated those I cared for most. Ada suffered terribly when she was accused of writing that dreadful letter. She was banished from the school's library for weeks, and she lived for her hours in the library. She never betrayed me or reproached me for imposing on her."

William vaguely recalled some narrowly averted scandal that had instead been taken for schoolgirl foolishness. "Then these challenges were what? Atonement? To prove something?"

"Maybe."

"To whom?"

"To myself." Kitty rose and untied the sashes holding the curtains back from the window. The result was a gloomier office, but sensible. Sunlight damaged upholstery, furniture, and wallpaper, after all, and the office would be vacant for at least a week.

"I had the means to help those who had once helped me," she said, smoothing wrinkles from the curtains. "I simply did what was right. Do you remember what you said to me when we first met? You told me that a selfish woman, regardless of her beauty, her fortune, or her title, would be a burden to any man."

He'd nearly shouted that at her, when she'd been holding forth about marrying any titled suitor she pleased to marry. "My words may not have been fair—"

"Don't apologize, William." She laid her hand on his arm. "What you said *was* fair, and it was honest."

She and he did not ever touch, except to share the most fleeting and inconsequential of courtesies. And yet, her hand remained on his sleeve, a small presumption he'd feel all the way to India.

"Kitty—"

"You alone have always been honest with me, William Carruthers. You have safeguarded my well-being and my fortune. No man could be … no man has been a better friend."

William took her hand in his, surely a permitted familiarity when two friends of long acquaintance were parting. What could he say, as a man hopelessly in love but determined to cling to his dignity for one more day?

"My lady, I will miss you." And wasn't that just brilliant oration from a highly trained legal mind? He tried again. "I will miss you terribly."

The cat rose from her perch on the desk and leapt to the sideboard. Her gaze struck William as pitying, then she commenced washing her paws.

"I hope you find happiness," Kitty said, smoothing her free hand over his lapel. "I hope you find your heart's desire. You deserve every joy life has to offer."

The cat paused in her ablutions and flicked her tail. *Get on with it, man. Bow and say farewell, why don't you?*

And therein lay the difficulty. A solicitor William surely was, but when it came to Lady Katherine Blackmore, he was first and always, a man in love.

"What if all I want is to have the woman I admire—have admired for years—at my side?"

Another pat to his lapel, but was that a tear shimmering on Kitty's eyelashes? "I hope your mother has chosen such a fine person for you. Someone who'll know how to draw you into long conversations and make you smile."

"Mother has probably found sixteen wonderful women, each more beautiful and accomplished than the last. None of those ladies will be you."

Kitty's hand went still on his chest. "What are you saying, William?"

He took both of her hands in his, lest she snatch up her gloves and cloak and flee before he could be honest with her one last time.

"You are my heart's desire. I wish to be the man worthy of your love."

Dignity be damned. He'd sail for India knowing he'd at least had the courage to face the truth, much as Kitty had faced the truth about her family's plans for her all those years ago.

"Say that again, William." She offered him not a command—and Lady Katherine Blackmore was very comfortable with imperative tones—but a plea.

"I love you. I have loved you since you first stormed into my office demanding to know why a lowly solicitor presumed to request a private audience on the topic of a client's nuptial plans. I will love you in some fashion until I'm an old man who can't recall where he's put his spectacles, though they are on his very head, but who will always know to whom he gave his heart."

She slipped her hands free of his grasp, and William steeled himself to be gently chided, perhaps even mocked.

Instead, Kitty slid her arms around his waist and leaned against him. "You need not fashion an argument for the jury, William. I considered buying the HMS New Hope so I could stop you from sailing."

The feel of her, warm, female, nestled so sweetly against him was intoxicating, and yet, William's legal mind had to parse the heretofores and notwithstandings.

"You need not have set up those challenges to convince me of your goodness or the depths of your generous heart, Kitty. I love you exactly as you are." He pressed a soft kiss to the back of her fingers. "But I have a challenge for you now."

"Do you?"

"Yes, one that comes with benefits, such as travel and love, but also demands."

Kitty leaned into him, and if ever a man envied the feline ability to purr, William was that man.

"What would be the conditions of such a challenge?" she asked.

"Allow me to love you for the rest of our lives. Marry me."

"I am headstrong, Mr. Carruthers. I am opinionated, obstinate, and incorrigible." The words were doubtless meant as a disclaimer, but William heard the vulnerability in them too.

"As your solicitor, I appreciate the disclosure of potential hazards, and in the same spirit of good faith and fair dealing, I warn you that my Mother is nearly as opinionated, obstinate and incorrigible as you are. You will get on splendidly. I must also advise you, though, to finalize the terms of this arrangement posthaste, that the benefits of the union might accrue to the parties with all possible speed."

Her hands slid inside his coat to loop around his waist. "When you talk like that, Mr. Carruthers, all legal and businesslike, I am only too happy to finalize the arrangement."

He cupped her face with his palms. "As am I. May I suggest you kiss me?" he whispered.

And Kitty, as ever, followed his advice to the letter.

ARCHITECT OF MY DREAMS

Originally published in No Dukes Allowed

DEDICATION

To those who dream big dreams

CHAPTER ONE

"How I envy you those new neighbors," Lady Alice said, smiling archly behind her tea cup. "All that masculine pulchritude parading before your very doorstep. You must promise to have more at-homes, Your Grace."

"One a week is quite enough." Given Eugenia's distaste for gossip, one at-home a week was more than enough. "Masculine pulchritude pales compared to the pleasures of a good night's sleep."

Lady Alice set down her tea cup. "Did you mean that the way it sounded? I know His Grace wasn't the most congenial of husbands, but one manages."

A fourth hammer—or fifth—joined the din coming from the property across the street. Men shouted back and forth amid the noise, and the jingle of harnesses sang a descant over the cacophony. Not fashionable coaches, of course. One delivery of lumber, stone, and nails after another, and all of it beginning before dawn and ending after sunset.

"One manages best with adequate rest," Eugenia replied. "What sort of barbarian disturbs his neighbors' slumber day after day, night after night?"

Lady Alice helped herself to another cinnamon biscuit. She was doubtless increasing again, else she'd stop at two. "He is a barbarian, you know."

"Who is?"

The noise grew louder, counterpointing the pounding in Eugenia's temples. This was the third week of incessant racket from the construction across the street, the third week of being roused scant hours after her head hit the pillow. The approaching full moon would doubtless result in noise round the clock.

"Your new neighbor is Adam Morecambe." Lady Alice talked around a mouthful of biscuit. "Francis says they call him More-coin in the better clubs."

Name-calling being the hallmark of adult gentlemen, of course. "Mr. Morecambe is taking up residence on my street?"

Eugenia lived in a corner of Mayfair that was more exclusive than fashionable. The families around her had been original investors on this square, and her town house was one of the ducal dower properties.

"Oh my, no. Morecambe isn't building *himself* a palace over there. He's converting the Campbell mansion into a gentlemen's club. Francis calls it the Blackball Club, because they're admitting only commoners, or that's the rumor."

A great crash sounded from across the street as a load of stone cascaded from the back of a wagon onto what had once been a tidily swept walkway. Mr. Morecambe had apparently devised some mechanism for tilting the bed of the wagon such that the contents, aided by gravity and accompanied by a horrific racket, delivered themselves to the ground.

"That's it," Eugenia said. "Even a duchess has limits. You are welcome to the rest of the biscuits, Alice. I have a barbarian to instruct."

"I want the recipe," Lady Alice said, swiping another treat from the tray as she rose. "I'm coming with you. Morecambe isn't a gentleman, and Francis says—"

"Enough of what Francis says, for God's sake. I am the Dowager Duchess of Tindale, and on my doorstep, what I say should matter."

"WORKS A TREAT, EVERY TIME," Rosenbarker said as the mason's apprentices began piling the stones onto the lifts. "Wish you'd thought of this tipping business ten years ago."

As the apprentice turned the crank, the wagon bed slowly returned to level, a sight that always gave Adam Morecambe pleasure. The mechanism was essentially a large screw with a shallow thread angle, rotated by a long handle. Thanks to Mr. Maudsley's screw-cutting lathe, an invention a mere two decades old, Adam was making other wagons like it.

"The gears sound like they need oiling," he said, "and the whole purpose of the tipper wagon is so work can proceed more efficiently, not so you can stand around admiring the results."

The bed settled, the apprentice threw the brace securing the crank handle, and the driver gave the horses the signal to trot off.

"I do hope you've built rest for the horses into the schedule," Rosenbarker said. "Nobody designed them any fancy mechanisms to ease their work, and when the stones were unloaded by hand, the horses got a half hour's respite."

"They need half an hour's rest for every load? That much?"

Rosenbarker took off his glasses and used a wrinkled handkerchief to clean them. Building was dusty work.

"You needn't allow the horses their rest, Morecambe. You can simply work them until they drop. Then the seasoned teams wear out faster, the nervous youngsters are put to in greater quantity, and we have more coaches galloping off across more village greens on market day. The choice is yours."

Solomon Rosenbarker's memory was one of his finest qualities—usually. "That was one team, three years ago, and I still contend a wasp was involved."

Rosenbarker widened his stance and stuffed his glasses in one pocket, his handkerchief in the other. "Two and a half years, and the cost in damages ate up twenty percent of—you have trouble, sir. The kind that wears bonnets."

Rosenbarker sidled away to supervise the sorting of the rocks, which needed no supervision. The old rascal was staying close enough to overhear the coming confrontation, but far enough away so that no stray verbal bullets would threaten him.

Trouble was a fetching pair of women in fashionable day dresses. The taller of the two wore the gaudier bonnet—two birds and an entire bouquet of silk roses. She also carried a lot of pink lace on a stick that was probably intended to resemble a parasol.

The smaller woman walked slightly ahead of her companion. Her bonnet was plain straw, her parasol unpretentious. Adam had no interest in women's fashions, or in most women for that matter, but he knew an angry swish of skirts from a flirtatious swish of skirts, and the small woman had no flirtation on her mind.

"You are Mr. Morecambe," she said, marching directly up to Adam.

"And you are angry."

She was also pretty, though quietly so. Brown eyes framed with brows heavier than was fashionable, regular features, and a full mouth pinched with ire. Her hair was dark brown, what he could see of it, and she eschewed cosmetics.

The lady's companion, then, charging forth at the behest of her more genteel associate. Somewhere on this street lived a dowager duchess, giving the neighborhood a dash of titled cachet. Had the street been burdened with a ducal residence, Adam would never have bought the Campbell property.

"I am not angry, Mr. Morecambe, I am exhausted and tormented by noise the livelong day. I refuse to suffer in silence any longer."

He knew better than to apply logic to an annoyed woman, and yet, he asked the obvious question. "How can one suffer in silence if the noise is incessant?"

She looked down her nose at him, quite a feat considering she was nearly a foot shorter than he.

"Be obtuse if your intellect is truly that limited, sir, but save your disrespect for those to whom such a slight would matter. I demand some quiet."

Rosenbarker was studying the pile of rocks. The other woman was pretending to be fascinated with the work site. Typical of London's upper class, she was allowing her minion to do the figurative heavy lifting.

"Then I suggest you go somewhere quieter," Adam said. "Nobody's stopping you."

"The common law of this great land says that you are the party who needs to go elsewhere," Plain Bonnet retorted. "A woman is entitled to the quiet enjoyment of her domicile, as are my neighbors. That is the law. You will either accommodate the law, or deal with the consequences."

Frilly Parasol was looking amused. Rosenbarker was blatantly staring.

Keep the lawyers out of sight was the first rule of sound business.

That was Adam's last thought before somebody three floors up called out, "'Ware bucket!" in a thick Lancastrian accent.

Adam reacted instinctively, grabbing the woman and snatching her six feet farther from the street as a deluge of mud rained down from the scaffolding. Rosenbarker commenced swearing at the offending mason's apprentice. Lady Frilly Parasol was laughing outright, and Adam was holding a small, curvaceous bundle of female closer than he'd held a woman in months.

"Let me go," she said in a low, furious voice. "By the father of all mischief, if that is your idea of a joke, I will set fire to your benighted boys club during the four hours each night when none of your fiends are at work upon it. I will tear down every brick and stone and turn loose a plague of rodents upon your foundations. I will implore the heavens to stop your work with forty days and nights of rain. I will take my crusade to the journalists, who are ever mindful that widows in the throes of plights sell broadsheets."

Adam turned her loose. "I am a plight?" He wasn't sure how he felt about being a plight, though the woman's creativity was impressive.

"We are airing our differences on the street, or I'd be more blunt. Suffice it to say that your project is a plight, a plague, and a pestilence upon the peace of my home."

If there was a second commandment in Adam's business bible, it was to keep the journalists farther away from all projects than the lawyers, and trailing behind those two eternal verities was some nonsense about not arguing with a lady.

Adam had always thought that prohibition disrespectful of the ladies. In his experience, they were more than capable of holding their own in a verbal sparring match. Arguing with *this* lady was downright invigorating.

"Renovations are noisy undertakings," Adam said. "Fortunately for you, our schedule will have us finished up by the end of the summer." He smiled, because antagonizing the neighbors was stupid. "A few more months, and you'll have an elegant façade where the Campbell's crumbling abode once stood. Your street will gain consequence, and—"

"Stop that at once," she snapped.

The hod carriers and masons weren't due for their afternoon break for another hour, and yet, work from the scaffolding above had gone oddly quiet.

"Stop what?"

"You have offended a lady. The proper response is to apologize, not to explain the obvious in overly simplistic terms. If I had somehow arrived to the age of eight and twenty in ignorance of the fact that renovations are noisy, the past ten weeks would have proved the point handily. I care not one crumbled brick what your schedule says. The schedule of every decent beast on the planet calls for adequate and regular periods of rest and quiet."

She'd jabbed his chest on the final three words: "rest"—*jab* —"and"—*jab*—"quiet"—*jab-jab*.

How could one small finger cause such a sharp pain? "We don't work at night."

"Mr. Morecambe, at this time of year, London enjoys almost eighteen hours of daylight, and that means your workers are already making a racket some two or three hours after polite society has gone to bed."

"Why should I care about polite society?"

She stepped back, her gaze assessing. "Why shouldn't you? Polite society will be your neighbors and, I assume, the membership of your little establishment, if not its investors. Do you really want the ladies on all sides up in arms against you before you open your doors?"

Adam was not much skilled at dealing with ladies. He shot a glance at Rosenbarker, whose expression conveyed foreboding.

"No," Adam said, "but neither do I want my investors up in arms if the project falls behind schedule. If we're not finished with the exterior by the end of September, we'll have to halt until spring, and that will be costly."

He cast a scowl at the crew now shamelessly goggling from their perches on the floors above. They grinned at him. One fellow saluted with his hammer. Another bowed over his bucket of mortar.

"If you do not allow me and my neighbors some rest," the lady said, "we will seek redress from the courts and enjoin you from working more than ten hours a day."

She spoke as if a judge stood ready to do her bidding, but then, spinsters—she was eight-and-twenty and loose on her own recognizance—were a particularly eccentric class of female.

"What exactly are you asking of me, madam?"

"I am departing from Town on Monday. I would like to begin my journey refreshed and rested. For the next three days, you will not allow your crews to start until nine of the clock."

Lose three hours of labor *per day per man* on a thirty-man crew? Fall back two hundred and seventy hours *in three days*?

"What you ask is impossible."

"Very well. Best call for the ratter, because you leave me no choice but to take matters into my own hands."

She looked as if she relished that prospect. "I cannot lose hundreds of hours of labor when the weather is fair and deliveries have already been scheduled."

"Then send your deliveries around back, for heaven's sake."

The other woman opened her lacy parasol and twirled it over her shoulder. "You seem to have the situation well in hand, my dear. I'll just be going." She kissed the shorter woman on the cheek, sent Adam a pitying look, and swanned off. Across the street, a footman opened the door to a fancy landau.

"She leaves you to fight this battle alone?"

"This is *my* battle, sir."

Adam's neighbor had faint shadows under her eyes, and her dress was of the pale gray usually worn in second mourning. No jewelry, not even a brooch, adorned her attire. Rosenbarker's warning about the draft teams wearing out faster if they weren't rested enough came to mind.

"You are the only person to complain of the noise," he said, "and you are soon to leave Town."

"Everybody is soon to leave Town, and then you can use the full moon to renovate through the night. I wish you the joy of that undertaking, but not until next week, please."

Long ago, Adam had danced attendance on a proper lady. He'd haunted Mayfair's ballrooms in hopes of a waltz with her, attended every Venetian breakfast and musicale in a vain effort to spend more time at her side.

He'd ended up numb with exhaustion and despair, which was probably the only reason he hadn't finished the Season by delivering a challenge to a certain duke. Not that His Grace would have met Adam on the field of honor. Peers did not accept the challenges of commoners, which worked very nicely for the peer and not at all for the wronged commoner.

"I can have the deliveries sent around back for the next three days. I'll tell the men not to start hammering until eight a.m."

"Thank you, and please do exhort them to use less colorful language."

She could exhort them to that end, and they'd probably listen. This small woman had presence, and she would be Adam's neighbor. He could afford to accommodate her wishes on this one occasion—he hoped.

"I'll make that request of the crews and wish you a pleasant respite in the country."

She offered her hand. At first, he thought she wanted to shake hands with him, as if solemnizing the beginning of a pugilists' match. He bowed over her hand after a moment of consternation.

She wished him good day and sashayed back from whence she'd come—a modest, tidy dwelling across the street.

"Get to work," Rosenbarker called to the crews. "Back to work, ye bloody dunderwhelps, or I'll know the reason why."

On her doorstep, the lady turned, her expression pained.

"Language, Rosenbarker," Adam muttered.

"What the hell's wrong with my bloody bedamned—? Oh." He swiped off his hat. "Beg pardon, missus," he called across the street.

She slipped into the house, and within seconds, somebody was pounding away with a hammer. A second and third hammer joined in, a hod carrier started singing about Barbara Allen, and one of the Welshmen glazing windows added harmony.

"We do make quite a racket, don't we?" Adam mused.

"That's the sound of progress," Rosenbarker said.

Noisy progress. The lady hadn't been wrong. Thank goodness Adam was also traveling away from Town, because some peace and quiet by the seaside would be much appreciated.

CHAPTER TWO

Because the seaside was the last place Lord Dunstable would look for Genie, to Brighton she did go. Then too, Diana and Belinda were joining her there, and the company of friends was a much-missed comfort.

"The scent here is always the same," Belinda said, linking arms with Genie.

"I've never been able to determine if that stink is gossip or rotten eggs," Genie replied, matching her steps to her taller friend. "Or court intrigue. Thank heavens the king's entire coterie has not yet arrived."

Neither had Diana, though she was expected that afternoon. Belinda and Genie were taking the air, one of the most popular activities in Brighton.

"How is Tindale?" Belinda asked.

Two gentlemen tipped their hats, though Genie recognized neither one. "His Grace thrives in the company of his duchess. I do believe they were a love match."

She managed that observation without sounding too envious. Genie and the previous duke had not been a love match. Charles had considered himself a decent husband, meaning he'd never taken his mistresses to the theater when Genie attended, and he'd never openly chastised her for failing to produce an heir.

The rhythm of the surf was punctuated by the cries of gulls overhead, and Genie finally began to relax. Brighton had been her haven, her respite from all things London. She'd come here to escape from the relentless burden of having married far above her station and to heal from the miscarriage. Tindale had left her alone in Brighton, one of the truest acts of consideration he'd shown her.

"You're quiet," Belinda said. "Was the trip down from Town tiring?"

"I'm a trifle fatig—merciful powers, he's here."

A gentleman approached, a lady on his arm. He was exquisitely turned out and so, of course, was she.

Belinda marched along, though Genie wanted to dodge behind the nearest hedge. Why, oh why, did Isambard Bentley, Marquess of Dunstable, have to be in Brighton now?

"Duchess!" he called, tipping his hat. "And Duchess." He bowed to Belinda and then to Genie, the dukedom of Winchester standing higher in precedence than the dukedom of Tindale. "What a pleasant surprise. I'm sure you're acquainted with Lady Naughton."

Lady Naughton was a sylphlike blonde who was no better than she should be, though she avoided outright impropriety. Genie silently commended the woman on organizing her life around who and what she wanted, though why anybody would enjoy having a parcel of randy men sniffing around her skirts was a mystery.

The ladies curtseyed, and Genie gave Belinda's arm a discreet tug. "We'll let you be on your way on this fine day," Genie said. "One must enjoy the sea air while the weather remains obliging."

Belinda, confound her, remained fixed to the walkway like a lamppost. "What brings you to the seaside, my lord?"

"The beauty," he said, treating both duchesses to calf-eyed mooning. "The excellent company, the healthful pastimes."

A ducal heir's notions about healthful pastimes did not include sea bathing and likely did include gambling, horse racing, and large quantities of liquor.

Genie tried another tug on Belinda's arm. "Taking the air is a pleasure on a day such as this, and I do so enjoy my constitutional."

"Oh, but the sun," Lady Naughton said, twirling her parasol. "One must have a care for one's complexion, particularly later in life."

God spare me. "With that in mind," Genie replied, "I won't ask you to tarry any longer." She hauled Belinda forward before her ladyship could observe that exercise was beneficial for the elderly.

"What an insecure, jealous cat," Belinda said before they'd gone far enough to be out of earshot.

"I find her impressive, insulting two duchesses at one go, but then, Dunstable was flirting shamelessly." The marquess and her ladyship rounded a corner, and Genie's pleasure in the outing fled with them.

"Are you considering him?" Belinda asked.

"For what? A posting to Gibraltar? Would that such a boon were in my power."

"Genie, we're widows. This ought to be when we finally have some say over our lives, some freedom. We're dowager duchesses, for pity's sake."

"And Dunstable is a fortune hunter. Everybody knows his papa is pockets to let, despite holding the Seymouth ducal title. Let's go back to the house, shall we?"

She and Belinda were sharing quarters with their friend Mrs. Diana Thompson, an arrangement that provided company, appeased propriety, and minimized expenses. Genie had a lady's companion, in theory. In practice, Cousin Daphne took advantage of Genie's hospitality during the Season and then jaunted off to make up the numbers and frolic at the house parties until winter.

On the way home, Genie and Belinda met two honorables, an earl's second spare, and a bachelor earl fallen on hard times.

"I should remove to Bath," Genie said. "Above all, I sought peace and quiet here, and it appears somebody has declared open season on wealthy widows."

"In Bath the bachelors have fewer teeth and more ailments. Safety in numbers, Genie. We'll fend off the more determined fellows, and the rest will soon take the hint."

A fine plan, except that as Genie and Belinda approached their own doorstep, a pair of strolling gentlemen managed to intercept them before they could turn up the walk. Mr. Purcell Vandameer and his bosom companion Mr. Trelawney Gaunt nearly climbed through the parlor windows in an effort to secure an invitation to tea.

Genie produced a headache from all the bright sun and a sour stomach from yesterday's travel and then shoved Belinda past the front gate before the gentlemen could wedge themselves through the very door.

"I cannot do this," Genie said as they waved the gentlemen on to their next quarry. "I cannot endure these strutting buffoons here, where I've come to rest and regain my wits."

"Give it a few days," Belinda said. "They like you because you're so approachable."

Not approachable—common, but lacking in the commoner's ability to reproduce in quantity. Genie had overheard Charles lamenting that shortcoming and had been heartbroken for days.

"Here comes another one," she said, though the gentleman coming down the walkway was alone and moving at a pace that suggested an actual destination rather than a need to be seen flaunting Bond Street finery.

"Yonder pedestrian is a sizable specimen of manhood," Belinda murmured.

Broad shoulders, height, hat sitting straight on a head of dark hair, rather than tilted at the prescribed rakish angle.

"That is not a fortune hunter," Genie said. "That is Mr. Morecambe."

"His features are not exactly refined."

No, but they were attractive. Genie had been married to a handsome fellow, one who'd spent more time with his tailor, hairdresser, and valet than most men spent at paying occupations. All the finery in the world wouldn't disguise the fact that Mr. Morecambe's nose had character, his jaw hinted of stubbornness, and his smiles were rare and more fierce than charming.

He had an air of purpose, and he was here in Brighton, looking formidable while simply traveling along the walkway. He'd plow over the fortune hunters without breaking stride.

"Mr. Morecambe!" Genie called. "What a surprise. Always a pleasure to meet a neighbor. Perhaps you'd like to come in for tea?"

"Oh, do," Belinda said, putting on her Delighted Duchess smile. She was an attractive lady, and her smile exuded genuine friendliness.

Mr. Morecambe looked more annoyed than enchanted. "Madam, we have not been introduced, though of course I recall our previous discussion."

"No matter," Genie said. "Widows are permitted a bit of eccentricity, and you and I are to be neighbors. This isn't a Mayfair ballroom, and we needn't stand on ceremony. Belinda, Duchess of Winchester, may I make known to you my London neighbor, Mr. Adam Morecambe. Mr. Morecambe, Her Grace of Winchester."

Belinda completed the introductions, though even as Mr. Morecambe bowed over gloved hands, he was sending appraising glances in the direction of the house.

"Is this Nash's work? It's in his style."

"The house has been renovated based on plans drawn up by Mr. Burton for another property," Genie said. "He's young, but quite talented. Perhaps you'd like to have a tour of the premises? The whole dwelling is lovely."

An offer of tea with two duchesses had produced only a scowl. The chance to inspect the house had Mr. Morecambe opening the gate.

"Most kind of you, though you needn't bother with the tea."

How refreshingly honest. Genie linked arms with him. "We're duchesses. We always bother with the tea."

He hesitated on the front step. "*Both* of you are duchesses?"

Hadn't they just boldly introduced themselves as such two minutes ago?

"Dowager duchesses," Belinda said, as if that was the most unremarkable status a woman could hold. Belinda was, in fact, the famed Double Duchess, having a second duke panting about her heels. She detested the nickname. Genie suspected Belinda detested her ducal suitor as well.

"We put out a hearty tray," Genie said, "and you will find the arrangement of the pantries ingenious."

The allure of the pantry layout appeared to intrigue him. He paused to study the knocker—a rampant gryphon rendered in brass—then followed the ladies into the house.

❧

ADAM HAD no use for duchesses.

They were merely a blight upon the social landscape, however, while dukes merited his unending ire. A duke had a legal right to consult with the sovereign, could not be arrested for civil wrongs, and any criminal charges against him were tried in the House of Lords—the original exclusive gentlemen's club.

Worst of all, dukes could not be jailed for unpaid debts.

Duchesses, however, were technically commoners and thus earned a vague resentment from Adam rather than unrelenting disdain.

Resenting these two ladies would be difficult. Her Grace of Winchester was lovely, with expressive green eyes, a flawless complexion, and a voice that conveyed equal parts refinement and gracious warmth.

She was, in other words, exactly as a fairy-tale duchess ought to be.

Her Grace of Tindale, however, was in need of some renovation if she sought to present herself as the former helpmeet of a duke. She wore the same plain bonnet she'd had on last week, her dress was several years out of date and loose about the bodice, and across her nose and cheeks appeared a smattering of freckles.

Adam liked those freckles. They put him in mind of goose girls and tavern maids, women who did honest work and didn't put on airs. Her Grace's eyes were brown, friendly, and intelligent, and what she lacked in stature, she made up for in unpretentiousness.

"What brings you to Brighton?" she asked.

Adam accepted his tea in a porcelain cup adorned with pink roses and gold trim. "Business."

Both ladies gazed at him expectantly. Making conversation with proper women felt like taking a sledgehammer to a plaster wall— sheer effort and slow going.

"I'm looking over some residential properties," he added. "For possible purchase."

"You're shopping," the Duchess of Tindale said. "I haven't the knack for shopping."

Adam set down his tea cup carefully. He'd smashed more than one porcelain delicacy by accident.

"Choosing real estate to invest in isn't the same as picking out a new pair of slippers."

"Oh yes, it is," Her Grace of Tindale replied. "You examine all the possibilities, consult your budget, consider the priorities control- ling your decision, then make a choice and hope for the best."

Her Grace of Winchester nodded. "Shopping, in a nutshell. Would anybody like more tea?"

Adam wanted to bolt from the tufted sofa and take his quizzing glass to the scrollwork running in two vertical columns above the mantel. The elaborate carvings framed a space occupied by a picture of a small boy standing beside a seated mastiff.

At the ceiling, the carving branched out into molding, which echoed a pattern of grapes and leaves interspersed with flowers. The transition from wooden carving to plaster molding was nearly invisible and exactly matched by smaller carvings on the underside of the mantel. The leaves appeared to be oak, the symbol for bravery, while the flowers—

"Mr. Morecambe?"

The duchesses were looking a trifle perplexed.

"Beg pardon?"

"I asked," said Her Grace of Tindale, "if you were in the market for any particular sort of property."

He was searching for a bargain, an overlooked jewel that wanted only a little care and appreciation to make it shine.

"I'm building a gentlemen's club in London, as you know. It has been suggested that we obtain smaller properties in Brighton, Bath, and Bristol for the convenience of our members."

"You'll want a residential property, then," Her Grace of Tindale said. "Close to the Pavilion and the beach, but not so close as to be prohibitively expensive."

"Recently refurbished," Her Other Grace added. "Not too recently. New construction is out of the question—a house newly built might start to leak or shift at any time—but those poky little medieval houses won't do either. The stairways in them are not to be borne."

The ladies commenced tossing back and forth the qualities of various streets—this one was near the market, that one had lovely neighbors—and Adam tried to listen, but it was no use. The scrollwork called to him, the mechanism for latching the windows wasn't one he'd seen before, and a vent at floor level along one wall intrigued him.

"If you'll excuse me," the Duchess of Winchester said, rising. "I've still some unpacking to tend to. Mr. Morecambe, a pleasure."

Then he was alone with the Duchess of Tindale and a house that cried out to be explored.

"I promised you a tour of the premises," she said. "Shall we start in the attics?"

"Always a fine plan." For the proof was in the roof, as one of Adam's master masons liked to say. If a house had been poorly constructed, the inferior materials, uneven foundation, and cut corners first took a toll on how the structure and roof joined. Water soon made an unwelcome appearance where water didn't belong—in chimneys, walls, attics, and so forth—and then the whole building was jeopardized.

"You will not find a water stain, if that's what has your gaze fixed to the ceilings," the duchess said as she led him into a dormitory under the eaves. "The present owner is my godmother, and she stewards her resources carefully."

The dormitory was both dry and airy, a comfortable place for the maids to sleep, with windows to let in light.

"Building properly is always the better bargain," Adam said, running his hand down the plaster wall. No subtle dampness, no unevenness better perceived by touch than sight. "Practice too many economies, take too many liberties, and you invite cracks, leaks, shifts, and poor workmanship."

"Rather like falsehoods in a relationship," Her Grace said, trailing a finger over the mantel. "An omission becomes a white lie, which becomes a well-meant untruth, that over time becomes a breach of trust."

She dusted her fingers together, rubbing away a fine smudge. Whatever had brought such a farfetched analogy to her mind had also chased the warmth from her eyes.

"Shall we inspect the attic?" Adam asked.

"Of course. I doubt there's much stored on the premises. Godmama mostly lends the house to friends or stays for only short periods herself."

The duchess spoke knowledgeably about each piece of art on the walls, each sideboard and reading chair. The dwelling was lovely, and the library a masterpiece in miniature. For those carvings, Adam did take out his quizzing glass to admire work so delicate, the hand of a master was obvious.

"These have to be Grinling Gibbons's work," he said. "Certainly from his workshop, but I'd be surprised if they weren't original to him." Personal woodcarver to both Charles II and James II, Gibbons had created works of genius for many a great house. His lintels of flowers were said to be so lifelike, a passing coach would cause them to bob in the breeze.

The duchess stuck her finger into a bouquet of daisies in a bowl of Delftware. The bird-pine-flower design suggested the vase was at least a hundred years old.

Her Grace shook droplets of water from her finger. "You've seen Petworth, I take it?"

"I've been marched through the long gallery once, by a house-keeper who clearly feared I'd be filching the valuables."

"That does sound like Mrs. Bryce. I can take you back there any time you please, and I can assure you, Mrs. Bryce will be more accommodating. What is the point of having such beautiful homes if they are admired and enjoyed by only a few? As an architect, you should have been welcomed."

The duchess used a pitcher from the sideboard to give the daisies a drink.

"You do know what the vase is worth?" When the Chinese had closed their porcelain export business in the early seventeenth century, the Dutch potters had created designs to compensate for the lack of imports. The work was exquisite, but when the Chinese resumed trading their wares, the Dutch had moved on to other inspirations. The container holding the mundane bouquet was a rare and beautiful antique.

"The vase is pretty enough to merit a spot in the window," she said, "so passersby can enjoy the lovely flowers too."

She was like no kind of duchess Adam had imagined, and as she led him all throughout this jewel of a house—the pantries were ingenious, the parlors exquisite, the bedrooms delightful—he admired everything, from the appointments, to the architecture, to the craftsmanship.

He admired *her* architecture, too, from trim ankles, to rounded hips, to hands that were both graceful and competent. She was not overly endowed in the bosom, but Adam had always preferred modest perfection to ample mediocrity.

He mentally dropped a hammer on his foot at that ungentlemanly thought.

"Would you like to sketch that scrollery?" she asked, crossing to the desk. "You've been staring a hole in it."

"Sketch it?" He would dearly, dearly love to make a drawing of the woodwork and to make enough notes to recall the layout of the whole dwelling. "If that wouldn't be too great an imposition."

She set paper, pencils, a penknife, and standish on the blotter. "I'll leave you to it. The bell-pull will summon the housekeeper, and I'll have the kitchen send you up a proper tray. Tea cakes and gunpowder will hardly be adequate for a man of your robust proportions."

Her gaze was frankly appraising. Not flirtatious, simply a hostess taking the measure of a guest and pronouncing him hungry.

Which Adam was—for food, but also to capture this house on paper. "Your hospitality is much appreciated."

"We're to be neighbors," she said, beaming at him as if being neighbors was the most enjoyable mischief known to humankind. "Make yourself at home, and I'll look in on you later."

She left the room after one more quick perusal of the accoutrements on the blotter, and Adam took a seat at the desk. The pencils were sharp, so he could set immediately to memorializing what he'd seen. The carvings, the floor plans, the window latches, the ingenious vent that let heat from the kitchen rise to the family parlor.

The image that took shape on the page was a homage to lovely architecture: gracious, pleasing, and—where was the harm in a quick portrait?—sporting freckles across her cheeks.

CHAPTER THREE

Genie sat in the family parlor and tried to ignore the fact that a man occupied the library only a few yards away. An attractive, intelligent man.

Mr. Morecambe had accepted the tray from the kitchen more than an hour ago, and Genie had spent the intervening time staring at the pages of Sir Walter Scott's *Ivanhoe*. The story was too much about brave knights hiding who they really were, getting wounded and killed, and acting like complete gudgeons. The ladies merely looked pretty and endured propositions, except for Rebecca the healer.

She possessed courage and lifesaving skills and doubtless had had wonderful adventures in far-off Granada.

"I am no Rebecca," Genie informed the marmalade cat. "I am merely a dowager duchess without offspring." The most pathetic creature in all of Debrett's.

One of few appointments in Godmama's house that Genie disliked was a stuffed nightingale arranged in a gilded cage amid silk roses. The little bird stared at her out of glass eyes, until Genie wanted to fling *Ivanhoe* at the wall.

Mr. Morecambe's interest in the house had been passionate. He'd traced the woodwork with his bare fingers, sniffed the dried herbal sachets—lavender for the library, rose for the parlor, jasmine for Genie's sitting room—and rapped on any number of walls. He'd engaged with the house more purposefully than some men engaged with their partners for the waltz.

"What could he be doing over there?"

He'd merely peered into her bedroom, an airy, high-ceilinged retreat featuring a bed large enough to hold most of Genie's six brothers. She'd been seized with an impulse to lock the door and fling herself into Mr. Morecambe's arms.

"There will be none of that," she muttered, rising. "Dunstable is underfoot, and any breath of scandal will reach his ears, and then where will I be?"

The one consolation left to Genie was that she was invited everywhere, had friends of varying degrees in most fashionable neighborhoods, and came and went as she pleased. She had worked long and hard and paid a very high price to be worthy of polite society's acceptance. Should Dunstable make good on his threat to drag her name through the sewer, even those comforts would be gone.

"But nothing says I must forgo an outing with a prospective neighbor," she murmured, hand on the door latch. "I am a widow and have earned my freedom up to a point."

She crossed the corridor and paused outside the library long enough to rap softly on the paneled door.

No response. Mr. Morecambe was likely absorbed in his sketching. What would it be like for him to focus on her? She had known one moment in his arms back in London, and those arms had been strong and sheltering.

"I'd likely need a roof and shutters before he took any special notice of me."

She pushed open the library door to find her guest seated at the desk, boots propped on the corner, arms folded, chin on his chest. A gentle snore wafted across the room, and as the cat stropped himself across Genie's ankles, she feasted on the sight of Adam Morecambe in shirt-sleeves, fast asleep.

~

A SHARP RAP on the door startled Adam from dreams of wooden flowers and freckled geese. His boots dropped to the floor, nearly clobbering an indignant orange cat.

"Where did you come from?"

The cat squinted, and the knock sounded again on the door, more firmly.

"Come in."

The Duchess of Tindale presented herself, looking as feminine and pleasing as she had in Adam's dreams, but wearing a good deal more clothing. He rose from behind the desk, holding his sketches in a manner intended to hide the evidence of his wayward imagination.

"Mr. Morecambe." She popped a brisk curtsey. "I'm looking in on you, as a hostess ought to. Do you have all you need?"

"I apparently needed a nap," he said. *And a thorough dousing in the frigid Channel surf.* "That is a diabolically comfortable chair." He shrugged into his coat as casually as he could, though Her Grace had been married. A man in dishabille would hardly shock her.

"I have remarked the same on the occasion of tending to my ledgers," she said. "The combination of accounting and that chair induces sleep even first thing in the morning. I've sent off a note to Petworth House."

Petworth was the finest collection of interior woodcarving in all of England, possibly in all the world.

"I beg your pardon?"

"I hope Friday suits. Godmama's gardener vows the weather will hold fair for the rest of the week. We can make a picnic of the outing."

She was inviting him on a tour of Petworth. Also, a picnic.

With her.

On the occasion of Adam's first encounter with the duchess, he'd swept her into his arms to spare her a soaking. The contact had startled him. He'd not held a woman closely for ages, hadn't wanted to. His every spare moment and thought went to building his business, and he liked it that way. Her Grace had tolerated the embrace for exactly two instants before she'd righted herself and shaken her skirts, but they had been lovely instants.

She was sturdy, lively, and friendly. None of which explained why Adam wanted to kiss her.

"I trust Lord and Lady Egremont will not be in residence?" he asked.

"Off to Paris. We'll have the place to ourselves."

To themselves and an army of servants. "Friday, you say?" Adam mentally rearranged lunch with friends as well as four other appointments to see properties for sale.

"Have you a conveyance?" she asked. "We can take my traveling carriage or the landau if the weather's fine."

"I'll drive," Adam said, lest he find himself plodding through the countryside when the time could be better spent marveling at the wonders of Petworth. "Shall we leave around eight in the morning?"

"Earlier than that," she replied, rolling up his sketches and handing them to him. "We have the long hours of daylight, we might as well use them. Leave the picnic basket to me and plan on a lovely day."

"The crack of dawn, then," he said, bowing over her hand as best he could with his sketches tucked under his arm. "I'll look forward to it."

The prospect of a day bouncing along the lanes of Sussex had her beaming at him, and her pleasure turned an unremarkable countenance luminous. Her eyes lit with such benevolence, that Adam held on to her hand longer than was strictly proper. She had a subtle beauty, not the boring, cameo-perfect appearance of the typical titled lady, but a personal loveliness that would make the hours until Friday morning long.

And busy.

She saw Adam to the front door, where no servant sat in attendance collecting gossip and spying on the walkway.

"Do you know," Adam said, "I do believe you are my favorite duchess in the entire world."

"How many duchesses do you know, Mr. Morecambe?"

"Two." Not strictly true. As a youth, he'd once been introduced to the Duchess of Seymouth, who'd regarded him as so much dung clinging to her slipper.

"You are my favorite architect."

"How many do you know?"

She went up on her toes and brushed a kiss to his cheek. "One, and I am looking forward to getting to know him better."

Adam tapped his hat onto his head, accepted his walking stick from her, and left the house without even taking the time to examine the fine Palladian window above the lintel.

THE HAMPER WAS PACKED—A hamper, not a mere basket— and Genie had dressed in her most fashionable carriage ensemble. The early hour was not a reflection of her enthusiasm for stately country houses, but rather, her need to leave Brighton unobserved.

Mr. Morecambe's chaise pulled up in front of the house before the sun had topped the horizon, while the world was still in that sweet, quiet, predawn gloom. Rather than make him come into the house, Genie met him on the walk.

"Good morning, Mr. Morecambe. You are punctual."

He bowed over her hand. "Are you running away from home, Duchess? That looks more like a wicker trunk than a picnic basket."

Genie had longed to run away, back home to Derbyshire, which guilty thought had her climbing into the vehicle unassisted.

"The day could be long, and who knows what fare will be available at the posting inns? Is this fine fellow yours?" The horse was a handsome bay, easily seventeen hands, no white on him anywhere.

"Caliban will eat my oats and pretend he's doing me a favor," Mr. Morecambe said, setting the basket behind the seat and taking the place beside Genie. "We can leave him at the first change, let him rest all day, and pick him up on our way home. Move, horse."

With a flick of a dark tail, the gelding trotted on.

Dunstable might have stayed at the Seymouth family property in Brighton, except his mama the duchess complained to all and sundry that the house was uninhabitable, a musty hovel built by an incompetent scoundrel.

Having no family residence at his command, Dunstable was thus biding with his friend, Viscount Luddington, heir to the earl of the same title. Genie had made it her business to know that the viscount's house lay on the opposite side of the Steyne from Godmama's. No telling from whose bed Dunstable might be stumbling home at daybreak, though, so Genie tied her straw hat with a scarf, securing it to her head like a brimmed bonnet.

"I should tell you that I am not highly regarded among some titled families," Mr. Morecambe said.

Interesting place to start a conversation. "Neither am I. I failed to produce a baby duke. What was your transgression?"

He glanced over at her as the horse gained the fields at the edge of town. They'd drive mostly north, toward the Downs, and being away from even the genteel streets of Brighton helped Genie breathe more easily.

"I am a commoner with airs above my station," Mr. Morecambe said. "How long were you married?"

"Five long years. You will think me awful, but becoming a duchess was not a pleasant adjustment. I was a gentry heiress—copper mining proved a very wise investment several generations back—and thus I was bound to marry a man with an impoverished title. My father was determined to see his progeny rise in the world, and I was determined to make my papa happy."

"That sounds like a fine ambition, to make your family happy. What does your father say now?"

"Not a word. We laid him to rest three years ago. This is such a beautiful time of day." Genie had forgotten how cheering, how fragrant with hope dawn was. She'd never quite lost the sense of having disappointed not only Charles, but also Papa, and to have this conversation so early in the day was especially painful.

"Do you miss your husband?"

The question was personal, also one Genie had considered many times. "Yes, and no. Charles was not a bad man, but he was an indifferent husband. He needed a duchess, a gracious, poised woman who could produce multiple sons in quick succession while making no demands of him that couldn't be met from her pin money. I was a disappointment, and it took me some while to realize just how egregious my shortcomings were. I exasperated him, he bewildered me. I wanted a marriage, he wanted a secure succession."

The sun crested the surrounding hills as Caliban trotted through the first crossroads, and Mr. Morecambe steered the chaise smoothly onto the northward turning.

"What could you miss about such a union?" he asked.

"Charles was not much older than I, and in odd moments, I'd see the man he could become. He could be funny, he was generous with his friends, and would never insult me or upbraid me publicly. In his way, he was honorable. He simply expected the world to do as he bade and hadn't much experience with frustration. Had there been a child, perhaps in time..."

"Your story confirms my conclusion that dukes are a blight upon society, and we'd be better off without them."

Mr. Morecambe's driving was deft and tactful, his opinion on dukes quite firmly stated. "You consign the entire senior branch of the peerage to perdition, Mr. Morecambe? Isn't that a bit harsh?"

The wind whipped the end of Genie's scarf behind her, and the sun warmed her cheeks. Why had she gone to Brighton instead of home to Derbyshire?

"I'd keep Wellington, and a few others, but a duke ruined my father. I haven't much patience for the lot of them."

He leaned closer to make that admission, bringing with him the scent of lavender. He favored clean linen, then, and made conscientious use of soap and water. Fine qualities in a man.

"Is there a scandal I should know about?" Genie asked, though any warning he offered was coming at least two miles too late, if that was the case.

"A quiet scandal, the worst kind, because then nobody champions the outcast. He's left to slink away, hoping the rumors die down along with his fortunes. Papa built a fine dwelling just as Brighton was becoming truly popular, and the duke not only refused to pay, he claimed Papa had done shoddy work. Papa was old-fashioned. He never built a house he wouldn't be proud to live in, and the work was anything but shoddy."

"But the damage was done," Genie said. "His reputation in tatters, and then nobody else felt compelled to pay him or to hire him. That is a dreadful tale, Mr. Morecambe."

"A tale you believe."

"Oh yes. When a man is seldom told no, or not now, or not at that price, he develops little patience or understanding. Such a man can either be grateful for the privileges of his station, or he can be a complete donkey's arse. Your papa's client doubtless had solicitors, barristers, and even judges in his pocket, while your father had a family to feed. I'm sorry your father ran afoul of a donkey's arse. Tell me how you came to build your gentlemen's club."

By degrees and questions, Genie drew him out, until it was time for the first change. She heard a tale of hard work, determination, sound investment, and more hard work, as well as several panegyrics to houses that had enthralled Mr. Morecambe.

"How can a house enthrall?" Genie asked as they trotted away from the posting inn. "A house is a place to get out of the wet, to take meals, or to sleep. A fine idea, but not... not enthralling."

He clucked to the horse, a gray this time. "Consider that vent in your parlor, the one that lets warm air waft up from the kitchen. That is genius, Your Grace. The bane of every soul in Britain the livelong winter is cold feet, and some mason, architect, or apprentice noticed that if a gap was allowed just so in a wall and a vent placed thus, the people in that one parlor in all of England would have warm feet, and without roasting their boots by the fire. I'm enthralled by such ingenuity."

And when he was enthralled, Mr. Morecambe became animated, charming even.

"Might I ask for a slight innovation where our dealings are concerned, sir?"

"You may ask."

Caution was usually a virtue, but Genie wasn't feeling cautious. She was feeling like herself for the first time in years.

"Will you call me Genie when we are private? This business of your-gracing and her-gracing, when I'm really not much more than a farmer's daughter, has long struck me as ridiculous. I'm Genie to my friends, and I hope we are to become friends."

He drove along in silence, and once again, Genie feared she'd blundered and failed to grasp soon enough the extent of her error.

"You truly do not like being a duchess, do you?" he asked.

"If I answer honestly, I'm the most ungrateful fool in the realm. Every little girl aspires to be a duchess."

"You are not a little girl, which fact gives me significant joy. My name is Adam, and I invite you to use it, Genie."

"YOU LOOK like the tomcat who got into the cream pot, Dunstable." Jeremy, Viscount Luddington, moved the teapot to his house guest's elbow.

Dunstable had come to the breakfast parlor from the front door rather than down the steps. His cravat was wrinkled, and his hair was styled *a la mare's nest*. One button of his falls was loose, and the chain of his watch fob had come undone from its buttonhole to flap about his waist.

"I need coffee." He ran a hand through his hair, creating further disorder. "You see before you a survivor of Lady Naughty's worst excesses."

Luddington motioned for the footman to pour the marquess a cup of coffee. "One doesn't romp and tell, Dunstable, particularly not with a married lady."

Dunstable slurped his salvation with all the delicacy of a thirsty coach horse. "If she's romping, she's not a lady, is she?"

"If you're telling, you're not a gentleman. Would you like some eggs?"

Another slurp. "Let's start with toast." Dunstable reached for the rack. "Some hair of the dog would likely serve a medicinal purpose as well."

Luddington passed over his flask, which held a fine Madeira. Dunstable was getting old to be sowing wild oats, particularly when he'd started on the project shortly after birth. The marquess's hand shook slightly as he buttered his toast, and he got a spot of jam on the tablecloth.

"When the hell is the rest of George's set coming down from London?" he asked. "The place livens up considerably when his toadies are in town."

"I honestly prefer Brighton when our dear sovereign is elsewhere. I did notice that the Double Duchess is among those enjoying the seaside."

Her Grace ought to be a double duchess because she was as gracious as she was good-natured, but the woman had married one duke and was rumored to be the intended of another. Luddington felt sorry for her—duke number two was hardly a prize—but she gave no sign of feeling sorry for herself.

Dunstable bit off a corner of toast. "That one. Doubly difficult. She's due for a comeuppance, I say. Did you know she's biding with Her Grace of Timid-dale?"

Luddington had never learned to appreciate the harsh charms of coffee. He poured himself another cup of tea and cursed Eton for the crop of inconvenient friendships it had produced.

"Her Grace of Tindale was kind to both of my sisters upon their come outs, and they are a provokingly shy pair of young ladies. I doubt they would have taken without the duchess's aid. You insult her at your peril."

Dunstable laughed, getting toast crumbs all over his cravat. "When did you become such a bishop, Luddy? If we didn't talk about who we've swived, who we'd like to swive, and who'd like to swive us, what conversation would remain?"

A note to Mama was in order. Both of Luddington's sisters were happily married, but Mama was quite the hostess. Her guest list needed to become shorter by one name. Luddington caught the footman's eye, and that good fellow took up the almost empty teapot and departed on a bow.

"Dunstable, allow me to presume on our long and amiable association. You are nearly penniless, which I gather is something of a family tradition. Not your fault, but there it is. Unless you want to be refused my hospitality effective immediately, you will cease to slander every woman who has granted you a waltz. We are no longer boys, trying to impress each other in the public school dormitories."

Luddington meant the rebuke kindly. There had been talk in the clubs of Dunstable playing too deeply and taking too long to make good on his vowels. His most recent mistress had left him for the company of a mere cloth merchant, and nobody had seen Dunstable's high-perch phaeton since April.

The marquess stirred sugar into his coffee. "No need to get up in the bows, Luddy. I'm still a bit cup-shot, not at my best." Dunstable smiled by way of further apology, and such was his inherent charm, that Luddington felt an iota of relenting.

"We're none of us at our best after a night of carousing, and if you're not inclined to sea bathing, Brighton can be a challenge."

Dunstable shuddered. "Sea bathing. Tried it once. My stones

were the size of raisins by the time the ordeal concluded. Never again."

Which raised a puzzle: If Dunstable wasn't in Brighton to enjoy the sea, and the Carlton House set wasn't present in any great numbers, what was the marquess *doing* here, and when would he be finished doing it?

"I find a dip in the ocean invigorating. Have some more toast. When are you off to the family seat? The countryside is ever a pleasant respite in the summer."

Dunstable finished his coffee and refilled his cup. "I dare not show my face at the ancestral pile, lest visiting heiresses pop out of linen closets at me. My parents think I'm in Brighton to refurbish the sole asset deeded to me on my twenty-first birthday. That abysmal excuse for an abode is not four streets from the Pavilion, but a sorrier dwelling you never did see."

Only a ducal heir could complain about owning such a prestigious address. "Have you inspected the property?"

"Had to. The solicitors would tattle otherwise. It's an awful place, all dusty and gloomy. Not a stick of furniture, not a potted salvia to be seen. Pater says the roof leaks, the cellars let in the damp, and the parlors are drafty. Not exactly what you call a bachelor establishment for one of my station."

"That was his idea of a birthday gift?" No wonder Dunstable was in the doldrums.

"For which I'm to be grateful," he said, rising. "You defend Her Grace of Tindale as the wife of our late friend, but Luddy, I could tell you a tale in confidence that would tarnish your regard for her considerably."

"If you told such a tale," Luddington said, "my regard for you would be tarnished as well. When you've finished breaking your fast, I suggest you have a bath and a nap. I'm off to call upon my aunt." He patted his lips with his table napkin and rose.

"It's easy for you," Dunstable said, brushing toast crumbs from his cravat onto the carpet. "Your papa doesn't meddle. Your properties send cash flowing into your coffers. You don't have four sisters beggaring the family exchequer while you try to make a pittance serve as a quarterly allowance. There's nothing I can *do*, Luddy. I'm not to have a profession, Papa doesn't want me mucking about with ducal properties, I haven't a head for academics, and yet, I'm to appear charming, well informed, and gracious at all times."

Was that such a burden? But then, Luddington had spent an occasional school holiday at the Seymouth family seat and did not envy Dunstable his parents. They were an arrogant, unsentimental pair who had high expectations of their son and little sympathy for his situation—or anybody else's.

"You bear up wonderfully under these hardships," Luddington said, "most of the time. Have that nap, and your outlook will be brighter for it." Luddington spoke to his four-year-old nephew in the same tone.

"I suppose I shall, and I'm working on a means of making everything come right. I intend to have a conversation with a certain dowager duchess, and then I'll not need to impose on your hospitality."

That did not bode well for the duchess. "If you need a small loan, Dunstable, you know you can count on me."

Dunstable waved a hand. "Small loans ceased to make a difference months ago, but thank you for the gesture. I'm for my bath and a bottle of that fine Madeira."

He sauntered from the room, his gait a bit unsteady, and Luddington sent up a prayer for his friend—and for any duchess upon whom that friend sought to call.

CHAPTER FOUR

"I am inebriated," Adam said, turning his chaise down the Petworth drive. "Drunk on the abundance of art and craftsmanship under one roof."

"Petworth has an enormous roof," Genie replied. "Would you like me to drive?"

He surprised her by passing over the reins. "A squire's daughter is likely more proficient at the ribbons than I am."

The horse in the traces was an inelegant piebald cob from one of the posting inns. A few adjustments with the reins revealed a surprisingly soft mouth and clockwork gaits. A duchess would never be seen driving such a lowly beast, which was silly.

"This is the best horse we've had all day," she said. "Not much to look at, but her trot is smooth and tireless. She has excellent conformation for the job she's doing, and that means she'll stay sound long after the flashier animals are in the knacker's yard."

"Shall I buy her for you?"

He wasn't joking. Adam Morecambe almost never joked, as far as Genie could tell. Never flirted either, drat the luck.

"Thank you, no. I'd rather buy her for myself." Her friends would consider the purchase eccentric, despite the mare's spanking pace in harness.

"Tindale doesn't manage your funds, does he?"

"My father negotiated the settlements, and I'm well provided for. If you think the current duke would meddle with my money, you don't know him."

"I don't," Adam said, bracing a boot on the fender. "Given the damage done to my father's reputation, I'm not likely to. You are a very skilled driver."

Something Genie herself had forgotten. "Thank you. What did you like best about Petworth?"

He was silent for a long time, while the harness jingled in rhythm with the mare's trot. "I can't choose a single item, but do you know the legend of the peapod where Gibbons's work is concerned?"

Genie had seen more fruit, flowers, fish, and game carved from wood that day than she would have seen offered fresh at most country markets, but she hadn't noticed any peapods.

"Enlighten me."

"He'd carve a closed peapod early on in a project and not carve it open until he was paid. Anybody observing the carving knew if the artist had been compensated for his labors. I like that Gibbons held his patrons accountable. I also like that so much of his work remains. I do not like that I must accord aristocratic families the compliment of having been the ones to commission and preserve it."

"They doubtless preserved his art because nobody else has matched it. The formal gardens of a bygone age were simple to rip out, and rebuilding them would take only time and money. Art can't be so easily reproduced."

"Good architecture is art," Adam said, sitting forward. "It takes into account everything from the local soil and flora, to drainage patterns, available materials, the owner's aesthetics, and, of course, budget."

He was off, expounding on the challenges of building a gentlemen's club in London. Done right, his current project would function as a restaurant, coffee house, subscription library, gentlemen's lodging house, and gaming hell. The club had to be both spacious and efficient, unpretentious and elegant, dignified and distinctive.

"You see it as a chess game," she said, when they'd traded the piebald mare for a rawboned chestnut. "Sacrifice a pair of pawns for a rook, stay out of check, while pressing ever forward."

The sun was low across the fields, and fatigue put a soft edge on the day. Genie spent many evenings talking among acquaintances in polite society at card parties, musicales, or balls, but she didn't *converse*. Those ladies and gentlemen did not argue that if London was to progress, then decent housing had to be erected for those who had only their labor to sell. They never stopped halfway down a corridor to stare at a ceiling while rhapsodizing about Michelangelo and Brunelleschi.

They chattered and gossiped and drove Genie nigh to bedlam.

Adam took the reins from her in a maneuver they'd perfected over the miles. His hands around hers, left and right, then she eased her grip on the ribbons, while the horse trotted placidly along.

"After the lunch Mrs. Bryce set for us," he said, "I thought I'd never be hungry again, but even that feast has become but a memory. Shall we investigate your hamper?"

The hamper was still mostly full, the Petworth housekeeper having insisted on feeding a visiting duchess and her escort. The meal had been lovely, but so too had been having an intelligent male companion with whom to share it.

"I did promise you a picnic, didn't I?"

"We're making good time. We can afford a short respite."

A longer respite would suit Genie. She wouldn't mind returning home as gathering shadows afforded privacy. The chaise's hood remained down, meaning anybody might note that she'd driven out with Mr. Morecambe.

"Let's make the last change," he said, "and then find a quiet spot for a quick meal."

"Would you like to see the Pavilion?" Genie did not want the day to end, though it must. The next best thing would be another day with Adam. If the weather held fair, King George would likely be out and about during the day, and thus Lord Dunstable would have no reason to haunt the Pavilion.

"Everybody wants to see the Pavilion," Adam replied. "That's the whole point of the place, from what I understand—to be seen, to make an impression. The roof is rumored to leak, and other rumors claim George is soon to pull down Carlton House altogether."

Their conversation became desultory as they traded the chestnut for Caliban at the last coaching inn. The sun was touching the horizon, and Genie was famished when Adam gestured with his chin to a grassy stream bank shaded by leafy oaks.

"How about over there? Caliban can have a drink, and if we spread the blanket on the far side of the oaks, we'll have privacy."

Genie saw to the hamper while Adam released the check rein and tethered the horse. She chose a spot along the stream out of sight of the road and spread two blankets over a bed of soft clover. The water babbled quietly, an evening zephyr carried the scent of scythed fields, and Caliban added to the bucolic peace by steadily munching the grass.

Why can't life be like this? Why couldn't life be peaceful and pretty, calm and relaxed? Why did life have to be stealing pleasures like a truant schoolgirl, hoping Dunstable or some other gossip wasn't watching?

"What has put the sadness in your eyes?" Adam asked, standing before her.

He did this—noticed what was around him. Observed and remembered. "I've been going about this duchessing business all wrong."

"You are my favorite duchess. How could you be doing anything wrong?"

"I'm not in a cottage in Derbyshire, watching the lambs frolic while the sun sets. As a girl, that's how I saw my dotage, and it was a happy picture."

He took her hand to assist her to the blankets, then came down beside her. "Sounds lonely."

The notion that even *he* saw Genie as already in her dotage provoked her nearly to tears.

"That cottage in Derbyshire is not as lonely as being a duchess. The first year of my marriage, I was so homesick, I wrote to a different brother each day of the week, then started the rotation all over again the next week."

"Did they write back?"

"They're brothers. Of course not."

Adam put an arm around Genie's waist, she let her head rest on his shoulder, and some of the sadness slid away.

While the determination to change, to take charge of her life remained.

ALL DAY, for every moment of this damned, wonderful, unexpected, unforgettable, grueling day, Adam had been torn between the marvels of a spectacular country house and the marvels of his companion. The Duchess of Tindale was so quiet about her accomplishments, they almost eluded his notice.

She knew her art, knew how to drive a fractious coaching hack so the horse was happy to do her job. She knew how to eat a sandwich without getting a single crumb anywhere, and she knew how to keep silent while Adam was moved beyond words by the woodcarving of a man long dead.

Genie didn't mock his passion for architecture, didn't grow bored when he waxed effusive about capitals and astragals, finials and stringcourses.

She also touched him. Casually wound her hand around his elbow, patted his arm, stroked his lapel as if to smooth a wrinkle. Her caresses soothed a restlessness Adam had long been ignoring, and they enflamed a desire as surprising as it was inconvenient.

She was a duchess. He could never move in her circles. His Grace of Seymouth had made that plain. Adam had approached the duke about unpaid bills at the time of Papa's death and had been escorted from the ducal town house under permanent threat of unending litigation.

"I don't want to climb back into that chaise." Genie put the cork in the bottle of lemonade and set it back in the hamper.

"Because the bench isn't sufficiently padded?"

"Because this has been a lovely day, Adam Morecambe, in lovely company. I don't want this outing to end." She leaned over on all fours and kissed him, and the moment became gilded with possibilities.

Rather than sit back on her haunches, she stayed where she was, her palm cradling Adam's cheek.

An invitation? She probably thought herself very bold. Adam thought her overture wonderfully understated. He kissed her back, smoothed her hair from her brow, and then she was on him, pushing him to the blanket, turning a polite kiss into a plundering of his mouth and wits.

"Your Grace, you needn't—"

She got him by the hair. "No more your-gracing."

"Genie, we have—"

He'd meant to say, *We have time to discuss this,* but the rest of his thought flew from his head as Genie loomed over him.

"I am inebriated too, Adam Morecambe. Drunk with the pleasure of a simple day spent in company I chose for myself. Do you know how long it's been since I was permitted to drive my own gig?"

Rather than let him answer, she kissed him again: *Too long. It has been much, much too long.*

She broke off the kiss and remained crouched over him. "Do you know how long it has been since I was permitted—permitted!—to climb in and out of a carriage without some man handling me as if I were a doddering granny?"

She wrestled her skirts—Adam helped—until she was straddling him. "Do you know how long it has been since I could *stay home* for three days in a row, no callers, no compulsory entertainments, no matchmaking mamas currying my favor, no *fortune hunters* complimenting my *fair gaze*?"

Her gaze was furious and determined, much as it had been when she'd scolded Adam into modifying his construction schedule.

"Genie, there is nobody here to tell you what to do. There's only me. Tell me what you want."

The ire went out of her like a balloon losing loft. "Hold me, Adam."

He rather was. He tucked her against his chest, wallowing in soft linen and softer curves. "What would make it better?"

"I can't think about that at the moment, though I *shall* think about it, now that I've engaged in strong hysterics."

Her hair remained in a neat bun despite miles and miles of driving. He set about freeing her braid.

"You merely expressed your frustration and shared a few delightful kisses with me."

She was sharing her weight as well, settling agreeably close to a part of Adam that was feeling interest and frustration.

"I can't even dress myself," she muttered against his throat, "without two maids interfering with my attempts to put a button through a buttonhole. I'd like to undress myself now."

Holy cavorting cherubs. Adam and his duchess were on a blanket on the outskirts of Lesser Cowclap, Sussex, and she wanted to undress.

But why shouldn't she? Why shouldn't Genie... Adam didn't even know her family name, though duchesses all but lost a family name... Why shouldn't she take a little joy for herself?

"Nobody is stopping you, Genie. If you want to dance naked under the rising moon, you're free to do that."

Her fingers went to the top button of her bodice. "You'll think me daft."

"I think you desirable." Also dear, and in the grip of some thorny issue Adam couldn't parse at the moment when every particle of him was longing to see the duchess unbuttoned.

He'd apparently said the right words, because Genie smiled at him with all the lovely mischief any man had ever longed to behold in a lover. She was still smiling eleven buttons later, and he was smiling too.

GENIE HADN'T ADMITTED to herself that morning that she'd set out to tryst with Adam Morecambe, but she had chosen front-lacing jumps instead of stays and a carriage dress that buttoned down the front. She wasn't wearing drawers—not all ladies did in warm weather—and in an astonishingly short time, she was sitting on a blanket under a darkening sky in her shift, boots, and stockings.

"These..." Adam said, scowling at her boots. "I can't nibble your toes if you're intent on keeping these on."

Nibble my toes. She shivered, not from cold. "Far be it from me to frustrate your appetite in any regard."

He started on her boot laces. "When you talk like that, all prim and tidy, I want to muss you."

"I want to be mussed." The desire—the need—to be wild and wicked had erupted of a sudden, driven by frustration and discontent Genie had been ignoring for most of her widowhood, if not most of her adulthood.

"I want to be naked," Adam said, setting her boots on the edge of the blanket. "I haven't the patience."

He undid his cravat, sleeve buttons, and watch, then peeled both shirt and waistcoat straight over his head. They joined the heap of linen Genie had started on one corner of the blanket.

His hands went to his falls, and Genie put her palm on his chest. "Might you pause for a moment? I'd like to admire the Creator's craftsmanship." Adam was no pale, pampered duke. He was closer to the heroic marble on such abundant display in the Petworth staterooms.

"I *like* manual labor," he said. "I like wrestling with stone and brick, I like digging foundations so I know they're level. I like…. I like *that* a lot."

She'd traced the muscles of his chest, then down the midline of his torso. Dark hair dusted the terrain, and he was everywhere warm. He watched her in the gathering gloom, watched her gently cup him through his clothes.

"Genie…"

"So serious." And so ready to indulge her on this adventure. Desire blended with something more complicated, not quite anxiety, but a sense of leaving the familiar forever behind.

"For a moment," he said, "I must be serious. Consequences can follow from what we're contemplating."

She shook her head. "In five years of marriage, I never bore a child, and Charles was diligent in exercising his marital rights."

They were kneeling on the blanket, face-to-face. Adam gathered her in his arms and lay back so she was tucked against his side.

"I'm sorry. Sorry you were denied the motherhood you sought, sorry your husband offered you mere diligence."

Adam had put his finger on some of Genie's frustration. Charles was the only man with whom she'd been intimate, but she'd heard enough frank talk among the ladies, caught enough muttered asides, to know that his efforts as a lover had been minimal.

"He'd come to my room after the candles were out, climb under the covers, lift my nightclothes, and fumble between my legs. He'd poke and heave and make odd noises, then flop upon me like a marionette whose strings had been cut. Sometimes he'd kiss my cheek."

This was not disloyalty to a deceased spouse, but rather, grief for a marriage mired in silence and duty.

"He was probably trying to be considerate."

"Do you think so?" Genie pondered that hypothesis, though

pondering anything except the bulge in Adam's trousers was hard—difficult, rather. "I never felt so empty as when he was inside me."

Adam swore softly, while Genie undid the buttons of his falls. Then she was on her back, a blanket of warm lover over her.

Adam was in the mood to dawdle, while Genie was frantic, and that was a wonderful combination. His deliberate caresses left her free to be wild. When he cupped her breast, she could arch and writhe into his hand. When he settled his weight on her, she could move against him with blatant yearning.

As desire escalated to craving, pity wended through all the other feelings Genie wrestled—pity for the late duke who'd owned assets beyond imagining, but had been impoverished for cash, and for courage and imagination regarding his marriage.

As Genie had also been impoverished.

Chasing that pity was a determination that she never again make the same mistake. She'd learn from this interlude with Adam, learn to take hold of courage and imagination with the hands of a skilled whip, and send her life in the directions she chose, on her terms.

She wedged a hand between her body and her lover's, got him in a firm grip, and showed him exactly where she wanted him.

Adam went still, dropping his forehead to her shoulder. "If you deny me some patience now, the pleasure will be too soon over."

His voice had acquired a growl, and his embrace enveloped her with the immutable strength of a masculine edifice.

"If you deny me the full measure of passion now—"

He moved, and words failed. Genie got one hand wrapped around his biceps, the other on his backside. She locked her ankles at the small of his back and endured such a thorough, relentless joining that the pleasure bordered on unbearable. She caught a glimpse of the night sky over Adam's shoulder, the stars emerging from their velvet darkness into a diamond-sharp illumination.

Then he gathered her impossibly close, and all the beauty and tenderness of the night sky filled her from within.

CHAPTER FIVE

Genie lay on her side, her cheek pillowed against Adam's belly. Her braid had come undone—not merely unpinned from its coronet—and a hairpin poked him in the ribs.

He was too well pleasured to care. Withdrawing had been a near thing, but he wasn't about to take unnecessary chances with the lady's future. His mind was like Caliban, munching on this grassy patch, then wandering to that clump of clover—all was lovely and delectable, in no particular order.

Genie's thighs were wonderfully muscular. She must enjoy frequent vigorous walks and good long gallops.

Her scent up close was like the jasmine of her bedroom. Subtle and spicy. Adam took a whiff of a lock of her hair and brushed it across his lips.

He wanted to taste her intimately, and she'd probably let him.

She patted his cock, then held his balls in a loose grip, which sent a buzz of anticipation in all directions.

"If you start that conversation," Adam said, "we'll be here until dawn." And what a night that would be.

"My friends would worry."

Being a fundamentally considerate woman, she would not give her friends cause to worry.

"And your reputation might suffer." Adam's too, though among the titled set, he had only the merest beginnings of good standing, and then mostly among the younger men whom Seymouth did not know well.

Genie let go of him and sat up. "My friends should be having adventures of their own. Moonlight does you credit, Mr. Morecambe."

An arc of shadowy gold had just crested the Downs to the east. Adam drew Genie onto his lap, and together, they watched the moonrise.

"I've never done this before," he said, though he hadn't planned on saying anything. Genie's hair tickled his chin. Her weight on his lap tickled his desire.

"Watched the moon come up?"

That either. "Not with a lover." Certainly not with a duchess. "Navigating the way back to town will be easy with all that moonshine."

Leaving their blankets would be difficult. Adam's peace was perfect—the grazing horse, the whisper of water over stones, and the lovely sense of having stumbled upon a lady in whom intimate trust could be safely reposed.

Genie kissed him, as if she sensed his thoughts, and then she climbed off his lap. She made dressing a cooperative undertaking, doing up Adam's sleeve buttons and allowing him to lace her jumps. She saw to her own buttons, and Adam tended to his, but she allowed him to assist her with her boots.

He did not trust himself to put her hair to rights, so he instead fetched the horse while Genie managed a swift braid and a tidy bun. They folded the blankets together—an excuse to share a few kisses— and then they were back on the road.

As Caliban trotted toward Brighton, the silence went from comfortable, to thoughtful, to... strained.

"You offered an invitation to tour the Pavilion," Adam said. "Were you merely being polite?"

"I'm through with merely being polite. I'd like to see the Pavilion with you, for you doubtless will notice what others miss."

Her tone was brusque rather than complimentary. "Are you cold?"

"I am quite comfortable."

Genie was also back to being the duchess. The proper, polite, unremarkable woman easily overlooked when among others of her rank. Adam missed his companion, missed the demanding lover.

The lights of Brighton glimmered on the horizon, and the air changed subtly, growing more humid and cooler with a tang of the sea.

"I won't soon forget this day, Genie."

She tied her bonnet down with a silk scarf, and thus her face was obscured by her hat brim. Adam had envisioned putting that scarf to other purposes, though perhaps his ambitions in that regard weren't shared by the lady.

"Petworth is impressive," she said.

What in the name of every marble saint was amiss with her? "Were we at Petworth? I must have missed it, so much did I enjoy our picnic."

She fussed with her skirts. "Truly, you did? You don't think me forward?"

Adam mentally whacked himself with a carpenter's mallet. He'd not given her the words, the flirtation, the reassurances, more fool he.

"Genie, I find you lovely, passionate, brave, and infernally distracting when I'm trying to think only decent thoughts and comport myself as a gentleman. How to be both lover and proper escort is a new challenge, though one I relish."

She edged closer on the bench, adding a hint of jasmine to the soft summer night. "Precisely. A new challenge. How to be a duchess and daring. I must think on this."

Adam was a builder, little more than an ambitious mason in good tailoring. Genie was a duchess. Of course, she'd regard him as only a partner for a dalliance, and he ought to be flattered to have that much of her consideration.

And yet, he was disappointed too. She was happy to build a folly with him, while he'd been dreaming of a permanent structure, complete with furniture, carvings, and clever vents—also a fine big bed in the largest apartment. His disappointment grew when, instead of offering him a peck on the cheek at her door, Genie was content to let him bow over her hand before she slipped into the house.

What had he expected? She was gracious and lovely and all that other, but she was still, above all, a duchess.

GENIE WENT about her days with two objectives in mind: First, to avoid the Marquess of Dunstable, and second, to cross paths with Mr. Morecambe. In all the hours she'd spent with Adam on the outing to Petworth, she had failed to get his direction.

And he had not offered it to her.

Brighton boasted rooming houses and hotels by the score, and even Adam Morecambe doubtless had friends with whom he could bide. Subtle questions to Genie's callers yielded no word of a large, taciturn architect down from Town. Diana and Belinda both made inquiries, but Adam had little use for the idle and titled, and his whereabouts weren't likely to interest them either.

"So much for embarking on a life of daring adventure," Genie muttered to the cat.

Rather than pause in his ablutions, he adopted a pose unbefitting of a lady's feline.

"I will keep to my plans nonetheless," Genie said, "for adventure won't find me if all I do is sit about and read Mr. Scott's works of fiction." Or stare at them without turning a single page.

She put on her bonnet and cloak, found a parasol, and waved off the footman who typically escorted the ladies of the house on their shopping expeditions. A proper widow could walk the streets of Brighton in broad daylight by herself.

Not that Genie ever had.

She nonetheless found her solicitor's office—her Brighton solicitor, not to be confused with her London solicitors (plural), or her Derby solicitor (only the one, but he was prodigiously long-winded), or her Paris solicitor (an outrageous old flirt).

Her request took some time to explain, while Mr. Vernon scribbled copious notes and promised to look into the matter straightaway. Genie took her leave without answering the question Mr. Vernon was too polite to ask: The Dowager Duchess of Tindale couldn't possibly be strolling a distance of three streets without a retinue, could she?

In fact, she was, and Genie was equal parts pleased with herself and anxious that she might run into Dunstable.

Derbyshire is looking better and better.

Though she had no lover in Derbyshire. Perhaps she had no lover in Brighton. What sort of man made passionate love and stirring declarations beneath the rising moon, then sent no word for days?

A wall of well-dressed male muscle interrupted her musing. "I do beg your—Your Grace."

"Mr. Morecambe. A pleasure." *Mostly. To some extent.*

Genie was blushing and trying not to smile. She offered her hand as he tipped his hat, then dropped her hand when he reached for her fingers.

"I was on my way to pay a call on you," he said, taking her hand in his. "Shall I walk you to your door?"

His grip was firm and steadying, as was the look in his eyes. He wasn't smiling, but his gaze said he was pleased to see her.

"An escort would be appreciated. I wondered if you'd returned to London."

He tucked her fingers around his arm, placing himself on the street side of the walkway. "I did, in fact. My master mason and builder got into a spat, and nothing would serve but I must mediate between them. I've missed you."

When had anybody ever missed Genie? Oh, her brothers occasionally dashed off a line or two at the bottom of a note sent by their wives. *Hope you're keeping well!* Or, *Come home when next you can—the children want spoiling!*

Those sentiments were casual gestures of affection from people whose lives had separated from Genie's years ago.

"Did I speak too boldly, Your Grace? Should I not have admitted to missing you?"

"You honor me with your honesty. I've missed you too."

They paused at a corner. "I'd thought to write," he said, "to send a note informing you of my travel, but does a widowed duchess receive correspondence from a single gentleman? Does *this* widowed duchess? Dithering is foreign to my nature, so I chose to pay a call upon my return."

"You've only just returned?" How lovely that he had come directly to see her—and told her he'd done so.

"I want that visit to the Pavilion," he said, leaning closer. "You did promise."

Was he teasing her? "I keep my word, Mr. Morecambe, but tell me, where are you biding on your visit to Brighton?"

"With friends who won't mind my coming and going at all hours. This time of year, many properties are to let, and others are under renovation."

"But you're looking to purchase, aren't you?"

He expounded on the benefits of owning over renting, and Genie realized he might be making a subtle point about the difference between a courtship and a dalliance.

"One has the security of a commitment," he said. "The building is wholly entrusted to the owner, the owner knows he'd best treasure the asset in his keeping. Renters break leases, landlords neglect maintenance. The more permanent arrangement seems the better bargain, if one can make the initial investment."

They crossed the street arm in arm. "True, if one chooses wisely and is a responsible property owner. If the choice was unfortunate, the owner is stuck with an ongoing liability, or the building with a negligent caretaker." And Genie did not care for any analogy that cast her in the role of property.

A permanent arrangement, however, was all too appealing.

The closer they journeyed to Genie's doorstep, the quieter the neighborhood became.

"Was your duke so awful as all that, Genie? Did he put you off speaking vows ever again?"

That Adam would admit to missing her, that he'd come straight to see her, warmed her heart. That he'd think to ask this question earned her respect.

"Ladies are to desire the married state above all things," she said. "Marriage to a duke is the best married state there is, supposedly, but I was lonely and often bored, despite being run off my feet with obligations. I'm only now realizing my late husband was likely in the same situation—lonely, bored, run off his feet with obligations. He was expected to marry profitably, and he accepted that duty, but failed to get all the consideration promised in the bargain."

To have some sympathy for Charles was a great and welcome relief.

"One doesn't think of dukes as merely mortal," Adam said. "But they are, I suppose. You've dodged my question."

His question about marriage. *Well.* "I am considering my answer and pleased that you'd put such a conundrum to me. How does your search for a property come along?"

"Slowly. Brighton is a busy market, in terms of properties changing hands, but merely because I have coin and know well how to care for a building doesn't mean I'm a suitable buyer in the eyes of many."

His London club was nicknamed the Blackball Club for a reason, apparently. "Use an intermediary," Genie said. She was about to offer her solicitor's services—hadn't she come from asking Mr. Vernon to look for a suitable property in Derbyshire?—but remained silent as Adam touched his hat to a pair of beldames daundering toward them.

"What day would suit for a visit to the Pavilion?" she asked, when she was sure she could not be overheard.

"Friday. I haven't any other appointments then, and you'll give me something to look forward to."

He was flirting. He was definitely, subtly, wonderfully flirting, and they were nearly to the gate. How on earth was she to flirt back?

"Could I tempt you into a cup of tea, Mr. Morecambe?"

"Yes."

"Splendid."

"I've also been plagued by a few questions regarding the wallpaper in your sitting room, Your Grace. I cannot recall the exact pattern, but think something like it would go well in the cardroom at the club. Perhaps you'd be good enough to allow me another peek?"

He held the garden gate for her, and Genie preceded him up the walk. "You may have more than a peek, Mr. Morecambe."

The housekeeper took Genie's cloak and bonnet, and Mr. Morecambe's hat and walking stick. Genie led him to the steps, and they got as far as her sitting room before she pinned her guest against the closed parlor door and kissed him witless.

ADAM HAD HAD a revelation on his London trip.

Journeying to Brighton previously, he'd resented the need to leave the London work site. The ring of hammers was music to him. A load of gravel or stone crashing onto the walkway was akin to the tolling of a steeple bell, summoning the faithful for the opening hymn. He loved being in the middle of a building in progress, loved the sweat and cursing, the gradual blossoming of a stately edifice where all had been disorder and noise.

He also loved Genie, Duchess of Tindale, and that was a problem.

In the normal course, he would have allowed his master mason and his builder to argue and discuss, and sit down over several pints to debate the need to switch plasterers. This time, he had given them fifteen minutes each to state a case and then chosen the plasterer who was available soonest. That his choice was more expensive than the alternative should have given Adam nightmares.

Instead, his dreams had been filled with images of Genie, curled on a blanket, moonlight gilding her smile. Genie, waiting patiently for him to finish sketching some pile of Mr. Gibbons's carved musical instruments. Genie, licking her fingers after finishing an apple, the core of which she'd fed to the lowly piebald mare.

And now, here he was, all but asking permission to court the woman.

And here she was, all but unbuttoning his shirt.

"The door..." he muttered against her mouth. "I'll not have your reputation put at risk—"

She smiled. "Diana and Belinda are away from home. Look to your own reputation, Adam Morecambe."

He picked her up and carried her to the bedroom, and she kept her arms around his neck when he settled her on the bed, drawing him over her.

The rest was a blur of loosened clothing, soft laughter, and pleasure every bit as intoxicating as he'd recalled. Genie lay on the bed, her legs over the side, her skirts frothed about her waist. Adam remained standing, and the fit was perfect. He wanted to linger and admire—he wanted to use his mouth on her—but she got her legs around his waist, and her urgency overcame his restraint.

Almost. He withdrew and spent into a handkerchief, while Genie lay panting with repletion beneath him.

He crouched over her, confounded by what had passed between them. He was an architect, a man of plans and diagrams, schedules and budgets. A boring fellow, but accomplished in his humble way. How much more pleasurable to be the lover of a duchess who all but dragged him into her boudoir and had her lovely way with him.

"I'm falling asleep," she murmured, fingers trailing through his hair. "You will think very ill of me, indeed."

"I think you serve a luscious cup of tea."

She laughed, her belly bouncing beneath him, and Adam smiled against her neck.

"Will you believe me if I tell you I honestly did want to see the wallpaper?"

Not until he'd been following her up the steps, her derriere at his eye level, had his wayward thoughts crested into the beginning of arousal. Until then, he'd merely been daydreaming.

"Will you believe me," she countered, "if I tell you that you're the first man I've kissed since my husband died?"

Adam straightened, took one last admiring look at the duchess in dishabille, then twitched her skirts over her knees and assisted her to sit up.

"Why would I have cause to doubt you?" Though a part of him did. She was attractive, widowed, had means, and moved much in high society. Aristocratic men were accustomed to having whom and what they wanted. As a widow, Genie should have been having whom and what she wanted too.

"Because polite society isn't always so polite," she said, hands in her lap. "The London newspapers would expire for lack of tattle if that wasn't the case."

He sat beside her, and the glow of the encounter faded. "I'll not be tattling, Genie. I'd rather be proposing."

She tucked her hands under her arms as if cold. "You hardly know me."

Lately, Adam hardly knew himself. "Every couple becomes better acquainted after the vows are spoken. I realize I am presuming to raise such a topic, but I cannot countenance sneaking about alleys or hiring some cottage in Kent for clandestine trysts. My intentions are honorable."

Are yours?

Adam had worked too hard to rebuild his father's business for anybody to cast his good name away on the basis of rumor—or fact. The other consideration was that he had fallen in love, and if his sentiments were unrequited, then he'd given a duchess the power to break his heart—a heart he would have said had been quarried of good English granite. Bad enough a duke had brought Papa's standing so low. A duchess dallying with Adam then tossing him aside wasn't to be contemplated.

"I had not taken you for an impetuous man," she said. "I like your boldness, but you must understand that I have never been impetuous."

She rose from the bed and stood by the window. Her hair remained tidily pinned, but for one lock curling over her neck. Adam sat on the bed while she repinned that errant curl in exactly the place it belonged.

"Never been impetuous?" he asked softly.

The smile she aimed over her shoulder was chagrined. "Before I met you. The common perception is that titled women produce heirs and then set about taking lovers. I never produced the heirs, I never saw a man who took my fancy, and I'd promised Charles both loyalty and fidelity. Then too, given my experiences as a married woman, why on earth would I—?"

A blush crept up her neck. She untied the curtain cord and retied it to exactly match its twin on the other curtain. Then she squeezed the sachets hanging from the cords, sending a hint of jasmine into the air.

Poor Charles had been an idiot. "Shall I speak to the present duke, Genie?"

"What has Augustus to do with this?"

"He's the head of your family." Also a complete stranger to Adam, who'd likely not spare an upstart architect so much as a nod in the churchyard. "If I seek to court you, then I should at least make his acquaintance." Distasteful though the prospect was.

"I leave Augustus and his new wife as much in peace as I can. A dowager duchess trying to hoard consequence she no longer has by hovering about the ducal successor is pathetic."

An architect proposing to a duchess might be pathetic as well, and yet, Genie's regard for him seemed genuine.

"I have been precipitous," he said, rising. "I apologize."

"You have been honest. I treasure your honesty, but you've also surprised me. For five years, I've been all but invisible, except to my friends. I encourage the nervous debutantes, intervene when I see a bad match in the making, and dance with the shyest of the bachelors. The old Genie, the one who sits smiling among the potted palms night after night, is not a confident creature."

A glimmer of understanding pierced Adam's disappointment. "You would like to be wooed?"

He could do that. More outings to bucolic locations, more strolls about town—*more picnics*.

"Charles and I never courted. His papa's solicitors met with my papa's solicitors. Charles and I were permitted to dawdle about the lime park on several occasions while at least three aunts all but followed us with spyglasses. Some wooing would be lovely, but you must tell me: How do I woo you?"

He did not dare join her at the window, for there was no telling who might glance up from the alley or garden and see a man side by side with the duchess in her very bedroom. Instead, he held the door for her.

"Wooing doesn't work like that. The gentleman does the escorting and paying calls and reading to his lady in the garden." Of that much, Adam was confident.

"We're discussing *my* wooing," Genie said, as they gained the corridor, "and I'm done sitting in the parlor with a book, waiting for the gentleman to run matters to his exclusive satisfaction."

He paused with her at the top of the steps, glanced about, then stole a kiss to her cheek. "I hope the lady was satisfied with our inspection of the wallpaper?"

"You are awful. I was not satisfied for more than two minutes. I want you naked in my bed, and I want to do wanton things with you."

"What manner of wanton things?"

She started down the steps, and she was blushing again. "I don't know. I've never done them before, and Charles declared certain shelves in the library unfit for a lady's delicate sensibilities. I do believe there are places a gentleman likes to be kissed other than on his lips."

"This gentleman does." As best Adam could recall when his mind was a muddled hash of desire, amusement, and hope.

Genie paused on the landing and turned a serious gaze on him. "You are concerned for your reputation, and I respect that. I have no wish to see my personal business bruited about, and you are every bit as private as I am. But I ask myself: What would make your situation right?"

The afternoon sunshine beamed through the window, bringing out her freckles. He wanted to kiss them—them too.

"My situation is enviable," he said, "in the eyes of many. I have means, an education, a thriving business, and a favorite duchess."

She fluffed the lace of his cravat. "Enviable, yes, and likely to grow more so, but you are also discontent—over that business with your father. What would lay that matter to rest for you?"

Adam offered his arm and accompanied her down to the family parlor, which looked out over the garden. All the while, he considered her question.

"You aren't asking about revenge."

She tugged a bell-pull and took a seat in a reading chair. "I might be. That's for you to say. I'm asking about how to untangle yourself from the harm done to you and your family. Resolving an injustice. Putting an old enemy in his place might be part of that."

Her question seemed to have significance beyond the obvious. "I cannot call out a duke, Genie. For one thing, the scoundrel did his damage almost fifteen years ago. For another, he's an old man, and he could ruin me with a curl of his lip."

"So the damage he did echoes to this day."

It did. Adam was having trouble even making appointments to see certain properties. Though the various agents and solicitors were polite, they were also subtly unwilling to do business with him. Perhaps they were unwilling to do business with any commoner. He had no way of knowing.

"To answer your question, what I'd seek in an ideal world is vindication—for the truth to be known. My father would never cheat a client, and the duke lied when he claimed otherwise."

Adam hadn't put that together for himself, that what he wanted was simply for the truth to be known—not such a radical outcome.

"The truth can be problematic," Genie said. "I agree in principle: Better to be judged honestly than pilloried by rumor and gossip."

As Adam swilled tea and inhaled sandwiches, he wondered idly if some aspect of the past still bothered the duchess. She seemed to have made her peace regarding her late husband, but she'd also spoken honestly: Adam did not know her well, not yet, and everybody had regrets.

Perhaps he'd learn some of hers when they spent an afternoon exploring the Pavilion, and perhaps he'd kiss her someplace other than on her lovely lips.

CHAPTER SIX

Genie was on excellent terms with the staff at the Pavilion, having lent her domestic staff to King George on any number of occasions when His Majesty was hosting some lavish entertainment. She knew her way around the building, or thought she did, and had already chosen several linen closets, dressing rooms, and stairways where she might have stolen a kiss.

Adam refused to oblige her.

If Carlton House was King George's personal art gallery, the Pavilion was his architectural peacock. Minarets and onion domes topped a palace both thoroughly modern—the kitchen was a marvel in itself—and luxurious beyond imagining.

"I do wonder about that roof," Adam said, taking one last look at the ornate ceiling doming the banqueting hall. "But I have reached the limit of what my sensibilities can absorb here. Shall I walk you home, Your Grace?"

The house steward stood by, having courteously escorted them from room to room—and closet to closet—answering Adam's endless questions.

"Thank you, yes," Genie replied. "One doesn't appreciate the size of this edifice until one traverses every corridor and stair."

Adam repeated his thanks to the steward and confirmed an appointment to tour the equally lavish stable the next morning.

"Will you come with me tomorrow?" he asked when they were strolling arm in arm along the walkway.

"I think not," Genie said. "My interest in a certain architect remains undiminished. My interest in ventilation, drainage, bearing walls, and supporting beams has been sated."

He patted her hand, a slow stroke of glove over glove. "My interest in those subjects is what keeps the roof over my own head, though I suspect even were my means abundant, I'd still be an architect. If you were not a duchess, what would you be?"

Happy. That reply would not do, not even for Adam's ears. "I would certainly bide in London much less than I do. I'd make more effort to see my family, rather than exerting myself to launch the daughters and nieces of every woman to claim an acquaintance with me. I would knit, and raise my own sheep, and spend more time by the sea and in the countryside."

"You enjoy Brighton?"

They wandered back to the house, with Genie expounding on the advantages of a simpler life, where gossip wasn't a constant threat to one's peace and expenses were reduced.

Adam held the garden gate for her. They'd come up the alley, in part because Genie preferred the quieter approach, but also because Dunstable was still in Brighton, doubtless up to no good.

"Does Tindale begrudge you your portion?" Adam asked.

"He would not dare," Genie said. "Augustus did not expect to inherit and couldn't care less what I do with my money. He was a mere cousin to the ducal line, and Charles was young and in good health when he died. Then Charles's younger brother got into that awful accident, and Augustus was left with the title. I am quite well fixed, but one doesn't speak of that openly."

Adam's gaze was serious—more serious than usual. "You are

circumspect about your wealth because of the fortune hunters. I'm not after your money, madam. I can provide comfortably for a wife and children."

"The fortune hunters are a constant plague." As was a certain marquess, who any day now would once again insinuate his hand into Genie's coffers. "Do you return to London soon?" For if Dunstable remained kicking his heels in Brighton, Genie would return to Town.

"I'm a failure as a suitor, aren't I? Shall we sit?" He gestured to a marble bench before a circular fountain with a swan eternally gliding at the center.

Genie let him assist her onto the bench—another lingering touch of gloved hands—and realized what all the holding doors, taking her arm, and standing near her the livelong afternoon had been about.

"You are a very attentive suitor. I am a failure as a blushing damsel. All I could think about was accosting you in a linen closet, while you were doing the pretty."

He took off his hat and set it on the bench. "The linen closet under the servant's stair? The one scented with jasmine and lavender? I nearly pushed you inside and closed the door in the poor steward's face. The scent of jasmine has become an aphrodisiac."

Why should—? "Because I use jasmine in my bedroom?"

"And in the morning, the fragrance clings to your person when you rise from your slumbers. Very clever, Your Grace. Maddening, even."

Maddening was lovely. "For me, the scent of fresh clover has become enticing. Puts me in mind of summer evenings and bucolic splendors."

They enjoyed a moment, not touching, but very much courting, while a pair of sparrows splashed in the shallows of the fountain then fluttered away.

"I depart for London on Wednesday," Adam said. "Locating a suitable property for purchase in Brighton will require, as you suggest, intermediaries. The houses that are fine enough for my purposes are not available to me, and I haven't time to undertake new construction."

"You mean the blue bloods won't take your money." The same members of polite society who would have cut a bumpkin like Genie without mercy, but for her husband's title.

"A gentlemen's club can attract enterprises of a less respectable nature. In London, that's tolerated or even expected, because of the influence of the gentlemen attending the clubs. The titled gentleman's convenience matters more than his neighbor's refined sensibilities, and nobody says a word. For a club catering to the untitled, different expectations attach. I was slow to grasp what was going unsaid."

He referred to the brothels that cluttered the streets of Mayfair, side by side with fine residences, respectable businesses, and venerable clubs.

"Do you mean to tell me Brighton has no such common nuisances?"

"Brighton has a history of promoting health rather than vice, despite His Majesty's efforts to the contrary. His court is aging along with him, and the town's residents look askance at any unknown quantity."

No, they did not. If that quantity sported a title, they looked at her graciously, even fawningly.

"I must ponder this," Genie said, "and you must accept an invitation to share a cup of tea with me in my sitting room. If I cannot at least kiss you, I will next be seen marching about the beach, ranting at the sea."

He picked up his hat and rose, extending a hand to Genie. "A cup of tea after our tour of the Pavilion would suit nicely. Would you march about the beach in bare feet?"

He'd seen her bare feet. Grasped them in his warm hands, caressed them. Pleasurable heat rose from Genie's middle.

"I'd remove both shoes and stockings," she said, taking his arm, "and even lift my hems a few inches to avoid the encroaching waves.

Then I'd come home and bathe thoroughly to get the sand and sea salt off my person."

He paused before the back door, his gaze fixed on the brass knocker, a gull with wings spread. "Bathe with jasmine soap?"

Genie used her parasol to shade them from view, then whispered in his ear, "I'd use that jasmine soap *everywhere*." Oh, this was marvelous fun. "We stock gunpowder tea scented with jasmine. Do you fancy a cup?"

He held the door for her, and as she swept past, he spoke very softly. "I fancy the whole, hot, delicious pot, with sweet honey drizzled into each steaming cup."

She needed to catch her balance on the sideboard after that remark. Adam presumed to take her parasol and close it for her, while she untied her bonnet ribbons.

"Allow me," he said, unfastening the frogs of her cloak.

This too was flirtation, for his fingers grazed her chin and throat, and when he drew the cloak from her, his palms stroked over her shoulders. Ye gods, she had not been done justice by her poor duke, and he had doubtless not been done justice by his copper heiress.

Genie would have stolen a kiss right there in the corridor, except that voices floated forth from the formal parlor at the front of the house.

"Guests," she said. "Belinda and Diana would use the family parlor if they were alone. We could simply duck up the back steps to my sitting room." *Please, please, please.*

"I leave that decision in your hands."

His expression had lost any hint of flirtation, and Genie recalled his words about skulking through back alleys and renting a cottage in some obscure village.

"One cup," she said, "and then I will find a way to extricate us from the clutches of strict propriety."

He kissed her in the deserted corridor, and that only made Genie's yearning worse. "You tease me, you fiend. I will have my revenge, and you may expect a few bars of scented soap delivered to your abode by this time tomorrow. I like cedar and cinnamon, though not at the same time. Do I look adequately composed?" Though she still didn't know his specific direction.

A masculine voice punctuated Diana's dulcet speech. Not friends, then, for Diana spoke freely with the few she considered friends and used that soft, amused tone only with bothersome bachelors.

"You look utterly demure, confound you."

Genie smoothed her skirts, taking a moment to savor the joy of having a suitor. She swept into the parlor, trailing streams of glee and smiling on all creation.

Only to see Lord Dunstable rising from the sofa like a spider crawling forward to greet the newest victim entrapped in its web.

IF THERE WAS one person Adam loathed more than he loathed the Duke of Seymouth, it was Seymouth's heir and only son, Lord Dunstable. That disgrace to manhood bowed over Genie's hand, and she curtseyed prettily.

"My lord, a pleasure," she said, with every evidence of sincerity. "May I make known to you Mr. Adam Morecambe, and Mr. Morecambe, I present to you Isambard, Marquess of Dunstable."

Adam managed a bow, while Dunstable wrinkled his nose and barely inclined his handsome head.

"I've made Mr. Morecambe's acquaintance, though I can't recall where." His lordship resumed his seat next to a lovely blonde, while a third woman, with auburn hair and green eyes, poured out for the marquess. Genie had introduced Adam to her. She was the other duchess—Warminster, Winchelsea, Wrexham. Some damned W or other.

"I don't believe I've been introduced to all of the ladies," Adam said. Nor was there anywhere for him to sit. The sofa held the marquess and the blonde, the auburn-haired duchess occupied one wing chair, Genie the other.

"I beg your pardon," Genie said, introducing Adam to Mrs. Diana Thompson. "And I'll have the footman bring us another chair."

"No need," Adam replied. "I'll be on my way. Ladies, your lordship, good day." Even that much civility directed at Dunstable was a tribulation, but he seemed to be on good terms with the women, and Adam would not embarrass Genie with poor manners.

"Not even one cup of tea?" the blonde, Mrs. Thompson, asked.

"The press of business calls me."

Dunstable saluted with his tea cup. "Don't let us keep you. Those who labor for their bread can't be expected to savor the company of their betters when coin of the realm calls."

Adam expected Genie to issue her guest a blunt set-down. She instead aimed a pained smile at the tea tray.

"I'll see you out," Mrs. Thompson said, springing from the sofa. She took Adam by the arm and all but dragged him from the room. "Count yourself fortunate, Mr. Morecambe, for his lordship has been swilling tea and decimating the tea cakes this past half hour."

"You don't care for him?"

She led Adam to the front door. "He's not the worst of his kind, but he's a trial, and Her Grace cannot abide him. She is too polite for her own good sometimes. Do call again, please, and I mean that."

Had she meant Her Grace of Tindale? If so, Adam had no call to doubt her, but then, here he was at the door, while Genie had chosen to remain in the company of a man she did not like.

"Thank you, Mrs. Thompson, and please give Her Grace of Tindale my special thanks for an enjoyable day."

"Might I ask how that day was spent?"

"Avoiding the near occasion of linen closets. Good day."

All the way back to his quarters, Adam wrestled with the possibility that Genie had been ashamed to be seen with him. Not ashamed before her friends, but ashamed before Dunstable. He was in line for a dukedom, well favored, smooth-spoken, moved in the highest circles...

"In short," Adam muttered, letting himself in the door, "he's everything I'm not."

"I beg your pardon, sir?" The butler was a dignified old relic named Fawcett. He put Adam in mind of erudite headmasters and advanced Latin tutors, and when Adam bided here, he always felt as if he did so at Fawcett's sufferance.

Adam handed over his hat and walking stick. "I'm lecturing myself. Will Cook have an apoplexy if I ask for a tray in the library?"

"Doubtless, sir. Her third of the week by my count. You have received a deal of correspondence, including an express from Town."

The day had taken a sour turn when Adam had beheld Dunstable in Genie's parlor, now sour threatened to turn rotten.

"Please ask Cook to send up a pot of jasmine gunpowder, if any we have. Otherwise, China black will do."

Fawcett bowed and disappeared down the steps. The third stair always creaked when Adam dared trespass upon the kitchen, but Fawcett's descent was silent.

Adam saved the express—from his builder in London—for last, because at this hour of the day, he wasn't about to start a journey north, no matter what emergency had befallen the work site. He instead plowed through bills, progress reports, membership applications, and offers of employment on other projects before slitting open the express.

"Damn, blast, and to perdition with the lot of them."

Fawcett paused at the door, a tray in hand. "Having a bit of an apoplexy yourself, sir?"

"My head mason has apparently quit, my builder is threatening to do likewise, and nobody has seen our tipper wagon since the day before yesterday."

"Shall I have the livery alerted that you'll need a horse?"

Adam would normally have bolted for the door, ridden through the night, and been at the work site before the sun came up.

"I'll depart for London tomorrow, after I've toured the royal stables at the Pavilion and paid a call on a certain duchess."

"Very good, sir. I regret to report that we have no jasmine-scented tea."

The scent of plain China black wafted up from the tray Fawcett set on the desk. A plate of sandwiches accompanied the tea, though abruptly, Adam wasn't hungry.

"My thanks for the tray."

Fawcett withdrew on a bow, and Adam turned to the remaining half-dozen items of correspondence. Each one was a polite note from some man of business or solicitor with offices in Brighton. They all thanked Adam for his interest in a very attractive property, then explained that circumstances—a recent offer to purchase, schedule conflicts, the owner reconsidering the decision to sell—made showing Adam the property regrettably impossible.

They wished him best of luck on his search, etcetera and so forth, but did not foresee the property becoming available for inspection in the immediate future.

And what a coincidence that Lord Dunstable should be in town, just as door after door was closing in Adam's face.

DIANA AND BELINDA had apparently been entertaining Dunstable for a good half hour before Genie had returned home. They had their revenge by all but abandoning her with him shortly after Adam had decamped.

And thus did a lovely day turn to mud.

To horse droppings, even.

"Duchess, let us sit for a moment in your lovely garden," Dunstable said, rising. "Old friends deserve privacy for the occasional chat about bygone times."

Dunstable had never been her friend. He'd been one of the countless toadies orbiting about Charles, most of them waiting to inherit a title, a fortune, or both. Charles had been patient with them, while Genie had dreaded the "intimate dinners" for thirty that came around at least once a month.

"I'll need a shawl," she said. "Enjoy the fresh air for a moment in solitude, my lord."

She scooted from the parlor and went in search of Diana or Belinda, anybody, who could ensure she wasn't left alone with Dunstable for more than a moment. Neither lady was to be found, and the kitchen staff was busy with dinner preparations.

Well, drat. Genie grabbed a shawl and found her guest helping himself to a pink rosebud from Godmama's bushes.

"If you have something to say to me, my lord, then best get to the point. We are observed from the house, and my lingering here with you will be remarked."

He threaded the rosebud into the buttonhole on his lapel. "You are a dowager duchess, my dear. Your conduct will be remarked regardless of how you behave, but none dare chide you for it... yet."

Genie waited, because she needed to know exactly what he was threatening. She could weather a little unkind talk, she could part with a bit of coin. She'd already paid Dunstable off twice, once with a diamond bracelet she'd inherited from her mother, once with a gold snuffbox passed down from her father. Even Augustus would notice substantial sums going missing from her funds.

"I adore a woman who can hold her tongue," Dunstable said. "Such a woman would make an admirable Duchess of Seymouth, particularly when she has already learned to wear a tiara."

Genie wrapped her shawl more tightly around her. "You are over-come with a violent passion for me, my lord? Perhaps you confuse me with my exchequer."

His rosebud was drooping at an odd angle. He attempted to reposition it. "And droll wit—I am ever amused by droll wit. I've done some investigating, dear duchess."

"Prying and gossiping?"

The rosebud hung all but upside down from his lordship's buttonhole. He took it out and swung it by the stem.

"We needn't be vulgar, Your Grace. Your late papa left you quite well to do, and he did a lovely job of protecting your inheritance in the marriage settlements. But then, you were bequeathed such an enormous pile of money that Tindale could have his portion and leave plenty for me."

Genie sank to the bench before the fountain, her knees going unsteady. In her wildest nightmares, she could not have foreseen Dunstable proposing to her.

"You needn't marry me, my lord. I'll give you the money. Just leave me alone."

He came down beside her uninvited. "Were you very upset when Cousin Augustus married his current duchess? That was bad of him, if you were still pining for his favors. He was supposed to marry you, wasn't he?"

"I will tell you this one last time, my lord: What you saw was an innocent embrace. Augustus is family, and I value his affection dearly. At no time did he, or have I, entertained untoward thoughts. I honored my vows."

Dunstable sniffed the rosebud. "I'm sure you did, but I'm also certain I saw you nestled quite close in the embrace of a man other than your husband. Within weeks, your husband was dead and that man had moved one giant step closer to inheriting the title. All quite distressing. If the wrong people learned of what I saw, then you and the current duke would be in enormous trouble. Your best option is to marry a man who can keep you safe from gossip and innuendo, and that man would be sitting beside you."

Looking so innocent, while impersonating the serpent in the garden. "Take the damned money," Genie said. "All I need—all I want—is a cottage in Derbyshire and my own sheep. I never wanted to be a duchess, much less a duchess twice over."

Poor Belinda faced that ordeal.

Dunstable's laughter was warm and friendly. "A cottage in

Derbyshire and your own sheep? Will you give them names? Will you hire a handsome shepherd to keep you and your sheep warm on those bitter Derbyshire winter nights?"

He smacked her lightly on the back of the hand with the rosebud. "You have brightened my day, Duchess, so I'll brighten yours. Present me with two sons—no, three, for we must be cautious, must we not?—and I'll allow you to retire to your cottage in Derbyshire each summer when I do my duty by the house parties. A fair bargain, if I do say so myself."

No sort of bargain at all, considering that many house parties were little more than discreet, rural orgies. All Dunstable sought was to pursue his debauches without a pesky duchess at his side.

"Why now?" Genie asked. "Why wait for years after Charles's death to wreak your mischief? Most would consider eight and twenty too old to be anybody's duchess, and I never bore Charles any children."

The money must be very important to Dunstable, and the supply of heiresses rapidly dwindling.

"I have a parcel of dreadful cousins who can see to the succession if needs must," Dunstable said, tossing the rose in the air and catching it. "But I will be diligent in attempting to fill our nursery. Make no mistake on that score."

The tea Genie had managed to choke down threatened to rebel. "What explanation will you offer for waiting years to spread these accusations? Nobody would have believed them at the time of Charles's death, and they won't believe you now."

He twirled the battered rosebud by the stem. "Ah, but your beloved Augustus became duke only earlier this year, and his good fortune brought to my mind the liberties he'd taken with you—a heated embrace, a passionate kiss, under poor Charles's roof!—and my conscience has troubled me sorely."

Augustus had kissed Genie on the forehead. "Your creditors have been dunning you sorely."

"We needn't belabor the obvious. A ducal heir must maintain a certain standard, which your settlements will allow me to do." He stood, looking quite, quite smug. "Don't spend too much time with your pet stone mason while I'm paying you my addresses. A little pity for the less fortunate is all well and good—was he your escort to Petworth?—but Morecambe is not good *ton,* according to no less authority than my own dear mother."

He tossed the rose skyward, and Genie snatched the beleaguered flower out of the air. "If you think to make this farce of an offer believable, you will court me *at length,* my lord. You will show me every courtesy, you will dote, you will pine, you will flirt with me and flatter me. No dowager duchess has any need of matrimony, with its attendant risks and obligations. Only after you have convinced the whole of polite society that the sun rises and sets in my eyes will you think of approaching Augustus to ask for my hand, or he will laugh you to scorn."

By which time, Genie would have a strategy for avoiding another tiara, even if it meant emigrating to darkest Peru.

Dunstable braced his walking stick against his shoulder. "You want to enjoy a dalliance with the stone mason, is that it? I could ruin him with a whisper, my dear, so please don't think to cuckold your intended with Morecambe's bastard."

"Once again, you quite mistake a matter of which you have very little understanding. It's time you left, my lord. You have a long and thorough courtship to plan."

He laughed again—Genie already hated his laugh—and bowed over her hand. "So I do, so I do. What a delightful prospect."

He was entirely too pleased with himself, and Genie was too distraught. "You will keep this scheme to yourself if you hope to see us wed, sir. I take a dim view of any suitor whose discretion cannot be trusted, and so will the rest of Society."

Dunstable tipped his hat to a jaunty angle with the handle of his walking stick. "Said the woman caught groping her husband's cousin on the stair."

"What does your mother think of your plan to make a widowed copper heiress your duchess?"

Dunstable's stick hit the paving stone. "We'll leave dear Mama out of this for the nonce. She knows the occasional heiress has kept many a titled family tree thriving."

Her Grace of Seymouth was an obnoxious old besom. Even Charles had had little patience with her, and for Genie, she'd served as an example of how not to be a duchess.

"Go plan our courtship," Genie said, gently placing the rosebud on the edge of the fountain, stem trailing in the water. "And do a thorough job of it."

Dunstable went chortling on his way, while Genie returned to the bench and contemplated a series of unfortunate choices. One certainty emerged: She could involve neither Adam nor Augustus in this tangled web. The one would be ruined, the other embroiled in scandal short months after inheriting his title.

"But I cannot marry that grasping, greedy idiot," Genie informed the swan at the center of the fountain. "One duke was more than enough, and two would be a penance I do not deserve. I hope there are some sheep farms for sale in Peru."

CHAPTER SEVEN

"Duchess Eugenia is from home," Mrs. Thompson said. "She departed three-quarters of an hour ago, unescorted, no word of her plans. I had hoped she was meeting you for a constitutional."

Adam held his cup of jasmine gunpowder under his nose. "She knew I had plans this morning. She did not know when I would call upon her." The tea was soothing and fragrant. He wanted to smash the cup against the wall.

"Shall I convey a message to her, Mr. Morecambe? She will be very sorry she missed you."

Is Dunstable bothering her? Tell her I love her. How much courting is enough? Adam could say none of that.

"Tell her the press of business sends me to London once again, posthaste. I will return to Brighton at the earliest opportunity."

He set down his tea cup and rose before he blurted out his frustrations. Where was Genie, what was Dunstable to her, and why couldn't one work site function smoothly for even a week at a time?

"Mr. Morecambe, the press of business seems to vex you greatly. Is there anything I can do to help? I consider Her Grace a dear friend, and I'm sure she considers you in the same light."

I do not want to be merely her friend. "Can you spare me a few spoonfuls of tea from the caddy?"

Mrs. Thompson peered into the little silver cannister. "We have plenty. Have you a handkerchief?"

Adam spread out his handkerchief—monogrammed initials, no coat of arms—and Mrs. Thompson spooned dry tea onto the linen. She tied it up in a knot and passed it to him.

"Safe travels, Mr. Morecambe. I'll tell your duchess you were very cast down to miss her."

Adam stashed the tea in an inner pocket. "I am not cast down. I am determined, and she is not my duchess—yet."

Mrs. Thompson stood and smiled, and such was her beauty that Adam, to whom aesthetics had long been a priority, should have goggled at her for a full minute. He offered her a hasty bow and nearly ran for the door, grabbing his hat and walking stick from a dismayed housekeeper.

Every two miles on the journey to London, Adam took a whiff of the tea sachet and schooled himself to patience. He should have left a note. He should send an express at the next change of horses. He should turn the damned coach around and let the work site sort itself out.

Except it wouldn't. Work sites never did.

Nonetheless, the situation had improved by the time Adam arrived. Rosenbarker and the head mason had turned up, though the wagon had been stolen.

"They wanted to study the tipper," Rosenbarker said, pacing Adam's small office as if a child had been kidnapped rather than a piece of equipment. "Held us at gunpoint, directed us to drive a good fifteen miles past the quarry, and if a friendly farmer hadn't happened along, we'd still be hiking home from Berkshire."

"They used deadly force to steal a damned wagon?" Adam asked.

"They both had pistols," the head mason said, his words bearing a thick Welsh accent. "Big, ugly pistols, the use of which I trow they grasped far more easily than they did the mechanism that works the tipper."

None of the tipper's various gears, screws, or levers had been stamped with a point of origin for this very reason. Adam could bear to lose a wagon, and he wasn't much concerned that others would learn how to use the mechanical advantage of a screw to raise one end of a wagon bed. Manufacturing that wagon involved a team that included carpenters, machinists, artificers, wheelwrights, and joiners, none of whom knew the identities of the others.

Until the patent on the wagon was approved, Adam would continue to exercise caution.

"You've both had an ordeal," he said. "Take the rest of the day off, and I'll hire a guard to... We don't have the damned tipper to guard."

"The first lot of new wagons are supposed to be ready by the end of the week," Rosenbarker replied. "We can unload the old-fashioned way until then."

Which would impact the schedule, and the payroll, and the dealings with the subcontractors.

"Do the best you can. I'll revise the schedule, hire guards for the site, and notify the authorities that my wagon has gone missing."

Though they would do little enough besides condole Adam on the loss. Doubtless the tipper was already in pieces in some barn or warehouse, never to be functional again.

"The blackguards also took a team of horses, guv," the head mason said. "That's a hanging offense too."

Forcing Adam to leave Brighton without offering Genie a farewell should be a hanging offense. Consigning him to spending the evening on schedules and budgets should be a hanging offense.

"Where do we get our tea?" Adam asked Rosenbarker when the head mason had departed for the nearest pub.

"Twinings on the Strand, because it's close and they don't adulterate the product with everything from grass clippings to hedge weeds."

"How late are they open?"

"Damned if I know. Where are you off to?"

Adam grabbed his hat and walking stick. "I'll be back within the hour. I'm off to report a crime." And buy some jasmine-scented tea.

GENIE HAD SPENT three days traipsing the length and breadth of Brighton, Mr. Vernon at her side. One property was too small, another had creeping damp freshly painted over in the basement, a third was going soggy about the cupola, a fourth was perfect but too far from a livery and lacked space to add a stable.

No wonder Adam had been frustrated.

Genie was growing frustrated. Dunstable had called on her twice and all but sat himself in her lap, he'd been so fawningly devoted. He'd sent flowers after the last call, a gaudy profusion of irises sure to be remarked by anybody who'd seen the delivery boy pounding on the *front* door before the housekeeper had shooed him around to the back.

Dunstable had proposed an afternoon constitutional for tomorrow, and Genie was thus praying for rain, and for Adam's safe return.

"I did hear of one other property," Mr. Vernon said.

The cat sat at the solicitor's feet, wearing an expression that suggested a pounce would follow when Mr. Vernon was least prepared to host a cat on his lap.

"I am interested in anything remotely suitable." Genie was also interested in one architect, to the exclusion of all dukes, titles, or fortune hunters. Instinct prodded her to follow her heart, but Dunstable was circling like a vulture and threatening the two men whom Genie esteemed most highly in all the world.

"Bit of old scandal attached to this property," Mr. Vernon said. "I happened to dine last night with my former partner, Mr. Bacchus Dingle, and informed him of Your Grace's present quest. Dingle's memory goes back to before Brighton became fashionable, for he was raised here. He told me that the Duke of Seymouth had a residence built not far from the Pavilion, because our then-Regent's interest in Brighton was well established. Lovely property, according to Dingle."

None of the inquiries Genie had made—and she had made dozens—had mentioned anything about a ducal residence being for sale.

"Go on."

"The duke took it into his head that the builder had been skimping on materials, cutting corners, and overcharging. His Grace refused to pay for the property, and the builder retired in debt and disgrace. The property has stood empty all these years, though the ducal heir became the owner on the occasion of his majority. What sort of papa deeds over a rattletrap establishment to his firstborn, I ask you?"

An instant of foreboding settled over Genie before recollections turned her foreboding to dread.

Adam's father had suffered a nasty turn at the hands of a duke.

Seymouth was a duke whose firstborn had come of age in recent years.

Dunstable imposed on friends when he visited Brighton, suggesting any residence he owned was not regularly staffed.

Oh dear. Oh damn. Of all the dukes in all the peerages in all the world...

"If the property was poorly constructed, Mr. Vernon, shouldn't fifteen years of neglect have resulted in its disintegration?"

The cat decided to be civil and stropped himself against Vernon's boots. The solicitor picked the beast up and scratched its hairy chin.

"Your Grace, as usual, makes a practical observation. If the property was poorly constructed, then it would be riddled with damp. The sea air is unforgiving of shoddy work and hard on even a solid edifice. If the property was in fact properly constructed—which theory Dingle supports—then it might be available at a bargain price. Would you like to see the house?"

"Above all things, and without alerting the present owner."

Vernon and the cat turned the same impatient expression on her. "Your Grace does not contemplate housebreaking, I hope?"

"Of course not. A duchess merely indulges in harmless, discreet curiosity. On no account is anybody to learn of my interest in the place. If I do make an offer, I want the owner to regard the sum tendered as a windfall from somebody ignorant of the building's tarnished pedigree."

Vernon set the cat down and rose. "I am your servant in all things, Your Grace. Will you at least comfort my conscience by assuring me that His Grace of Tindale will approve the expenditure before you saddle yourself with an uninhabitable abode?"

Genie got to her feet. "Who employs you, Mr. Vernon?"

"You do, Your Grace."

"Then as your employer, I encourage you to refrain from dragging any unnecessary dukes into my affairs. I'm available tomorrow at any hour to view this property."

She accompanied Mr. Vernon to the foyer and passed him his hat and walking stick. He was approaching his prime, no longer a boy, his wisdom beginning to catch up to the abundance of a young man's animal spirits. He was a fine solicitor, but England was full of fine solicitors, and Genie could not afford to be sentimental.

"We'll use the servants' entrance," he said. "Dress accordingly, for the place hasn't any staff in residence. I'll come by for you in the alley in a closed coach and return you by the same means."

Genie beamed at him. "You've done this before. I'm impressed, Mr. Vernon."

"Don't be impressed, Your Grace. Be very, very discreet. Good day."

She closed the door behind him and allowed herself a moment of hope. She'd spent years being discreet, and what had that earned her but Dunstable yapping at her heels and filching her heirlooms? Now he wanted to filch her future and get children on her, three boys, at least, with no guarantee that he'd keep his word to cease threatening Augustus—or Adam.

A SMARTLY TURNED-OUT gentleman climbed into an equally smart town coach, which rolled away from Genie's doorstep at a smart pace. Adam had paused only long enough to wash the dust of the road from his person and wasn't feeling smart in any regard.

The gentleman might have been calling on one of the other ladies. He might have been an old friend, or a garden-variety fortune hunter. Adam resented him on general principles, though, because he'd been crisp and attractive and full of energy.

"Mr. Morecambe, a pleasant surprise," Genie said, ushering him into the formal parlor—not her private sitting room.

The leavings of a tea tray sat on the low table, and the cat, balancing on its back legs, was making designs on the cream pot.

"I was called to London again. Did Mrs. Thompson tell you?"

"She did. Shall we go upstairs? I've had about as much tea as I can tolerate for one day, but I will never tire of good company."

Genie's words should have reassured Adam, but her manner was merely friendly, and she looked tired. He followed her up the steps, long hours in the saddle making even that slight exertion an effort.

She left the door open and settled on the sofa. "How goes the work in London?"

Adam remained standing. "Somebody is trying to steal my tipper-wagon design. They won't get far without knowing how I put the thing together. Screws have been around for millennia. Might I sit?"

"Of course. I gather the tipper wagon is very clever?"

Adam took the place beside her on the sofa. "Very valuable, because it saves time and labor." *Who was that man?* "I've missed you."

She rose and took the wing chair when Adam had hoped she might instead close and lock the door.

"I've missed you as well, but in your absence, my situation has become complicated."

"In what regard?"

She tried for a smile and ended up studying the carpet, a fine Dutch weave of flowers and leaves in red, green, blue, and gold.

"Another suitor has presented himself, a most unexpected and ardent admirer."

Adam knew all about competing bids, and they didn't intimidate him. "Your expression suggests that admiration is not mutual."

"Admiration can take many forms."

He would have bet his tipper-wagon patent that Genie had not admired this rival in the privacy of her bed or on any picnic blankets.

"Are you showing me the door, Your Grace?" Part of him accepted that possibility as inevitable. His version of courting had been to drag her all over the backstairs of two large houses between disappearances to London. Not very impressive.

But his heart—his purely human heart—ached to think she'd give up on him so easily.

"I am not showing you the door, but if in the coming weeks, I am less available to you, or you see me in company that you cannot condone, then you must not take it amiss."

Adam rose, for he refused to take such a reversal of his dreams sitting down. "This is called letting me go gently. My spirits will soon be level with the pavement, but nobody will be troubled by a loud, impolite crash. I am to pretend your announcement has not devastated me, pretend my affections were only superficially engaged. That is what an almighty duke or a marquess or an earl—"

She flinched at the word *marquess*.

Dunstable, then, the pestilential spawn of a posing, prancing, lying old scoundrel of a duke.

"You fancy to become like your friend," Adam asked, "the Double Duchess? I read the papers, Your Grace. Has ducal consequence once again exerted itself to crush the aspirations of the lowly Morecambes?"

Say no. Say of course not. Say anything honest.

She shook her head. "Mr. Morecambe, I consider you a dear friend. I am not at liberty to say more, but please believe that my regard for you is genuine. I simply need time…" Her breathing caught, an odd hitch that she tried to cover by rising. "I simply have a few complications to sort out. I hope that one day soon, I might again be able to welcome your attentions."

She was tossing him out on his ear, ejecting him like a tavern regular who'd overimbibed.

Adam's pride demanded that he make a dignified exit, before overimbibing in truth. He was exhausted, furious, minus his tipper wagon, and soon to be minus his intended. Minus the woman who'd sat for hours while he'd sketched woodwork at Petworth.

Minus the lady who'd cheerfully driven through miles of countryside so he could spend a day admiring parts of Petworth he'd never be admitted to without her.

Minus the high-born friend who'd earned him a peek at every royal pantry in Brighton.

Minus his lover.

Minus his favorite duchess, whose first marriage had been bewildering, grueling, and, above all, *lonely*.

She was staring out the window, a pillar of unshared confidences and private woes. How stubborn she was, and how he loved her.

His father had slunk away from the prospect of holding a duke accountable. That course—bitter retreat—was unthinkable for Adam.

"Do you know," he said, "how strong a man becomes when he spends his youth wrestling good English stone? Do you know how determined that man learns to be when turning stone into art?"

"You should go. For your own sake, Adam, you should go."

She confirmed his suspicions with that warning, bless her proud, obstinate heart.

"I'm not going anywhere until you put aside your tiara long enough to tell the man who loves you which varlet has set himself against us and why he has you so frightened."

Genie didn't take a seat on the sofa, but rather, she deflated onto the cushions, from a proud duchess to a woman overwhelmed.

"I hate tiaras," she said. "My tiaras are heavy and old, and they give me awful headaches. I'm frightened—you're right—but I'm also bitterly, mortally angry."

Adam shifted to the sofa and put an arm around her shoulders. "Angry is good. With a little anger and a trusty sledgehammer, you can bring down almost any edifice. Now tell me where I need to swing my hammer and why."

CHAPTER EIGHT

The parlor door was open, and Genie did not care. She cared only that Adam had his arm around her and wasn't put off by a rival suitor.

Not by anything.

She could make another attempt to dissemble, to persuade him to give her time to deal with Dunstable on her own, but she'd been dealing with Dunstable, and her efforts had only made the cad bolder.

"I have been dissembling since the day I became betrothed to a duke," Genie said. "Wearing a tiara forged of lies. I'm a sheep farmer's daughter, and I am proud of that."

Adam kissed her hand. "No tiaras, I promise, but you have to tell me the rest of it."

A tiara of truths, then. "You cannot swing your hammer at a ducal family," she said. "Seymouth takes his consequence seriously, and though he might not respect his son, he'll take any affront to Dunstable as a slight to himself."

"As he should. An affront to my father, even fifteen years ago, offends me still." Adam scooped Genie into his lap, an exceedingly comfortable perch. "An affront to my intended will see me laying about with any tool I can grasp."

His intended. Not his duchess, thank the kind powers.

"Dunstable wants my money," Genie said. "I've rather a lot of it, and I gather his debts are enormous. He can't afford to open the house your father built here in Brighton, which has been deeded to Dunstable. I've seen the interior, Adam. It's a jewel of modern convenience and excellent taste, worthy of a ducal family trying to discreetly rival the sovereign."

Adam's hand on her back went still. "You've seen my father's house?"

She withdrew the pin from his cravat and snuggled closer. "Toured it from top to bottom. Dunstable's man of business attempted obstinance, but duchesses have reserves of stubbornness mere lawyers cannot hope to achieve. I found no hint of damp, not a whiff of subsidence, not so much as a stuck window. Seymouth would have known this if he'd bothered to inspect his own premises."

Which dukes rarely did. They relied on stewards, men of business, solicitors, and an overworked duchess to keep all running smoothly. Augustus would not be such a duke, but Seymouth exercised every privilege of his station.

"Thank you," Adam said, kissing her temple. "I knew my father would not cheat a customer, but I haven't been able to prove it. Your eyewitness testimony erases my last doubt."

She sat up to peer at him. "You would doubt your own papa?"

"Not his integrity, but the best architect can be hoodwinked by a dishonest builder, the best builder can be taken advantage of by a lazy master mason, and the best mason can be cheated by the quarry. Constant vigilance is impossible when an architect's practice is going well."

"You sound like a duke." Adam smelled like himself, though, mostly cedar with hints of linseed oil and sawdust in the far corners of his fragrance. Genie loved the scent of him, loved the feel of his arms around her.

Loved him for telling her to put her tiara aside.

"I have not the resources of a duke," Adam said, "but I have the ability to take a bare patch of ground, and from nothing more than a sketched elevation, I can build an edifice that will last for centuries. Tell me why you haven't laughed in Dunstable's face on the dance floor at Almack's."

Delicious thought. "He has threatened me, which would be of no moment, but he's also threatened Augustus, and—lest that not be sufficient—he's thrown a few vague aspersions in your direction as well."

Adam kissed her cheek. "He's promised to ruin me."

"Promised with a casual cheer that makes me uneasy."

Adam was quiet for a moment, his hand resuming a soothing rhythm on Genie's back. "Do you esteem the present Duke of Tindale?"

"Augustus? I adore him. He danced with me at my presentation ball, a great, growling brute of a man whom nobody dared cut, but nobody wanted to acknowledge. He was the cousin they had to invite and wished to never see. He told me not to let a parcel of prancing ninny-hammers send me to bedlam. He also told me we were to be family, and I was entitled to his unquestioning loyalty for the rest of my days."

"I like him already, but you are a woman of great sense, and you feel you have to protect Augustus from Dunstable. What is the rest of the story, Genie?"

Genie wiggled from his grasp and rose, an undignified undertaking. Adam made no move to thwart her and had sense enough to remain on the sofa.

"I betrayed my husband in one sense and in one sense only."

"You failed to conceive a child, which is hardly your fault."

Any other man would have dodged that topic, brushed it aside with platitudes about the will of God, the futility of dwelling on the past. Adam started his enterprises from bare ground, though, and planted his foundations securely on truth.

"That is not quite accurate. I did conceive. I'm almost sure of it." Even now, Genie had to leave herself a reprieve, a hope that her sorrow had been unfounded. "The early signs were there, the very early signs, that is. I hadn't said a word to Charles, on the advice of the midwife. She suggested I wait at least another two months to be certain. I was counting the days, my hope nearly eclipsed by my anxiety."

The hope had been excruciating, and the sorrow proportional.

"You lost the child."

"If a child there was. We were having a dinner party, and I told myself the discomfort I was experiencing was from the wine, the candle smoke, anything. When I found a moment to use the retiring room, I learned my courses had started. Augustus came across me sitting on the stair, unable to speak, unable to return to my guests. I could not cry—duchesses don't cry in the middle of their own entertainments—and the tale came out. I never told Charles, but I hoped desperately to conceive again."

The weight of that hope had dragged at every moment of her marriage, added to her grief, and still threatened to overwhelm her. She braced herself on the mantel, and then Adam's arms were around her again and she was sobbing against his shoulder.

She cried not simply for a barren marriage, but for a happy Derbyshire girl who'd come to London with stars in her eyes and been handed a cold, heavy parure. She cried for all the girls and all the busy, self-important men casually crushing their spirits because those men had never been taught better. She cried for her widowed self, looking after those young women and spreading graciousness in all directions, while longing for the rural splendor of the north.

"I told Augustus," she said, her voice made low from tears, "and he has kept my secret to this day. Dunstable saw me in Augustus's arms, saw Augustus kiss my forehead, and has made a great salacious interlude out of it. Nobody would have cared if I discreetly dallied with my husband's cousin—though I ought by rights to have produced sons first—but now that cousin has the title, and Dunstable has debts."

Adam walked her to the sofa, came down beside her, and tucked her close. "So Dunstable threatens a woman who has done him no wrong rather than take up an honest profession or tell his father he's in dun territory. If he'd stolen from the poor or turned the elderly out of their homes, I might not hold him in greater contempt."

"He's threatened you and Augustus. He sought to marry me, but he can ruin you and make false accusations to the authorities regarding Augustus. Augustus is not a typical duke."

"For which we must commend him. I need to think."

While Genie needed to be quiet, recover her composure, and for once let somebody else consider her situation while she dozed against his side and dreamed of chubby lambs and lush meadows.

"LUDDY," Dunstable said, taking a seat at the luncheon table, "you see before you a man in anticipation of matrimonial joy. Pass the wine."

The earl obliged, though he took the precaution of pouring for himself first. Dunstable started his serious drinking with the midday meal, and Luddington had no reason to believe today would be an exception.

"Has the young lady accepted your addresses?"

Dunstable filled his glass to the brim. "She's not young, but her fortune compensates for a host of shortcomings. I do fancy a hearty merlot, though not usually so early in the day."

"Jones," Luddington said to the footman at the sideboard, "please serve his lordship some of the soup, and then you may be excused." Not that Dunstable would bother with excellent beef and barley stew when he could instead be swilling wine. "What does your papa think of your choice of bride?"

More to the point, what would the Duchess of Seymouth think? Dunstable's dame could make any young woman's life merry hell on a good day, and bachelors regarded time in her company as durance vile.

"Haven't told Papa yet, but he's been after me for years to 'start conducting my affairs like an adult.' To hear him tell it, he was meeting with his stewards before he was breeched, and Mama was stitching prayer samplers before she could read. Why do we teach women to read anyway? All they do is correspond with each other the livelong day and tattle on their menfolk."

By which means, family and social ties were preserved despite great distances and years of separation. "Are you drunk already?"

"Believe I am. Drunk with joy at the prospect of putting aside the lonely tedium of bachelorhood and accepting the responsibilities I was born to shoulder. Certain funds will come under my control when I marry—certain needed funds—and my lady wife will add to those funds nicely. Should have married long ago, but never met the right sort of female."

"What sort would that be?" Besides desperate.

"One wants a wife whom one can control," Dunstable said, downing half his wine. "I need look no farther than my dear parents to see what havoc a female can wreak when she don't know her place. I won't have that problem."

"You'd marry a simpering featherbrain?" Luddington shuddered to contemplate the offspring of such a union.

"I'd marry a mature woman who knows how to respect her duke. Fortune is smiling on my choice. I've had an omen." He nodded sagely and finished his wine.

"You've taken to reading bird entrails."

"Mock me all you please, Luddy." Dunstable helped himself to another bumper of merlot. "That dreadful property Papa tried to foist upon me when I came of age has caught the interest of a buyer. Have you another bottle of this vintage? It's quite good."

Luddington set aside his empty soup bowl. "I generally buy by the lot when I find a wine I enjoy. I didn't know your Brighton property was for sale."

"It's not. The damned solicitor said I'd have to load it up with furniture and art and servants to get a decent price for it. I'm letting it go for a mere bagatelle, but between us, the construction ain't sound. Papa said. Damned place will be somebody else's problem. Caveat empty, and all that."

"*Caveat emptor*," Luddington murmured. *Let the buyer beware.* "I congratulate you on your good fortune, both as regards the real property and the marital prospects. Might I know the name of your intended?" He asked out of simple expedience, for he himself was in the market for a spouse. No need to court another man's prospective duchess.

"You may ask, though you are sworn to secrecy. Have to inform Papa of my choice, and he'll have to talk Mama 'round. I intend to offer for none other than Eugenia, Dowager Duchess of Tindale."

Luddington nearly got a snoutful of merlot. "You think *she* will make you a biddable and docile duchess?" The lady had brooked no nonsense from her haughty husband and was held in very high esteem by the matchmakers. The fortune hunters had learned not to approach that citadel, and King George was said to owe her favors.

"I'm certain of my ability to maintain the upper hand in the marriage. For me, the duchess will be the epitome of domestic subservience."

"Have some more wine," Luddington said, though clearly poor Dunstable was already either half-seas over or showing signs of early dementia. "Did I mention that I'm removing to London at the end of the week? You're welcome to bide here as long as you please, but I must look in on my sister."

For under no circumstances did Luddington want the task of consoling Dunstable when the duchess sent the marquess packing with a flea in his ear.

WITH GENIE TUCKED against his side, Adam could think more efficiently. She was snoring gently, spent from unburdening herself, while he mentally constructed a project schedule complete with elevations, landscape plans, and a budget.

He would need the services of one duke and one duchess—possibly two of both—and the timing would be delicate. Funds would be required and some luck.

The most critical asset, however, was determination. "My love, wake up." He kissed Genie's temple, because he could.

"Chocolate."

"I can think of many ways to wake a lady that are more enticing than chocolate."

She straightened to peer at him. "You are a resourceful man. I must look a fright."

"You look splotchy and tired, also lighter in spirit and very dear. If you can gather your wits enough to plot a strategy with me, I have need of your keen intelligence and remarkable powers of observation."

She kissed his cheek, lingering near enough that the scent of her addled Adam's wits. "Nobody has ever valued my keen mind before."

"When you are the wealthiest sheep farmer in Derbyshire, they'll learn of their error." For she would be. She'd see which flocks prospered in which fields, which ewes produced the most twins, which shepherds truly loved their occupation, and soon, fat, fluffy sheep would dot every hillside she owned. Adam would build snug byres for the sheep and model cottages for the tenants...

"We will own property in Derbyshire?"

Why hadn't anybody, not her damned ducal cousin, not her brothers, not her man of business, bought her an estate in Derbyshire?

"You will own property in Derbyshire. We'll tie it up in a trust for our daughters, and when you are wroth with me, you will remove there to torment me. I won't dare trespass, or you'll have me ejected and bound over for the assizes, and your neighbor, His Grace of Devonshire, will see me transported."

Genie curled down to rest her head in his lap, as she had on their picnic blanket. "Your vivid imagination is surely why you are such a success as an architect, but before I become a sheep nabob, might we decide what to do with Lord Dunstable?"

Might we decide. Adam had never taken a partner for his building projects. He suspected that was about to change.

"What is needed," he said, "is truth, and somebody with enough consequence to make that truth compelling, for the same source authored my father's downfall as can author Dunstable's."

"His Grace of Seymouth."

"*Their* Graces of Seymouth. I know not what role Her Grace played in Papa's troubles, but if she'd taken so much as a single tour of the Brighton property, she might have intervened. The house was built to her specifications."

Adam closed his eyes, the better to learn the curve of Genie's cheek against his palm, the better to savor the texture of her skin. Her face was warm, her hair silky. For the first time in years, he felt the urge to take up a mallet and chisel to craft cold stone into a living form.

Instead, he must sculpt a solution to Genie's troubles, and to his own.

"Her Grace is formidable," Genie said. "Quite the force of nature. I've arranged to buy that house. I'd thought to sell it to you for your gentlemen's club."

An odd effervescence cascaded through Adam's heart. "You bought my father's house for me?"

"You needn't get all masculine and affronted. The business called for some subtlety, and nobody suspects a duchess of anything other than self-indulgence. I will charge you exactly what I paid for the place, and you may do with it as you please."

She'd bought the property, protected Adam's pride, and done so with Dunstable prancing about her parlor. She was a terror in a tiara, and if Adam hadn't been in love with her before...

He was in love and he was in awe, a stirring combination of sentiments. "What are you paying for the house?"

She named a figure, perhaps one-tenth what the dwelling was worth, and Adam just had to hug the stuffing out of her.

"The Duchess of Seymouth might be intimidating," he said when he had stopped laughing, "but you are the more formidable, for you bring the element of surprise to every battle. You are so gracious and charming that others miss your determination and strength. I must learn to be formidable as well."

Genie patted his thigh. "You can be grouchy and direct. That's a fine start on formidable, and an aptitude for numbers helps."

"Anybody can work an abacus and eschew idle talk."

"I've done what I could, Adam, but Dunstable will now have the funds from the sale of the house, and he'll be pleased with himself for having liquidated an asset his father could not. He means to offer for me and to create serious trouble for Augustus and for the man I love if I refuse."

The man I love.

"I cannot have a mincing dukeling vexing the woman I love with threats of marital servitude."

Genie sat up and situated herself in Adam's lap, her arms around him. For a long, lovely moment, Adam reveled in their mutual declarations. His breeding organs clamored to celebrate the occasion intimately, but first he must conclude the strategy session.

"You have kindly given me the means to make the truth of my father's situation known to all and sundry," Adam said. "I need only execute the task I dread most in the entire world—other than losing you—to see the plan put in motion."

Genie left off teasing his earlobe with her tongue. "What task is that?"

"I must give aid to a duke and ask him to aid me in return."

"A BEAR in morning attire is pacing about in the formal parlor," Anne, Duchess of Tindale, said. "I like the looks of him."

Augustus more than liked the looks of his duchess, a circumstance which weeks of marriage hadn't changed. Anne passed over a silver salver with a single card on it.

"I intercepted Jenkins," she said. "He would not have offered this visiting bear tea. What manner of ducal household fails to offer hospitality to all who call?"

"One recovering from years of priggish posturing. Shall you join me in receiving"—Augustus glanced at the card—"Mr. Morecambe?"

"He's an architect. I'm not in need of any buildings or renovations, while you own property in six counties and the City. I'll leave you to it."

She sashayed from the room, grinning over her shoulder as she passed through the doorway, because of course, Augustus had watched her departure with a worshipful devotion that only grew the longer they were married.

He tucked Mr. Morecambe's card into his pocket, buttoned his morning coat, and prepared to set down a presuming fellow who should have made an appointment rather than stormed the ducal residence. Augustus appreciated initiative wherever he found it, though, so he'd at least hear the bear—the fellow—out.

Anne hadn't exaggerated regarding Morecambe's appearance. He was large, dark, and possessed of shoulders worthy of a blacksmith. His countenance was far from refined, and his blue eyes held not a hint of deference.

"Mr. Morecambe." Augustus bowed. "I don't believe we have been introduced."

Morecambe bent from the waist. "I'm madly in love with your cousin by marriage. We can discuss that later."

Being a duke was tedious. One wasn't to brawl, not physically, not verbally, not financially, not ever, and as Mr. Morecambe turned an imperious glower on his host, Augustus realized how much he'd missed brawling.

"We'll discuss it now, sir. Who the hell are you to fall in love with the Dowager Duchess of Tindale?"

"I'm the man who will get her free of Lord Dunstable's clutches, and you are the man who will listen to what I have to say before you summon footmen to do what you yourself don't dare attempt."

"Toss you out on your presuming ear?"

"*Attempt* to lay hands on me. I'm not very toss-able, Your Grace. I suggest you take my word on that, for your duchess doubtless values the present arrangement of your features."

Augustus nearly burst into whoops, but he was learning to be a duke—to be Anne's duke. "Before I return the favor and rearrange your features, would you care for some tea, Mr. Morecambe?"

"No, thank you. I'd care to enlist your aid in ensuring that Lord Dunstable is shamed for his presumption."

"You have a pretty way of asking for help."

Morecambe smiled, and his resemblance to a large, hungry, wild beast was complete. "The Dowager Duchess of Tindale finds my ways pretty enough."

Genie hadn't thought to warn Augustus of Mr. Morecambe's call. She must finally be recovering from her marriage to Charles.

"The dowager duchess was gracious to me when the rest of my family barely acknowledged me. Trifle with her, Morecambe, and I will kill you."

"As well you should. Lord Dunstable is attempting to trifle with her, but she won't let me call him out. A fate worse than death is to live with dishonor, and I'd like to sentence Lord Dung-stable to at least that."

Augustus held out his hand. "Welcome to the family. What have you in mind?"

Morecambe's grip was crushing, though Augustus knew that Genie's pet bear would be the soul of tender delicacy with her. Anne would be so pleased, and Augustus was damned happy for Genie too.

CHAPTER NINE

Genie's nerves were in a state, balanced between hope and despair. She received her guests with the Duke and Duchess of Tindale at her side, for she'd appropriated the ducal town house in Brighton for her ball.

Her guest list had skimmed the cream of summer Society from the seaside towns, and no less personages than the Duke and Duchess of Seymouth had bestirred themselves to accept her invitation. Dunstable had called upon her nigh daily, while Adam had taken himself back to London with every appearance of having ended their association.

"You have the document?" Augustus asked during a lull in the receiving line.

"Adam sent it by express earlier today," Genie replied.

"And where is your Mr. Morecambe?"

"On his way." Though Genie had no idea if that was the case. Construction at the club had been plagued by the usual sorts of delays and setbacks, and cold weather would arrive without regard to an architect's schedules. Horses went lame, coaches overturned, and plans went awry.

"I saw the house you purchased for your architect," Augustus said. "Lovely property."

"The ceilings," Anne murmured. "I want those ceilings. Tindale, you are warned."

"Our ceiling renovations will start in the bedroom." Augustus and his duchess exchanged a look that confirmed where the couple spent most of their time when at home.

"The eighth biblical plague approaches," Genie said, pasting her own darling-duchess smile in place and curtseying to Her Grace of Seymouth. "Your Grace, welcome. So glad you could join us."

Genie endured the same sniffy perusal she'd been treated to a thousand times before, a copper heiress's lot when she aspired to become a duchess. Now, though, she was not only a duchess, but also soon to become Mrs. Adam Morecambe.

She returned the older woman's rudeness.

"Dunstable told us to expect an announcement," Her Grace of Seymouth said. "I'd best not have spent three hours in a coach only to learn one of your protégés has snagged a mere honorable, madam."

"We assure you," Augustus said, "this evening will figure in your memories for years to come."

The greetings proceeded at the pace of a turtle navigating a sandy beach, with Dunstable all but licking Genie's glove, and still, no Adam. The time came to open the dancing, and fortunately for Genie, the Tindale dukedom had nearly a century's precedence over the Seymouth dukedom, or she would have been forced to dance with Dunstable's papa.

"This feels right," Augustus said as he escorted Genie to the center of the dance floor. "I danced with you at your presentation ball, and now you dance with me at my first formal appearance in Society as a ducal host. Where the hell is Morecambe?"

"Adam will not fail me," Genie said, sinking into the requisite curtsey, "and Dunstable has already appropriated my supper waltz, exactly as planned."

The next two hours were spent in the usual fashion for Genie—

matching wallflowers with bachelors, diffusing spats among the ladies in the retiring room, monitoring the punch and those who partook too often from the men's bowl.

Dunstable's gaze followed her everywhere, and when Genie spent a few minutes visiting with the Duchess of Anselm, a friend from the days of Genie's court presentation, Dunstable went so far as to stand in Genie's line of sight and pat his pocket.

Wherein a ring doubtless nestled.

The supper waltz arrived, and nothing would do but Genie must dance with Dunstable.

"Do I mistake the matter, my dear, or are we to make an announcement when our guests have sampled the buffet?"

His gaze dropped to Genie's décolletage; she tramped on his foot.

"I have not the gift of seeing into the future, my lord, but I do hope Augustus will make an announcement by the end of the evening."

"I suppose His Grace of Tindale is the host, though Papa does a fine job of commanding the attention of a large company. I thought we'd make our wedding journey to Paris, but then, everybody goes to Paris."

"You have creditors waiting for you in Paris, and they will seize your coach and horses, if not my jewels, to settle the debts you've run up." Adam had passed that tidbit along. Dunstable's situation in London wasn't much better, which explained his weeks by the sea sponging off of Lord Luddington.

Also his desperation to plunder Genie's fortune.

"If Tindale has been looking into my finances, then I must assume he has raised no objection to our match. I thought a special license would suit, so we can be married at Seymouth House."

He tried to twirl Genie under his arm and ended up clipping her on the jaw with his elbow. The blow stung, not her first in the course of a polite waltz, and he had the grace to look horrified.

"Too much punch," he said. "I do apologize."

"If it happens again, Augustus will doubtless provide you instructions on how to properly stand up with a lady, though by the conclusion of his lesson, you will be hard put to stand without assistance yourself."

The waltz came to an end, and Dunstable clamped his hand around Genie's. "Tindale doesn't plan to be an interfering sort of relation, I hope."

"You know how fond I am of Cousin Augustus," Genie said. "I expect if I remarry, he'll be very much in evidence until he's satisfied the union is happy. I did the same when he and his duchess were courting. Family looks after family, you know."

"Any more looking after you with close embraces on secluded stairways after we're married, and His Grace will become an outcast, his duchess with him."

You will become the outcast, God willing.

They took their places in the buffet line, though Genie had no interest in the food. The Duke and Duchess of Seymouth were looking bored and impatient—also tired—and Augustus was nowhere to be seen.

Anne, however, caught Genie's eye over the offerings of *soufflés à la vanille* and smiled like the cat who'd divined how to open the canary's cage.

"He's here," she whispered.

Genie wanted to dump her plate over Dunstable's head, but instead comported herself as a proper duchess, nibbling this and that, tasting none of it. All the while, Dunstable chattered about Continental destinations he'd never seen and sat so close his knee constantly bumped against Genie's.

She felt sorry for him, despite his bullying and arrogance, for he'd very likely be living in one of those far-off cities unless his papa agreed to again pay off his debts.

At the top of the steps, the herald was consulting with a late arrival, a tall man with broad shoulders, his evening attire accented with a red rose *boutonniere*.

"I have a late-arriving guest," Genie said, setting her plate aside. "Perhaps you'd like to greet him with me?"

Dunstable stuffed another strawberry into his mouth and rose. "Of course. My duchess is the soul of graciousness, and then we can find some library or parlor and get the bended-knee bit over with. Paid a damned fortune for the ring. Had to sell my Brighton property because the jeweler would only take cash."

Good for the jeweler.

Adam smiled faintly as she approached.

"I don't recognize him," Dunstable said. "Looks familiar, though. Probably got some of his blunt at the gaming tables. Are you sure he was invited?"

"He is the guest of honor," Genie said, gaining the top of the steps. "Mr. Morecambe, a sincere pleasure to see you here tonight. Have you met Lord Dunstable?"

Adam sketched a bow. "I have had that honor. My lord, good evening." Adam was breathtaking in his formal clothing, and the mere sight of him settled Genie's nerves.

"Morecambe. Suppose you've come for the free food and drink. Don't bother the women, or this will be the last ball you attend."

"Do you promise?" Adam asked, taking Genie's hand and tucking it over his arm. "To be spared the tedium of Society balls would be a great blessing."

Dunstable looked like his cravat had abruptly grown too tight.

"Shall we repair to the formal parlor?" Genie suggested. "Mr. Morecambe has some news to pass along to you, my lord."

"Mr. Morecambe's news had best not take long," Dunstable said, starting down the corridor. "I have plans for that formal parlor that do not include him and his clumsy attempts at flirtation."

Adam bent close to Genie. "You are well?"

"I will be. The letter is in the parlor, and I hope Augustus awaits us there with Their Graces."

"Two dukes, a duchess, and a presuming disgrace of a lordling. Promise you'll not abandon me in such company, Genie."

"Never."

"Then all shall be well."

DISASTER HAD STRUCK, in the form of bad eel pie served at the pub nearest to the club's construction site. For most of a week, Adam had had barely half a crew at barely half strength. He'd carried hod, he'd laid brick, he'd wielded saws, mallets, and hammers, while His Grace of Tindale had passed along each debt and bet Dunstable owed money on.

The sum was astounding and showed a capacity for industry, albeit mischievous industry. Adam ached in every particular as a result of the past week's exertion, but sore muscles and scraped knuckles faded from his awareness at the sight of his Genie.

He'd never seen her in a ball gown, and the shimmering russet velvet showed her off exquisitely. She'd chosen rubies for her jewels—fittingly precious—and gold settings. By candlelight, she glowed, while Dunstable looked pallid and effete.

When Adam arrived at the formal parlor, Augustus was serving the Duke and Duchess of Seymouth glasses of wine. A missive sat on the escritoire's leather blotter, the red seal unbroken. Augustus was looking severe, while Her Grace of Seymouth appeared dyspeptic.

"There you are," she said when she caught sight of Dunstable. "Have you an announcement to make? I came all this way, braved the dust of the road and the heaving of that dreadful coach, because I was promised by your father that the evening would result in cheering news. The sea air does not agree with me, I can tell you that straightaway, young man, so you'd best be about your business."

"Lord Dunstable will appreciate his parents' support, I'm sure," Adam said, withdrawing a folded paper from his pocket. "He's considering paying his addresses to the dowager duchess, but sought to compel her agreement to his proposal by force."

The Duke of Seymouth was on his feet in the next instant. "Who the hell are you, and what gives you the right to make any accusations against a ducal heir?"

"I am the lady's intended," Adam said. "I make no accusations, I state facts. This is a list of your son's debts, Your Grace. If you ask him, he'll tell you he sold his Brighton property to satisfy a few of his creditors. In fact, he spent a pittance with the jewelers on Ludgate Hill, then gambled away the rest."

Dunstable sank into a chair. "Every gentleman has debts. His Grace knows that, and the Brighton property was falling in on itself."

Dunstable's mother glowered at Adam. "The Brighton property was an eyesore, which you'd know if you'd ever set foot inside it. Nothing was done as it should have been, because the architect was a cheating scoundrel who thought to ill-use his betters. Be off with you, whoever you are, and don't think to show your face among polite society again."

Adam bowed. He did not withdraw. "I am Adam Morecambe, son of the man who designed, financed, and oversaw the building of your Brighton property, madam. My father died in penury and disgrace because he was cheated, lied to, and taken advantage of by a pair of high-born scoundrels whose perfidy will soon become common knowledge. If Your Grace of Seymouth will please read the letter awaiting you on the escritoire?"

Seymouth stalked over to the desk and slit the seal. "To whom it might interest," he began...

I HAVE HAD the pleasure of recently examining the dwelling located at the corner of Monmouth and Exmoor Streets, Brighton, which dwelling first became known to me when a late associate in the architectural profession, one Peter T. Morecambe, consulted with me on plans for this property more than fifteen years ago. My inspection was undertaken in anticipation of the sale of the dwelling by Lord Dunstable to a dear acquaintance of longstanding, the Dowager Duchess of Tindale. Though the house was in want of a thorough cleaning, I found all appointments carried out exactly according to the plans signed for by the late Mr. Morecambe, which plans I did examine in detail prior to visiting the premises.

A better example of domestic elegance on a tasteful scale does not come to my mind, and several of the innovations—plumbing on the upper floors, speaking tubes to accompany the bell system, a solarium on the uppermost floor—have been incorporated into my own subsequent designs.

I cannot fathom why such a lovely and commodious home suffered so many years of disuse and neglect, but I hope that in future, the prospective owner will do justice to this jewel of architectural art.

John Nash, Architect to King George IV

SEYMOUTH TOSSED the letter onto the desk. Tindale took it up.

"What do you want of me, Morecambe?" Seymouth asked. "The house has been sold. Your father is long dead. Take the matter to court, for all I care, but don't expect me—"

"Seymouth." The duchess spoke softly. "I told you not to believe a man of business who knew nothing of building. I told you to have a look, to get another opinion."

"Your Grace," Seymouth retorted, "now is not the time to air old and much-wrinkled linen."

Dunstable looked from one parent to the other. "You mean to tell me that I sold a house John Nash has deemed *a jewel of architectural whatever?* Sold it for a *pittance?*"

The duke and duchess spoke at the same time. "Hush."

"You did," Adam said, "and I now own the property. I'll convert it into seaside quarters for the members of my gentlemen's club, once it has been cleaned and refurbished. My wife will oversee the decorative scheme once we return from a protracted wedding trip to Derbyshire."

"Derbyshire is lovely this time of year," Augustus observed.

"Derbyshire is lovely any time of year," Genie added.

"What's the rest of it?" Dunstable's mama snapped. "There has to be more, or you wouldn't have gone to all this trouble. Your father has been exonerated of cheating us. What else can you want?"

"Your son has attempted to extort not only an enormous sum of money from my intended, but also to force her to join him at the altar. In an effort to placate his ambitions, she has surrendered at least two personal heirlooms. Dunstable saw, years ago, an embrace between cousins by marriage during a private moment of grief and chose to misconstrue that memory for his own advantage. He is no gentleman."

"Now see here," Dunstable began, "I cannot be responsible for the foolish fancies of a widow whose recollections are as inaccurate as they are unflattering to me. I never threatened, implied, or intimated in any way that what I saw was anything other than—"

"You did," Genie said, marching up to him. "You promised me that not only would the present Duke of Tindale suffer the brunt of gossip and rumor at your hands, but you'd inform the authorities that he schemed with me to gain the title by nefarious means. You further threatened Mr. Morecambe and made it very plain that my fortune was the motivation for your proposals, threats, and plots. You extorted Papa's snuffbox and Mama's diamond bracelet from me. You are the proverbial blot on the family escutcheon, and I never want to see you again."

This magnificent set-down was followed by a ringing silence. Adam wanted to applaud, but he'd save his expressions of admiration for later, perhaps on a picnic blanket.

"Do you contradict Her Grace of Tindale, my lord?" Adam asked.

Dunstable's gaze slewed about the parlor, from parent to parent, to the door, which Augustus happened to be casually leaning against.

"Apologize," the Duchess of Seymouth said. "For God's sake, boy, apologize if you ever want to set foot in England."

"Do as your mother says," the Duke of Seymouth added tiredly.

"One ignores her advice at one's peril. You will return the snuffbox and bracelet as well."

In the looks exchanged between duke and duchess, Adam understood something that hadn't until that moment been clear: Seymouth had swindled Papa because the duke had *lacked the funds* to pay for the house and had been too proud to admit to his poverty. Seymouth had married an heiress and run through her money, and his son had expected to do likewise.

"I most humbly apologize," Dunstable said, bowing to Genie. "I do think we'd have rubbed along tolerably—"

"Get out," Genie snapped.

Augustus held the door. "Your valet is packing your effects, and you're to be on a ship for Calais by this time tomorrow."

"But I haven't—"

The Duchess of Seymouth waved her hand, and Dunstable was gone. When Augustus had pulled the door closed behind him, the duchess aimed her next question at Genie.

"How much do you want? I warn you, the Seymouth dukedom is perennially pockets to let, but we have properties in abundance, and some of them even produce income."

Genie took the place at Adam's side. "What I want—what *we* want—is for the wrong done to Peter Morecambe to be put right."

Adam slipped an arm around Genie's waist. "What *I* want is to thrash your son within an inch of his useless, titled life."

"I want to watch," Augustus added, straightening his cuffs.

"If thrashing had done any good," the Duke of Seymouth said, "Dunstable would not have made such a pest of himself. You have Nash's letter. What will you do with it?"

"The letter will become part of the club archives," Adam said, "available in our Brighton property for any to see who have an interest. I won't hide it, but I won't bruit it about either. Reparation to my intended for Dunstable's bullying is another matter."

Genie folded her hand over his where it rested on her waist. "I want Your Graces to remain for the rest of the evening, and when

Augustus makes his announcement at the conclusion of the supper break, you will be visibly pleased at the news."

"Very visibly," Augustus added.

"And Dunstable?" the duchess asked.

Adam and Genie hadn't discussed this. He'd been too busy keeping his construction project moving forward, totaling Dunstable's debts, arranging Nash's visit, and missing his beloved.

"I have two requests," Genie said. "The first is simple: Make him pay his debts. He's left everybody from tailors to bootmakers to haberdashers to finance his excesses. Don't allow him to perpetuate a legacy of dishonesty and irresponsibility."

Seymouth looked pained. His duchess looked vindicated. "What else?"

"Keep him away from England for at least two years," Genie said. "My menfolk need some time for their tempers to cool—as do I. Dunstable was a nasty, vile, conniving disgrace and had I been just another young heiress in from the country, I'd likely be shackled to the likes of him for life."

The duchess rubbed a gloved hand across her forehead. "We will remain for the rest of the evening. We will rejoice at any announcement. We will leave Dunstable to sell his coaches and rings and snuffboxes to pay the trades. We will send him abroad for a good long while."

Seymouth assisted the duchess to her feet. "And we will apologize. By the time I could have made things right with Peter Morecambe, he had gone to his reward. I will recommend your services to all and sundry, Mr. Morecambe, and admit my part in the misunderstanding that sent your father into retirement. Honesty from me now won't give you back your father, but it will allow me a very small measure of self-respect."

He bowed and withdrew, his duchess at his side.

"That went well," Augustus said. "I do believe Seymouth and his duchess consider themselves in your debt, Morecambe."

"Honor is not the exclusive province of the titled," Adam said.

Genie kissed his cheek. "Nor of those who wear breeches. Away with you, Augustus. Adam has something he wants to ask me."

Tindale stayed right where he was. "If it has to do with capitals and astragals, then an estimate would be the first—"

"Out," Adam said. "Now."

Augustus scampered from the room—in as much as a largish duke could scamper—and Adam took Genie by the hand and led her over to the sofa.

"Your Grace," he said, lacing his fingers with hers. "Would you do me the very great honor of reserving all of your future picnics for me and me alone?"

"Yes," Genie said, wrapping her arms about his neck, "or yes, unless children come along, in which case, we will have to let them accompany us at least some of the time."

Oh, that was the best, best answer. Adam kissed her and kissed her and kissed her, and only Augustus rapping on the door prevented Genie from holding their first picnic as a betrothed couple on the rug before the formal parlor's hearth.

EPILOGUE

Genie mapped out a wedding journey that wandered from Yorkshire to Lancashire, then down to her beloved Derbyshire, the better to inspect properties for purchase. She also frequently inspected her husband's unclad person.

She settled on a lovely estate in Derbyshire and promptly named it Farmdale. The lintel over the drawing room was Gibbons's work, and the portrait gallery included plasterwork by Bradbury and Pettifer.

"I do so love my sheep," she said, lounging back on the blanket. "They seem happy."

Adam, upon whose chest she reclined, propped his chin on her crown. "They seem woolly and happy."

She turned in his arms, feeling like the luckiest woman in the realm. "Are you happy?"

Adam nuzzled her ear, which gave her the shivers in the best possible way. "Not quite."

Oh dear. She'd worried. She had never quite felt like a genuine duchess—and thank heavens she no longer had to try—but would Adam ever feel comfortable as the husband of a dowager duchess?

"What's amiss?"

"Another viscount has petitioned for membership in the club." The gentlemen's club in London was simply named Morecambe's, nicknames notwithstanding.

Adam had the loveliest steady heartbeat. "How many is that?" Genie asked.

"This will be our fourth if we approve of his application. He's an earl's heir."

Three months ago, Genie might have scampered off to the nearest copy of Debrett's, where she'd research the courtesy lord in question and all of his family connections. The Farmdale library held no such volume.

"Is he a decent fellow?" she asked.

"Seems to be. Two current members vouch for him. He pays the trades on time."

Genie struggled into a sitting position as an inquisitive lamb sniffed at the blanket. "But you don't want his business?"

"I want the business of any decent man who appreciates a place to spend time with others of like temperament, but this man will be an earl someday. Viscounts can be relatively unassuming, but an earl..."

Genie waited, because Adam considered his words and what he had to say mattered.

"Life was simpler when I could resent the entire peerage and dukes in particular," he said. "We've been invited over to Chatsworth for dinner."

"His Grace of Devonshire is a lovely man," Genie said. "He's a bit hard of hearing, but a great patron of the arts and sciences." He was also their neighbor, by country reckoning, and a genial host.

The lamb grew bolder, sniffing at the wicker basket on one corner of the blanket.

"He's a duke," Adam said. "This part of the country is positively infested with them. I'm an architect."

"My favorite architect, who is wrestling with some conundrum which you've yet to share with me."

Adam distracted the lamb by scratching its woolly forehead. "Devonshire's invitation included a note. He'd like my opinion on some renovations."

"Ah."

He scooped up the lamb and cradled the lucky little creature against his chest. "Am I a tradesman, a respected professional, a neighbor?"

"What would you like to be?"

"Mostly, I'd like to be your husband." The lamb leaped off of Adam's lap and gamboled away. He watched it go, and Genie took the lamb's place.

"You are concerned," she said, pushing his hair back from his brow, "that a gentleman does not engage in trade, much less in commercial undertakings. As an architect, you were a gentleman with a profession. Now you are in the middle of Derbyshire, with me."

"My favorite place to be."

He meant that, and he'd given up much to make it so. "Adam, you don't have to choose. You don't have to remain penned here at Farm-dale like one of my rams. You can be Devonshire's neighbor and consult on his renovations. Chatsworth is a perpetual work in progress and enormous. If the duke isn't modifying his house, he's tinkering with the stables, the gardens, the conservatory, the land-scaping, the fountains... I'm sure you will assist him if you can, and if he offers a professional arrangement, and you'd enjoy the work, then do it."

Adam passed her a clover plucked from the grass. "For pay? You would not object to my taking commissions?"

He'd found a lucky clover, hadn't even had to hunt for it.

"You trained long and hard to develop your expertise, and Devon-shire has pots of money. Why should you work for free? I don't intend to give my wool away." That Adam would trouble over this decision and discuss it with her was all the morning gift Genie would ever need.

"I never want you to regret marrying me, Genie. You learned to move in circles I never aspired to reach, and I…"

"You love to build things." He'd built her the most marvelous barn, for example, with winches and trapdoors and chutes and clever lifts.

"Mostly, I want to build a life with you. I'll have a look at the renovations at Chatsworth." He fanned his hand over the grass again, as if he could feel the four-leaf clovers. "Worksop apparently needs some interior redesign as well."

"That's the family seat of the Dukes of Norfolk."

Adam was smiling. "His Grace of Newcastle has invited us to Clumber House at a time of your convenience. I think your peers are rallying to your cause, madam."

Genie tackled him, because what were blankets—and husbands—for? "They are rallying to *your* cause, you daft man. Not all dukes are like Seymouth or Dunstable. They are the exceptions, in fact. Most dukes are simply gentlemen with complicated estates."

"I am a gentleman," Adam said, frothing Genie's skirts up. "I am *your* gentleman."

He was so much more than that. He was Genie's partner in every regard, her lover, her companion, her favorite architect.

"You will be very busy," she said, kissing his nose. "I might have to hire you to ensure our home is kept in good repair."

"You will come with me on reconnaissance," he said. "I don't intend to take on these dukes without you."

"We'll take them on together, just as you assist me to manage my flocks, and—oh, Mr. Morecambe." Adam had situated himself behind her, so they lay spooned on the blanket. His hand had found its way between her legs, and Genie's thoughts went scampering off like spring lambs.

"We should reply to Devonshire's invitation, Mrs. Morecambe." He called her that when they were private, and it was Genie's favorite endearment. "Also to Newcastle and Norfolk. You'll help me compose my replies?"

"No dukes right now, please, Adam. Not on my picnic blanket, please." What he could do with his big, talented hands...

He leaned closer and kissed her temple. "No dukes , then, only the architect of your fondest wishes and most intimate dreams."

TO MY DEAR READERS

I hope you enjoyed these little tales of amor vincit-ing omnia, because I certainly had fun writing them. ***No Dukes Allowed*** and ***Love by the Letters***, the anthologies where these stories first appeared, remain among my favorite group projects. Writin' buddies are the best buddies... (so are readin' buddies).

I will soon have all of my backlist novellas re-published, and that means.... It's time to write some new ones! I have a Christmas tale planned for November of this year for my ***Rogues to Riches*** series, ***A Rogue in Winter***. If you're looking for a novel-length happily ever after, my second **Mischief in Mayfair** story, ***Miss Delightful***, will be available from the web store in late August, and from the retail stores in mid-September. (Excerpt below).

If you'd like to stay up to date with all of my new releases, discounts, and pre-orders, following me on **Bookbub** is a simple way to do that. I also have a **Deals** page on my website, updated about monthly, that details web store early releases, special sales, and web store exclusives. I also send out a **newsletter** when I have something worth sharing, and if you sign up, I promise I will never sell, swap, or disclose your addy or private information—word of a Burrowes!

Happy reading!

Grace Burrowes

Read on for an excerpt from *Miss Delightful*...

MISS DELIGHTFUL—EXCERPT

"That is a baby." Alasdhair MacKay stood back lest the woman holding the infant knock him over as she sailed across his threshold and into the foyer.

"How astute you are, Major MacKay."

"*Former* major." Alasdhair closed the door because the day was chilly and babies were fragile. Also because this situation needed no witnesses among the nosy neighbors. "And who might you be?"

He turned his signature commanding office glower on the woman, and allowed his burr to deepen to the consistency of a growl. He did not so much as glance at the wee bundle in her arms.

"Miss Dorcas Delancey." She dipped a curtsey, baby and all. "This good fellow appears to be your son, so I will leave him with you—"

"He is not my son." Of that Alasdhair was emphatically sure.

She turned earnest gray-green eyes from Alasdhair to the baby and back again. "Perhaps not your legitimate son, but there is a certain—"

"That child is not my son, and you and I have not been introduced Miss Delancey." Alasdhair would recall an introduction to a such a woman. She wore propriety like a Sunday cloak, and could probably deliver whole sermons on mankind's fallenness.

She was no classic beauty, from eyes which were neither slate nor emerald, to hair that aspired to auburn but stopped just past dark brown. Her features were elegant, though any emotion in them was diluted by an air of briskly unsentimental detachment.

She would be difficult to shock, and even harder to impress.

As was Alasdhair, did she but know it.

"You recall your activities from well over a year ago?" she asked. "The child is a good six months or thereabouts. He's beginning to teeth, you see, and that is a good thing. The landlady heard him yelling and realized his mama was not with him. He was having rather a bad time of it."

A coldness assailed Alasdhair, the same coldness that had come over him in battle. His body would function with heightened efficiency, his mind would leap along paths of strategy and intuition, while his heart turned to granite.

But there was no battle here. No enemy. Only this demurely dressed female with her drawing room English and earnest gaze, along with that... that bundle of trouble.

"I am sorry for the lad's misfortune, but he is not my son."

"He is still your responsibility." She unfurled the word *responsibility* like a pristine banner of righteous certainty. "Melanie Fairchild named you as his guardian, and as she is no longer extant, and her will is quite clear, that makes you—"

"*What?*"

The coldness had never made Alasdhair light-headed before. "I saw her just last week. She was in great good health." Melanie, like so many of the women offering themselves on London's streets, had been a good girl once, the kind to suffer terribly when deemed no longer worthy of that appellation. She'd been quiet when last Alasdhair had called on her, perhaps tired. Only that. "She cannot be dead."

"I am sorry," Miss Delancey said. "You cared for her."

"Of course I cared for her." Alasdhair cared for them all, fool that he was. "She had come so far, against such odds. She had a cousin or auntie who was helping her, though the rest of her family was a worthless pack of pious hypocrites. She doted on that baby, went on and on about him."

What a smart lad he was, how merry, what a good sleeper. Melanie had rhapsodized about one tiny infant and foreseen a great future for him.

"I apologize for being the bearer of sad tidings, Major, but you will have young John here to console you."

"No, I will not."

The baby gurgled, a happy sound accompanied by a tiny fist flailing in the direction of Miss Delancey's not-quite-dainty nose.

"Might we continue this discussion somewhere warmer, Major MacKay?"

"Plain MacKay will do." Manners required that Alasdhair take the lady's burden from her, but he could not. "This way."

He led her through a townhouse that was more of a roofed camp-site than a dwelling. London was not his home, God be thanked, but he bided here from time to time and had cousins here. No siblings, and certainly not a son.

"My study," Alasdhair said, opening the door reluctantly. "My guest parlor is unheated." Equally important, the guest parlor had windows visible from the street, and the draperies on those windows were tied back, the better to display Alasdhair's social life to any passerby.

Fortunately, he had no social life.

Based on the lady's merino wool cloak, matching blue gloves, and nacre buttons, she was one of those women who thrived on going from friend to friend collecting gossip. She would expect a tea tray. Where were her chaperone, lady's maid, and footman for that matter?

"It's half-day," Alasdhair went on, "which is why you find me answering my own front door and without help in the kitchen."

"You will need a wetnurse," Miss Delancey said, taking a place in the middle of Alasdhair's favorite napping sofa. "I'll have Mrs. Sidmouth send along Melanie's effects, and I'm sure the baby's dresses and whatnot will tide you over for a time. He's taking some cereal, but he wasn't yet weaned."

Alasdhair remained on his feet, pacing the length of the carpet. "Miss Delancey, I care not which society for the oppression of beggars you represent. I have no need to know what variety of meddling fool you are, but I must observe that your hearing appears deficient. I cannot take in that baby. I am a bachelor. I have no staff to care for a child. I have no wish to care for a child."

Not quite accurate. Alasdhair would save them all if he could, and their mothers, but he had no *ability* to care for a child. "Has anybody seen to Melanice's final arrangements?" He could not bear the thought of her lying in a pauper's grave, nobody to mourn her, nobody to leave a single flower.

"Please do sit, Mr. MacKay. You have had a shock."

Why were women such as Miss Delancey always telling others what to do? "How did she die?"

Miss Delancey adjusted the blanket swaddling the baby. "She surrendered herself to the embrace of Father Thames. No inquest has been held because we have no body. A woman fitting Melanie's description made her way to the Strand Bridge last night, and Melanie's favorite bonnet and slippers washed up on the morning tide."

The proper name for that newly-opened bridge was Waterloo Bridge, an irony when many of the women who chose to die there were war widows. Alasdhair perched a hip against the battered desk. He'd have a word with the river police, and see what the mud larks had to say.

First, he had to get this woman, *and that baby* out of his house. She would see to the lad, come fire, flood, famine, or Frost Fair.

"Send the lad to his mother's family," he said. "They can pretend, as all the best families do, that he's the offspring of a widowed cousin in Scotland with too many mouths to feed. Make him into a badge of virtue for the very Christians who all but threw him to the lions."

One do-gooder spinster relation had taken pity on the child. Melanie had never mentioned her by name, but the pittance that auntie or cousin had regularly sent along had been enough. Alasdhair had made sure of that.

"With you named as legal guardian, Melanie's family would have no authority to raise the child."

"I will cheerfully give my permission for them to do just that."

"Are you ever truly cheerful, Mr. MacKay?"

She tucked the child against the corner of the sofa, banking pillows around him. Swaddled in his blanket, the baby could hardly crawl off across the cushions, but still, the lady took precautions.

Did the lad even know how to crawl?

"I will be very cheerful," Alasdhair said, "when I contemplate this boy growing up in the bosom of his nearest and dearest. I am a stranger to him. No relation at all. I have no children and don't expect I will ever be so blessed. Take him away, Miss Delancey, and I wish you best of luck with him."

The words hurt, like telling a wounded man he was bound for the surgeon's tent. A boy barely shaving was to lose a limb, if not his life, and all Alasdhair had been able to do was stop by to offer a nip from his flask if the soldier survived the day.

"Melanie chose you to raise him, Mr. MacKay. You had best reconcile yourself to that honor." The woman rose, and though she was not tall, she carried herself with dignity. She undid the frogs of her cloak and draped it over the sofa.

Her figure was a trifle on the lush side, somewhat at variance with that ruthlessly reserved expression.

To be a plain creature of mature years in a society that valued beauty, youth, and malice equally was a tribulation, a battlefield of sorts. Miss Delancey had chosen aloof dignity and virtuous meddling as her weapons. An interesting combination.

She inspected the framed copy of the dispatch mentioning the *notable gallantry* of Major Alasdhair MacKay, Lieutenant Colonel Orion Goddard, and Captain Dylan Powell. From there she moved to a landscape of the River Tweed, and Alasdhair realized he was being lectured with silence.

"I am no relation to that child, Miss Delancey, but I suspect you are."

She smiled, a sweet, surprisingly impish curve of her lips. "I am indeed an exponent of that tribe of pious hypocrites who turned their backs on Melanie. She and I were cousins. We grew up together, and when she ran off with her handsome soldier, I knew exactly what her fate would be. We lost touch for a time, but then she wrote to me, and I thanked God for that."

"Why not take in the boy now?"

The lady folded her arms. Perhaps in deference to her cousin's passing, she was attired in a blue so dark as to qualify as mourning attire, or nearly so.

"What do you think his fate will be, with my father angling for a bishopric, and my great-uncle already in possession of one? Do suppose John will be permitted to dine with us at table? Will he be made to say the grace and quote all the nasty proverbs and passages about ungrateful children, Jezebels, and Magdalens? I can assure you that will be the least of the tender regard to befall him, and heaven help the boy if he's given to running in the house, yelling, or talking back. He still be bread-and-watered to within an inch of his sanity—for his own good, of course."

"You will intercede for the lad."

Miss Delancey regarded Alasdhair steadily, and his insides went squirmy.

"Babies cry, Mr. Mackay, a lot. They make messes and drool and refuse to sleep when it's dark outside. Babies cannot tell us what hurts or frightens them. They can only squall and whimper or go off their feed. If they are lucky, they grow up. Don't delude yourself that I would be free to meddle much on John's behalf as he matures."

Miss Delancey stalked over to Alasdhair, her bootheels rapping against the carpet. "If you cannot take in this child, then arrange for him to be fostered someplace safe. Not one of those dreadful baby farms, not the foundling homes. Take responsibility for him, or you are wishing upon the boy a fate no child should endure. Melanie asked this of you, and I demand it."

The squirmy feeling acquired the dimensions of resignation. Defeat was imminent, retreat a certainty.

"You may leave him with me for now," Alasdhair said, "but use your charitable connections to find a proper place for him. Your father's household might not be appropriate for an illegitimate child, but a soldier's bachelor quarters aren't much better."

Her smile returned, a benevolence so palpable and good-hearted that basking and wallowing came to mind.

"I knew Melanie's faith in you was justified. I will return tomorrow morning, Mr. MacKay, with a wetnurse if I can find one. John can make do with warm, thin porridge until morning, though you will also need a supply of clean clouts."

Alasdhair eyed the bundle waving chubby fists at nothing in particular. "Why will I need a supply of clouts? He's only one boy."

Miss Delancey's smile acquired a hint of mischief. "Use your nose, sir. It's a very fine nose, and I'm sure you will deduce the situation soon enough. I will see myself out. Until tomorrow."

She shook out her cloak and swept it around her shoulders with a graceful flourish, then marched for the door. She had a good, sturdy march, probably a result of the robust health of the inveterate crusader.

Those thoughts hummed along at the periphery of Alasdhair's mind, while the reality of the child's presence occupied the center of his mental stage. The front door closed, and the ticking clock on the mantel exactly matched the cadence of Alasdhair's thumping heart.

"You and me, lad," he said, "for the nonce. Only for the nonce." His brisk tone of voice apparently did not fool the child, who regarded him with owlish caution.

"The lady has gone, and we're to make do on short rations until she comes back. I'm MacKay." How was the boy to learn to speak if nobody talked to him? Alasdhair came to within two feet of the sofa and bent to take up the child.

He straightened, assailed by a spectacularly foul miasma. "That woman. That woman ambushed me. That infernal woman *ambushed* me."

The baby flailed his fists, and tried to kick against his blankets. His little face squinched up, and Alasdhair had no choice but to lift him off the sofa.

"I will court martial her," Alasdhair muttered, trying to cradle the child closely, but not too closely. "I will have her drummed out of the regiment. I will strip her of rank and see her reduced to private. Put me on latrine duty, will she?"

He kept up a similar patter—the boy seemed to enjoy it—until they reached the laundry. Alasdhair set the baby among a basket of folded towels, and took a knife to the first clean length of linen he found.

ORDER your copy of *Miss Delightful*!

9 781952 443701